PHANTOM DELUSIONS

OTHER TITLES BY
CARRIGAN RICHARDS

Standalone Titles
Pieces of Me
Black Dove

Elemental Enchanters Series
Under a Blood Moon
Under the Burning Stars
When Darkness Fell
Under a Winter Sun
Under an Onyx Sky

January Dreams Series
January Dreams
Silent Dreams
Shattered Dreams

PHANTOM DELUSIONS

CARRIGAN RICHARDS

Cover Art by Jake @ J Caleb Design
Edited by Sophia Jimenez

Library of Congress Control Number: 2025911589

ISBN: PB: 9798990514713; ASIN: eBook: B0F6V2Y6N8

Printed and bound in the USA

For the ones who feel too much, think
too deeply, and fear they'll never be
believed.

This one's for you.

Chapter One

Rain streaked down the coffee shop window in jagged lines, blurring the world outside into something unrecognizable. The coffee shop smelled of freshly brewed espresso and warm pastries. Becca had chosen the corner booth, the one with the best view of the rain-streaked windows and the street outside. The low hum of conversation filled the air, mingling with the faint clinking of cups and saucers. My half-empty latte sat on the table, growing colder with every passing minute, while Becca stirred the remnants of her chai with a long spoon.

"It's just one week. What's the worst that could happen?" Becca's voice was sugarcoated persuasion, but something in her tone made my stomach knot.

Her presence was magnetic. Becca Patterson was a burst of energy and personality in human form. Her long, blonde hair, a cascade of lively curls, framed her face with an untamed charm that she somehow made look effortless. Her vibrant green-blue eyes reflected her free-spirited nature, like tiny kaleidoscopes of chaos and charm. Today, her outfit screamed "look at me" a bright pink jacket over a plain white T-shirt, ripped jeans, black feather earrings, and the tiniest stud in her nose.

I, in comparison, felt like a shadow—a smudged outline of a person sitting across from her.

"I don't know." I wrapped my fingers around my mug, letting its warmth seep into my palms. A cabin in the mountains with Becca, Jax, and a couple of their college friends for an entire week. It sounded like the setup for a murder mystery novel. Or maybe one of those horror movies where everyone makes stupid decisions.

I wasn't sold.

"I'm just getting used to my schedule." I sighed. "Wake up, school, pick up Casey, homework, dinner, study, bed. Weekends are messy enough without a routine. Next week is fall break, and I haven't even figured out how I'm going to manage."

"You've been cooped up for weeks, Hazel. This is exactly what you need. A change of scenery, fresh air, and some actual fun." Becca leaned forward, her voice dropping conspiratorially. "Besides, you'll love Logan. He's ... different. But he's sweet, kinda quiet, and hot. You'll like him. I promise."

I raised an eyebrow. "Remember the last guy you wanted me to meet?"

"Okay, maybe I owe you an apology for *that* one," she said, twirling her spoon dramatically, "but Logan's nothing like Matt. Ugh. So glad you got rid of his sorry ass."

The mention of Matt's name was like a dart to my chest. I shifted in my seat, uncomfortable. "Can we not rehash that?"

"Are you still upset? I mean, come on, Hazel, I think it's for the best. He's not all that great."

"Maybe I want to wallow. Is that okay?"

"Okay, but like, it's been six months."

"Four."

"Please. He ghosted you well before he"—she lifted in her fingers in air quotes—"*officially* broke up with you."

"We were together for nine months."

Becca threw her hands up in exasperation. "And he treated you like crap. Especially when he didn't even come to see you—"

"Can we stop talking about it?" I snapped, cutting her off. I didn't want to talk about my hospitalization. Or the fact that Matt had never visited.

She gave me a look, her lips pressed into a thin line, but then she smiled again, quick to move on. "I'm telling you, once you see Logan, you'll definitely stop wallowing."

I rolled my eyes. "Then why don't *you* date Logan?" Becca's solution to everything seemed to involve a guy, but in her case, it was always the same one.

"You know Jax is my person."

I knew all too well that Jax was *her* person. We'd grown up with Jax, and he'd been like a brother to me. That's why I couldn't stand the on-again, off-again mess between him and Becca. She'd chased him all the way to college like he was the sun and she was Icarus, and I was just waiting for the inevitable crash.

I shook my head, knowing Becca wouldn't listen to me, especially when it came to Jax. I'd never understood the two of them. It was like they couldn't stand to be together, yet they couldn't stand not to be together.

"Why is this so important to you?" I asked, narrowing my eyes.

Becca hesitated for the briefest moment. Her fingers fidgeted with the edge of her napkin. "Because you're my best friend. I want you to have a good time for once."

Her words were sincere, but I couldn't help the creeping doubt that always lingered in the back of my mind. Becca made everything sound so simple, but "simple" wasn't a word I trusted anymore. Not since my mind started splitting reality into jagged little pieces.

I glanced out the window. The rain had let up, but the clouds were still a heavy gray, promising more to come. The idea of a cabin in the mountains, surrounded by nothing but trees and the people Becca swore I'd have fun with, made my chest tighten.

"You'll get to see Jax," Becca said, her smile spreading wider, a flicker of excitement dancing in her eyes.

I felt my chest tighten, not with anxiety this time, but with something lighter. "I haven't seen him since ... June." At the graduation party I hadn't wanted to attend. "I miss him. Wait. Are you two back together?"

Becca shrugged, but her grin betrayed her. "It's not *official* yet."

"How did this happen?"

She twirled a strand of her golden curls, feigning nonchalance. "We've just been talking more. He said he was excited to see me."

"Well, maybe it'll work this time." I tried to sound optimistic, but my voice faltered, and Becca didn't miss it.

While I was happy to see Jax again, the invitation still puzzled me. Becca and Jax had their own rhythm, their push and pull, and I knew I'd end up an afterthought once they started orbiting each other. "So ... why bring me along?"

"What?"

"Why bring me if Jax is gonna be there?"

"...So all of us can hang out?" Her answer felt rehearsed, like she'd prepared for this exact question.

I nodded but raised an eyebrow.

She sighed, dramatically. "Oh, come on. Just because we're getting back together doesn't mean I'll ignore you."

"Okay." I tried to believe her, but doubt settled in anyway.

"Seriously, Hazel. What's it going to take for you to leave? Take a week off from … life."

"I have to stay and watch Casey." It wasn't exactly a lie, but it wasn't the truth either. Gary, Casey's dad, could handle him for a week.

Gary. Just thinking of him tugged at something bittersweet inside me. He was the closest thing I'd ever had to a real father. When Mom got pregnant with Casey, I thought we'd finally have a real family. Stable, whole. Gary was kind, funny, the kind of person who made you feel safe. But Mom, being Mom, got bored. She always did. She pushed him away, and eventually, he moved out. I was devastated when he left, but he never disappeared from my life. Casey was ten years old now, and Gary was still there for him and even there for me, in ways my own mom never was.

But without Gary around full-time, it had been up to me to fill in the gaps. I loved Casey more than anything, but sometimes I needed a break. The idea of being away for a week tugged at me, a mix of guilt and longing. Could I really leave them behind?

Four months. That's how long it had been since I'd clawed my way out of the darkest place I'd ever been. Two weeks in the hospital. Two weeks of sterile white walls, fluorescent lights that never turned off, and the unbearable feeling that I was a broken piece in a world that only accepted perfect ones.

I could still feel the heaviness of that first night. The hospital bed was stiff and cold, the blanket scratchy against my skin. The faint hum of lights and footsteps echoing in the hallway felt like a taunt, reminding me that I didn't belong there. My chest tightened at the memory of how I'd cried myself to sleep, the tears choking me as I fought to keep from falling apart entirely.

By the third day, a nurse had brought me a journal to write in. "It helps," she'd said softly, and I'd nodded, not because I believed her, but because it felt easier than speaking. I wrote everything that night: the way I felt like a stranger in my own body, how afraid I was of disappointing everyone, how I didn't know if I'd ever feel normal again. The pen dug into the paper as I scrawled the words, like if I pressed hard enough, I could force the pain out of me.

Now, the thought of leaving Casey, leaving home, and stepping into the unknown for an entire week left my throat dry. The cabin sounded remote, quiet, isolated. A place where your mind could run wild. A place where you could lose yourself.

"I don't know," I said finally, staring into my now-cold coffee.

Becca groaned dramatically, resting her chin on her hand. "You know damn well Gary would take care of Casey for a week. Hazel, come on. You need this. Besides, I can't wait for you to meet Logan."

My chest tightened at her insistence. But maybe she was right. Maybe I *did* need this. A week in the mountains, away from the monotony of school and the constant reminder that I was the only one there repeating my senior year. It sounded almost appealing. The thought of escaping everything, even for a little while, tugged at me like a thread I wasn't sure I wanted to pull.

But then there was Becca and Jax. I could already picture them, tangled in their on-again, off-again whirlwind, leaving me on the sidelines to figure out how I fit into the picture. Would I really be part of this trip, or just an afterthought?

I bit my lip, feeling the weight of her expectant gaze. "Fine. Tell me about Logan."

Becca's eyes lit up as she leaned forward in excitement. "Okay, first of all, his dad used to play for the Braves. Like, actual MLB. He plays baseball too at his college. And it's his family's cabin we're going to. Logan's sweet and smart, but he's kinda closed off."

I raised an eyebrow. "Then why do you want me to meet him?"

"Because maybe you can open each other up! I mean, you're both kinda closed off."

"And that bothers you?"

"Well, yeah. Why hide?"

"Not everyone likes putting their whole life on display."

Becca shrugged. "Life's messy. No one's perfect. Who cares?"

"People are judgy, Becca. You *know* that."

"Yeah, but I don't care."

"Well, some of us do." My voice dropped, quieter now. I hated how people saw me. The second they found out I was bipolar, or worse, that I'd spent time in a hospital, their perception of me shifted. Suddenly, I wasn't Hazel anymore. I was fragile. Unstable. Dangerous.

"You shouldn't care what people think," Becca said firmly, reaching across the table to grab my hand. "You're not crazy, Hazel. Don't let anyone make you feel that way."

Her words softened something inside me. Even after everything, Becca always had my back. "Thanks. Okay, so Logan's closed off. What else How old is he?"

"Nineteen. About to turn twenty."

"How long have you known him?" I asked.

She shrugged, looking away. "A while. Jax and I used to hang out with Logan at parties. You probably don't remember, though. You were ... dealing with a lot."

Her words stung, not because they were meant to, but because they were true. I'd spent so much time drowning in my own chaos, my illness, my breakup with Matt, that I hadn't even noticed parts of Becca's life were moving on without me. I hadn't realized just how disconnected I had been over the last few months. More than that. I'd been a terrible friend when I started dating Matt. He was my whole world back then, and I'd spent more time with him than I ever did with Becca.

"I guess I missed a lot," I admitted.

"It's okay." Becca's voice was gentle now. "You've had a lot going on. Anyway, Logan's funny, a little broody, but ... you'll see. You'll like him."

"You're really selling this guy."

"Just wait."

"Does he know about me?" I asked, my voice faltering.

"No. No one knows except Jax."

Good. I wasn't ready to be *that* girl in their eyes. "Who else will be there?"

"Marcus," Becca said.

"Who's that?"

"Logan's best friend. He's a sweetheart. Super smart and caring. His mom died when he was young, and he and his brother got adopted separately. Honestly, I don't know how he's such a good person with everything he's been through."

"Sounds like you're crushing on him."

Becca grinned. "Not my type. He's into this guy on his baseball team. But the guy's straight."

"That's gotta suck."

"Yeah, but anyway, Marcus is a good guy. You'll see. They're all cool, Hazel. I promise."

I wanted to believe her. Maybe being around new people would distract me from everything I'd been through. But the thought of leaving my routine, my stability, still made me hesitate.

She took my hand again, her expression soft but insistent. "Please. You've had such a shitty year. Let me do this for you. I promise it'll be harmless fun. I got you."

And I knew she did. Even after everything—after my diagnosis, my breakdown, the times I shut her out—Becca had never given up on me.

I sighed. "Okay."

She squealed and pulled me into a hug. "Yay! We're gonna have so much fun! Oh, and bring your camera. You can take pictures of Jax and me by the fire ... or of Logan."

I laughed. "Or the mountains."

"Sure. That, too. But trust me, once you see Logan, you won't care about the mountains."

My stomach flipped at her words, but I rolled my eyes to hide it. "What is he, some kind of model?"

"No. But think Jacob Elordi meets Glen Powell. Dark and intense, but when he smiles, he's cocky in a good way."

My face grew warm. "Sounds out of my league."

"Hazel Marie Williams. Don't you dare think you are not worthy. Don't let Matt's stupidity make you think you're less. You're amazing. Don't forget that."

"Thanks," I mumbled.

"Anytime. Now, we gotta pick out your outfits for the week!"

I rolled my eyes, but a small smile tugged at my lips. Ever since she'd gone to Paris to study fashion abroad during our junior year summer, Becca had been treating me like her personal Barbie doll. I let her because it made her happy, even though it was just another reminder of all the things she had that I didn't.

I was happy for her, truly, but the truth was, I'd been jealous. Paris was everything Becca loved: bright lights, art, beauty, a world full of possibilities. I couldn't afford Paris. I couldn't even afford to dream about it.

But as I watched Becca's excitement spill over like it always did, I wondered if this trip to the mountains could be my Paris. Maybe it wouldn't change everything, but maybe, just maybe, it could change something.

For now, I would let her plan my outfits, because for the first time in a long time, I felt like I had something to look forward to.

Friday

Chapter Two

I had never been one to fear the unknown, even though my mind sometimes played tricks on me. But the faint, creepy laughter I kept hearing sent goosebumps rippling down my arms. I couldn't ignore it.

"Do you hear that?" I asked Casey.

"Hear what?" he mumbled from the center of my bed, his face lit by the glow of his Nintendo Switch. His fingers danced over the buttons, his teeth clenched in frustration.

"It sounded like a laugh. Was it from your game?"

"Not unless zombies laugh," he said without looking up.

I tried to shake off the creeping unease, turning back to my suitcase. "Maybe I'm just hearing things again."

"You should get that checked out."

"Funny," I muttered, though the comment reminded me to pack my medicine. Casey always had a way of making me feel normal, like hearing things wasn't some huge deal but simply another part of me. He never treated me like I was fragile. I was just his big sister who could take a joke.

The laughter sounded again, faint and distant, raising the hairs on the back of my neck.

I froze, glancing toward the hallway. "Seriously, Casey, you don't hear that?"

"Nope."

I narrowed my eyes at him, knowing he loved trying to scare me, but he was still staring at his game.

I couldn't shake the unease. As I resumed packing, I kept an ear out for the sound, folding flannel shirts and tucking my hiking boots into the suitcase. Becca had convinced me that spending a week in the mountains over fall break was exactly what I needed, but the thought of leaving my routine, leaving Casey, still gnawed at me. Would I really be okay for a week? Closing my eyes, I took a deep breath. The medicine had been working, and I felt good. And Becca would be with me. No matter what, she'd always had my back. And like Casey, Becca still treated me the same. She never tiptoed around me. This week would be good.

I checked the time on my phone. 1:46pm. *Good.* I still had time to finish packing before Becca picked me up.

Cramming my makeup bag into my overnight pack, I mentally checked "makeup" off my list. *Don't forget medicine.* I grabbed it from my dresser and put it into the bag, then tossed my current romance book into the top of my suitcase. I grabbed the camera I'd inherited from my grandmother, excited to take shots of the beautiful landscape. Finished packing, I stood up, brushing a few strands of hair from my face.

"Do you really have to go?" Casey asked.

"It's only for a few days," I said, more to reassure myself than him. *Did I remember my brush? Medication?*

"I wouldn't go this week," he said, his eyes still glued to the Switch. He shifted onto his knees and then flopped back down on the bed, a habitual move when he was immersed in gaming. He cried out again in frustration.

"Why don't you play something else? Or go play in your room?" I said, trying to keep my frustration in check.

Casey finally paused the game and looked up at me, his wide eyes filled with energy. "But I like it here! And I'm almost about to beat the boss!"

I rolled my eyes but couldn't help the small smile that tugged at my lips. Casey always managed to find a way to be both annoying and endearing at the same time. "Fine, just ... try to be quieter, okay?"

"Okay!" he chirped. "I still wouldn't go this week. Full moon and all."

I laughed, but the unease lingered. "What's that supposed to mean?"

"Weird stuff always happens with a full moon. And a week in the mountains during a full moon? That's just asking for trouble."

"You've been watching too many scary movies," I teased, though his words stuck with me.

Casey shrugged, muttering boss-fight strategies under his breath as he flopped onto his stomach. "What if some guy with a mask comes and terrorizes you?"

"You've *definitely* been watching too many scary movies. Maybe it's time for some Disney."

"Disney's for babies," he scoffed.

"No one's too old for Disney," I said, brushing his wild chestnut hair back affectionately. "Maybe I'll meet a sexy werewolf. Then he can turn me into one, and I'll come back all hairy."

Casey made a face of mock disgust. "You'd make a terrible werewolf."

"Why?"

"You're too nice." He grinned. "And you're scared of everything."

"I am not!" I lunged at him, tickling his sides. He squealed with laughter, squirming away from my grip.

As I pulled back, catching my breath, the eerie laugh sounded again, louder this time, and unmistakable.

I froze, staring toward the door.

Casey sat up, wide-eyed. "You heard that, right?"

I nodded.

Another noise. A thumping, like heavy footsteps crossing the living room floor. My pulse quickened, each beat thudding in my ears.

I hesitated at the edge of my room. "Mom?" I called out, but the muffled sound of her music from her room drowned out my voice. Mom was getting ready for her date, completely oblivious.

I turned back to Casey, still sprawled across my bed with his game. "Stay here," I said, trying to keep my voice calm.

Creeping down the hallway, my heart raced with every step. It wasn't a big house. There weren't many places someone could hide. But the shadows seemed longer than usual, stretching into dark corners where they didn't belong.

I reached the living room and scanned the space, my eyes darting to every shadow, every inch of darkness. Nothing. My gaze drifted to the kitchen, and I let out a frustrated sigh.

The counter was a disaster: an open loaf of bread, jars of peanut butter and jelly with their lids discarded, and a butter knife sticky with jelly. Most of the cabinets and drawers were open like Casey had torn through them in a frenzy.

"Seriously, Case? You left a mess," I yelled.

"Sorry." His voice floated back lazily.

Shaking my head, I started putting things away, my movements brisk and irritated. The normalcy of cleaning steadied me for a moment. Maybe I'd imagined the thumping noise.

Then came a knock at the front door.

I froze, my hand hovering over the jelly jar.

The knock was deliberate, loud enough to cut through the stillness. I glanced at the microwave clock. It blinked an hour behind, because no one had bothered changing it to daylight savings time. Becca wasn't supposed to be here yet.

My mind flickered to Gary. Maybe he'd arrived early to watch Casey. Or was it someone else?

Crossing the room, I approached the door slowly, each step making my pulse pound harder. I hesitated for a moment before swinging it open.

"You're—" I started, but the doorway was empty.

I blinked, stepping out onto the porch. The air was cool and crisp, carrying the faint scent of damp leaves and pine. The late afternoon sky was a muted gray, the kind that hinted at an early sunset. No cars. No footsteps. Just an empty stretch of road and the soft rustle of wind through the trees.

Frowning, I shut the door and locked it, unease settling over me like a heavy blanket. I made my way back to my room.

"Casey?" I called.

Silence.

I poked my head into his unlit room. The bed was empty, the Nintendo Switch abandoned on the covers.

"Casey, where'd you go?"

My irritation was giving way to worry, but before I could call out again, I heard the laugh.

It echoed through my room, faint but unmistakable. High-pitched. Mocking.

A shiver crawled up my spine as I stepped inside. "Casey, this isn't funny!"

Something cold brushed against my ankle.

I glanced down, and my heart leaped into my throat.

Hands. Pale, thin hands clawing at my legs, their grip icy and desperate.

A scream ripped from my throat as I stumbled backward, crashing into the wall. My chest heaved, my vision swimming as I stared at the floor where the hands had been.

Nothing.

Chapter Three

Laughter erupted from beneath the bed as Casey and Becca crawled out, their amusement clear in the gleam of their eyes.

Becca doubled over, clutching her sides. "You should've seen your face!" she wheezed, barely able to get the words out.

Casey giggled uncontrollably beside her. He was clearly overdue for a ban on horror movies.

Relief washed over me, quickly replaced by annoyance. "I'm going to kill you both. Becca, how did you even get inside the house?"

Becca wiped a tear from her eye, grinning. "I knocked on the front door and then climbed in through your bedroom window. Casey was more than happy to let me in."

I shot a glare at Casey, but my lips twitched despite myself. "And the creepy laugh?"

Casey held up his phone, still giggling. "It's an app. You can play scary sounds and all kinds of stuff. I got you good!"

I rolled my eyes. "Yeah, you did. Congrats."

Becca squealed and threw her arms around me. "I'm so excited for this week!"

"Me, too. Just no more pranks, okay?"

"Scout's honor," she said with a mock salute.

"You ready?"

"Yeah." I swung my bag onto my shoulder.

Casey groaned. "What am I gonna do for a week without you?"

"Like you'll even notice I'm gone with that game. I'll text you when I get there." I kissed his forehead. "Say hi to Gary for me."

"I'll take good care of her, monkey," Becca said, ruffling Casey's wild hair.

"Mom!" I called, cracking open her bedroom door. The music blaring inside was deafening. "I'm leaving!"

"Okay! Have fun."

As we headed outside, Becca pulled me into another hug. "A whole week!" she squealed.

"Yep, just don't let me regret it," I teased, though nerves prickled at the edge of my excitement. Meeting new people wasn't my strong suit, but I needed this. A break from school, home, and everything that weighed me down.

Becca's tiny car was surprisingly clean. The usual clutter of chip bags and water bottles was gone, replaced by a cheerful duck with a disco ball dangling from the rearview mirror. A rainbow of scrunchies decorated the gearshift.

"Did you clean your car for me?" I asked, sliding into the passenger seat.

"Maybe," she said with a grin.

The engine roared to life, and electronic dance music blasted through the speakers. The bass vibrated through my chest.

Becca turned down the volume and backed out of the driveway. "Whoopsies."

"Still love this noise, huh?" I cringed.

"Don't judge me. You're the reason I'm not boring, you know," she said, merging onto the interstate.

Our friendship had always been a balancing act. In first grade, we were teased mercilessly for our matching *Sesame Street* lunchboxes—her with Elmo, me with Cookie Monster. But somehow, we'd survived it together. Becca always said I gave her the confidence to be herself, but the truth was, she'd done the same for me.

Becca switched the music to Taylor Swift, which wasn't my favorite but at least didn't make my ears bleed. "This weekend is gonna be lit." Her excitement was infectious, even as my own nerves lingered.

"I hope so," I said, watching the trees blur past the window.

"What's up with Casey begging you not to leave?"

I shrugged. "I dunno. Probably just wants a normal week. He's not used to me being gone this long." At least not since my hospitalization.

"What's he gonna do when you go to college?"

Another shrug. I didn't know if I'd be going to college. Most of the subjects in school didn't interest me. My lack of motivation led to mediocre grades. And missing a lot of days lowered my grades even more. I couldn't afford college without a scholarship, and neither could my mom. Recent events made me certain that no college would want me anyway.

"Knowing your mom, she'd probably send Casey off to college with you," Becca laughed.

Becca's laughter was infectious; it resonated with the energy of the EDM concerts she loved. I went with her once, and that was all I could handle. Hundreds of people. Bright, flashing lights. Bodies dancing. Scantily clad girls. Glowing sticks and whips. But Becca thrived in that environment. She moved with a natural grace, embodying the rhythm of the music. She always lived life to the beat of her own unapologetic drum, one of the many reasons I loved her. Becca always attributed her energy to me because if it wasn't for me, she said, she probably would've been too afraid to show off her Elmo lunchbox and too afraid to be herself.

The Blue Ridge Mountains were only two hours north of my house, but I'd never been. As we drove along the winding roads, the world seemed to slow down, allowing me to soak in the beauty of the fall afternoon. There was something magical about the way the sun filtered through the trees and the way the leaves glided through the air. I felt a sense of nostalgia and a calm, and a new certainty that I'd survive the breakup with Matt and other things.

To the right, a gap in the dense thicket allowed me to catch a fleeting glimpse of the majestic mountains that stretched out in layers of red, orange, and gold, their rich colors rivaling any postcard. I grinned, my heart swelling with happiness. "Wow."

"It's pretty, isn't it?"

"Why haven't we done this before?"

Becca shrugged.

The last time I'd spent any time away from home was when I was in the hospital. The thought hovered in my mind as Becca drove, the hum of the engine lulling me into uneasy reflection.

The trees blurred past the window, their shadows stretching long across the road in the late afternoon light. I shifted in my seat, staring at my hands. The trip was supposed to be a break, but part of me couldn't shake the fear of leaving the fragile routine I'd built for myself. The last time I'd let everything spiral, it ended with sirens and an ambulance ride.

The memory crept in before I could stop it—the night of the graduation party in June.

Matt had ghosted me weeks before. Mom was spending as much time away from home as she could. And then the blow from the school counselor: I wasn't graduating.

All of it had broken me.

Becca had begged me to go to the party, so I did, hoping to see Matt, hoping to fix everything. Instead, the night had crumbled around me. Matt ignored me. Becca and Jax fought. And when Oliver kissed me, Matt exploded.

I ran after him, apologizing, begging. But he just walked away, leaving me standing alone, choking on my own humiliation.

The day after the party, I had gone into a spiral, staying in bed all day watching TV, ignoring my phone and locking my door so no one would bother me. Including Casey. I listened to sad songs on repeat, feeling gross and pathetic. I felt like I'd ruined everything. Like I was a failure. I had let everyone down.

The shadows in my room stretched long into the corners, and every creak of the house seemed to grow louder, sharper. I sat on the edge of my bed, clutching my knees to my chest, convinced that someone, or something, was watching me.

Then, Gary knocked on the door, his voice muffled through the wood. "Hazel? Dinner's ready."

I flinched. Was it really him? My chest heaved, my pulse racing. *What if it's not him? What if it's them?*

The second knock made me bolt to the door, yanking it open.

Gary stood there, his face etched with concern. "What's wrong?" he asked.

"They're watching me," I whispered, my eyes darting over his shoulder, scanning the shadows.

"There's no one here," he said gently. But I couldn't believe him.

The house had become a prison, every sound a threat, every shadow an enemy. I tried to explain, but the words tangled in my throat. My mind spiraled faster and faster until it all became too much.

Hours later, the paramedics came, their voices calm but distant. I barely remembered being led to the ambulance, but the sight of my reflection in the hallway mirror had stuck with me. My pale face, my wild eyes. I barely recognized myself.

"Hazel?"

Becca's voice jolted me back to the present. I blinked, realizing the car had stopped. The grocery store loomed ahead, bright and bustling.

"Logan said we're in charge of snacks, paper towels, and coffee," Becca said, cutting the engine.

The store was packed, noise and movement pressing in from all sides. My chest tightened as I tried to focus on Becca weaving through the aisles ahead of me.

This week was supposed to be different. I wasn't going to let my past ruin it.

"I'll grab the paper towels," I mumbled, barely meeting Becca's eyes before slipping away.

Navigating through the sea of shoppers, I kept my head down, to avoid the overwhelming chaos of people darting around me, gripping the handle of the shopping cart like it was the only thing keeping me steady. My hands trembled slightly as I reached the paper towel aisle and grabbed the first rolls I saw.

As I waited for Becca near the front, I found my gaze wandering to the community bulletin board. Flyers cluttered the space. Ads for pottery classes, dog walking, local festivals. But my eyes locked on the section I always tried to avoid: missing child posters.

My stomach twisted. Casey had gone missing once. Not for long, but long enough to terrify me. He'd just been at a friend's house down the street, but for those few hours, I'd imagined the worst. The fear of not knowing had been paralyzing.

One poster caught my attention. A girl exactly my age had disappeared ten months ago in January. I swallowed hard, a chill creeping down my spine. Did she run away? Was she kidnapped? Killed? The questions clung to me like cobwebs, impossible to shake.

"Ready?" Becca's voice jolted me, pulling me out of my thoughts.

I nodded quickly, tearing my gaze away from the posters and following her outside.

The rest of the drive to the cabin wound through tunnels of autumn leaves, their vibrant colors glowing in the late afternoon sun. Becca hummed along to the radio, the music a steady backdrop to my thoughts. I tried to focus on the scenery, but my unease from the store lingered like a shadow.

As the road climbed higher, the cabin came into view, perched on a hill and bathed in warm sunlight. It was beautiful, almost postcard perfect.

Becca pulled into the gravel driveway, parking next to two cars already there.

My gaze drifted over them, and my breath caught when I recognized one.

The smile slipped from my face, replaced by a heavy, sinking feeling in my chest.

Frozen, I stared at the car, my pulse quickening. All hope of a happy, relaxing week vanished in an instant.

Chapter Four

"Is that—is that *Matt's* car?" My heart raced.

Memories of our painful breakup flooded my mind.

Becca let out a sigh.

"Did you know he'd be here?" I looked at her in disappointment and shock.

"No. I swear I didn't know."

I crossed my arms and let out a bitter laugh. "I'm not staying."

"Come on. We just drove two hours to get here. The best way to get over this is to act like it doesn't bother you. The second you leave, he'll have won."

I knew Becca was right, and I hated it. I hadn't seen him since the day he dropped by my house unannounced and said he was sorry he never visited me in the hospital. Sorry I didn't graduate. Sorry, but he had to break up with me, because our paths were going in two different directions and we really needed time apart. Or something stupid like that.

"Besides, Jax really wants to see you. And Logan and Marcus want to meet you." Becca nodded at the two guys playing cornhole in front of the house.

I tried to push down my anger, knowing I needed to put on my game face.

As Becca emerged from the car, she yelled, "Who's ready to party?"

The dark-skinned boy laughed and shook his head. "Of course, you are."

While Becca jogged toward the two guys, I got out of the car and grabbed my bag and the items from the store. I meandered after Becca while gawking at the enormous cabin. It was bigger than my house, though that didn't mean much, since a lot of houses were bigger than mine.

Towering, ancient trees enveloped the cabin, their leaves ablaze with vibrant fall colors. Sunlight filtered through the dense foliage, dappling the ground with a mosaic of light and shadow. A thick carpet of pine needles and leaves covered the ground, offering a soft and silent pathway through the woods. I inhaled the sweet scent on the air—pine, earth, and the occasional waft of wood smoke.

I reached the three of them and stood idly by as Becca gave both boys a hug.

"This is Marcus." She motioned toward the dark-skinned boy. "And this is Logan."

Logan stood tall, holding a red plastic cup in one hand and a cornhole bag in the other, and a genuine smile lit up his face. His short, dark hair was tousled in that effortless way guys seemed to pull off without trying.

"I've heard a lot about you," Marcus said. "Glad you could make it." He had a warm and expressive face, with dark brown eyes.

"Yeah. Becca's told me a bit about you guys too."

"All good things, I hope," Marcus said.

"Like I would ever say anything bad about either of you."

Logan extended his hand, his eyes, a captivating gray, locked onto mine. "Nice to finally meet you, Hazel. Becca's told me a lot about you."

Becca shot a mischievous glance at me.

I shook Logan's hand, a polite smile on my lips. "Yeah. She talks a big game."

He chuckled. "She said only the best things, I assure you. Here, I'll take that bag." He had a charming and alluring smile, with a confident curve of his lips.

While Marcus went to the car with Becca to grab her luggage, I bit my lip, trying to push the stupid butterflies out of my stomach.

"You okay?" Logan asked. "Did Becca's crazy driving make you sick?"

I let out a small laugh. "No. It's nothing. Just didn't know my ex would be here."

"Wait, who?"

"Matt."

"Damn." He paused. "Becca didn't mention it?"

Shocked, I snapped my eyes to him, my mouth agape. *Becca knew?* "No."

"Sorry." With a glimmer of mischief in his eyes, he offered me his drink. "Warm apple cider? With a slight twist." He gave a sly grin.

I let out a defeated sigh. "Sure." I downed it, feeling the warmth of the cider tingle in my throat and the hint of alcohol settling nicely in my veins. I wasn't supposed to drink with my medication, but I was letting loose. What could it hurt?

His grin widened. "Let the games begin."

I playfully punched his shoulder.

"Come on. I'll show you the inside," he said.

I inhaled deeply and followed Logan toward the cabin door. Stepping inside, a cozy, open living space greeted me. The lingering fragrance of burning wood in the fireplace permeated the air. The place was astonishing. But I suppose that when your father is, or was, a professional baseball player, your finances are quite generous. Professional photos of scenic mountain views and wildlife adorned the walls. The floors, wide-plank wooden boards, creaked under my shoes. An enormous stone fireplace dominated one wall, the fire in it crackling and radiating warmth into the room. The furniture was a mix of handcrafted wood and comfortable, worn-in upholstery.

"Wow," I said. "How did you convince your parents to let us all stay here?"

"Please," said Becca, stepping through the door with Marcus. "He's got them wrapped around his finger. We've hung out here lots of times, and we all behaved." She batted her eyes.

"If you say so," Logan said under his breath.

Becca's laugh was quick, but it didn't quite land right. "Oh, come on. Don't make it sound like we trashed the place or something." Her voice was light, but there was a strain to it, her smile too wide, too bright.

Logan's gaze lingered on her, his expression cool. The silence stretched between them for a moment, charged with something I couldn't place. Finally, he turned back to me. "Anyway, there are eight bedrooms. Two downstairs, three on the main floor, and three upstairs. Each has a full bath. Game room is upstairs with a pool table and air hockey. Downstairs has a home theatre and hot tub."

His voice was steady, but the tension in the air hadn't dissipated. I could feel it pressing against my chest, making my stomach twist.

I glanced between them, sensing an unspoken history. Had something happened here? Something they weren't talking about? I felt like an intruder, as if I'd just walked into a private moment I wasn't supposed to witness. My gaze flicked to Becca, who was already moving on, her laughter coming too quick, too forced, as she walked farther into the cabin.

I hesitated, stealing a glance at Logan. His jaw was tight, his eyes following Becca for a second longer before he turned away without a word.

"You can take any bedroom, except the master," he said, his voice quieter now, almost resigned. "There are two open ones on the main floor." He hesitated. "Matt's upstairs, by the way."

The mention of Matt sent an unwelcome jolt through me, but I nodded, pretending it didn't. I spotted a door to my right. "Looks like I'll take this one."

Becca appeared at my side and gestured to the door across from mine. "Perfect! I'll be right here."

I stepped into the room and let out a soft breath. The rustic wooden scent hit me immediately, warm and earthy.

Then I looked up, and my jaw dropped.

The room enveloped me in a comforting golden light, accentuating the rustic yet elegant interior. A king-sized bed made of rich, dark wood dominated the space, its intricately carved headboard adorned with pinecone and leaf motifs. The soft light of the bedside lamps cast elegant shadows that danced across the walls, and the plush bedding looked so inviting that I had to resist the urge to sink into it immediately.

A stone fireplace stood against one wall, its presence grounding the room with warmth and charm. My gaze drifted to a cozy seating area near a large window, where two armchairs, draped with textured throws, flanked a rustic wooden table. The thick curtains softened the sunlight streaming in, and when I pulled them back, the breathtaking view of the dense forest stretched before me. Outside, a firepit surrounded by chairs added to the cabin's allure.

The room felt like a sanctuary, a retreat carved out of nature. For the first time in what felt like forever, I let my guard down, a small smile tugging at my lips. Becca might be overwhelming at times, but this moment made me grateful for her.

"Do you like it?" Logan's voice came from the doorway, pulling me from my thoughts.

I turned to face him, leaning lightly against the window frame. "Yeah, it's amazing."

He stepped farther into the room. "This is usually my room, but I figured I could take advantage of the master this week. Uh..." He gestured toward another door. "The bathroom's in here."

I followed as he flipped on the light. The bathroom was as luxurious as the bedroom, with tiled flooring, a marble countertop, and a glass-enclosed shower that gleamed in the soft light. Logan opened a closet, pulling out a neatly folded stack of towels.

"Here are towels and washcloths. Um ... there's extra soap and shampoo in here too," he said, glancing at me over his shoulder.

I smirked, tilting my head. "Are you trying to impress me?"

A faint blush crept up his neck, and he chuckled, rubbing the back of his head. "Just making sure you're comfortable."

I crossed my arms, raising an eyebrow. "You do this with everyone else?"

His blush deepened as he fumbled for a reply. "They've all been here before. Many times, actually." He paused, his gaze flicking to mine. "So ... what made you decide to come?"

I hesitated, unsure how much to reveal. "Becca insisted. Said I needed a break."

He nodded, leaning casually against the doorframe. "She's probably right. This place can be ... good for that."

There was something in the way he said it, a quiet sincerity that caught me off guard. For a moment, I thought he was going to say more, but he just offered a small smile and stepped back. "Anyway, let me know if you need anything."

"Thanks."

With a small nod, he left the room, his footsteps retreating down the hall.

As the door clicked shut, I exhaled, leaning against the bathroom counter. There was something about him, quiet and steady beneath the surface. And for the first time in a long time, I found myself wondering about someone in a way that I hadn't let myself do in months.

Shaking the thought away, I stepped back into the room, letting my eyes roam over the cozy interior. My gaze landed on a weathered wooden shelf tucked against the wall of the seating area. The shelves were neatly arranged, adorned with trinkets, framed photographs, and an assortment of books. But one book stood out.

Its leather cover was cracked and faded, its title barely legible. Unlike the others, which were perfectly aligned, this one leaned slightly out of place, as though it had been waiting for someone to notice it.

I hesitated, drawn to it for reasons I couldn't explain. The air felt heavier, like the room was holding its breath. When I reached out, a shiver ran down my spine, and my fingers brushed the worn leather.

Before I could grip it, the book slipped from the shelf and fell to the floor with a soft thud.

I froze, my breath catching in my throat. The room seemed unnaturally still, as though it, too, was startled.

I let out a breath and tried calming my racing pulse. *Okay, the book did not just fly off the shelf. I must've knocked it over.*

But even as I tried to rationalize it, the atmosphere in the room felt... different. I crouched down to pick up the book, carefully flipping it open where it had fallen.

The words on the aged paper seemed to shimmer in the dim light, as though they carried a weight that demanded attention. My gaze settled on a line that sent a chill through me: *"There are two ways of seeing: with the body and with the soul. The body's sight can sometimes forget, but the soul remembers forever."*

The quote sent a flicker of recognition through me, though I couldn't immediately place where I'd read it before. I frowned, glancing at the worn title pressed into the cracked leather cover. The letters were faint, but I could just make them out.

The Count of Monte Cristo.

Suddenly, the door burst open with a loud thump, the sound shattering the fragile quiet of the room.

I jumped, the book slipping from my hands again as my pulse spiked. Whirling around, I saw Becca standing in the doorway, her grin wide and unapologetic.

"Oops! Did I scare you?" she asked, feigning innocence.

I rolled my eyes, bending down to pick up the book again. "What do you think?"

She laughed, leaning casually against the doorframe. "I'm going outside to play cornhole. You wanna come?"

Her words barely registered. I placed the book back on the shelf, my hands lingering on the worn leather cover. My voice was steady, but my stomach twisted as I asked, "Why didn't you tell me Matt would be here?"

Becca's smile faltered. She sighed, biting her lip, her guilt visible in her expression. "I know.

I'm so sorry. I just ... I knew you wouldn't come if you knew he was here." She crossed the room, her tone softening as she took my hand. "But I promise we'll have fun. We'll have so much fun you'll forget he's even here."

I gave her a knowing look, raising an eyebrow. "Becca."

"I know, I know." She squeezed my hand. "I suck. It's just ... it took so much to convince you to come, and I really wanted to spend this week with you. You've been so stressed, and I thought this would be good for you. Forgive me?"

Her eyes pleaded, and I couldn't stay mad. Not really.

"Yeah," I sighed.

Becca squealed, throwing her arms around me. "Thank you! Come on, let's go play cornhole."

"In a sec. This place is incredible, though." I gestured to the room around me. "I can see why you like it here."

"Right?" Becca's face lit up again. "I love coming here. And I'm so glad you're here." She pulled me into another hug, this one tighter, as if trying to squeeze all her excitement into me.

"Me too." I pulled back. "How come you didn't tell me you'd been here before?"

Her smile faltered a little. "I did," she said, her tone overly casual. "I was here a couple of times this summer. Remember? And a few times last year."

I shook my head. "No. Has Matt been here before?"

"A couple of times."

Interesting.

Becca placed her hands on my shoulders, her tone more insistent now. "Don't spend any time thinking about that prick, okay? We're here to have fun." She paused, her grin returning. "And besides, looks like Logan's already trying to impress you. See? I *knew* you two would hit it off."

Heat rose to my cheeks, and I quickly looked away. "What are you talking about?"

"Oh, please." She laughed, nudging my shoulder. "Don't even try to deny it. He's already being all helpful and charming. Trust me, Hazel, he *never* does that for anyone."

"Becca," I warned, trying to keep my voice steady, but the way her words lingered in my mind made it hard to stay unaffected.

She kissed my cheek lightly and grinned. "I'll leave you to it. But don't make him wait too long." She winked and darted out the door before I could argue.

I sat on the edge of the bed, pulling out my phone. Casey's name popped up in my messages, and I typed out a quick update.

Me: Made it. Cabin's incredible.

Casey: Watch for bears and werewolves.

Me: Ha ha.

I set my phone aside, but my gaze lingered on the bookshelf. The book seemed to stare back at me, its crooked position now corrected. My fingers itched to open it again, but I shook the thought away.

Becca's teasing words echoed in my mind. *He never does that for anyone.*

I rolled my eyes, pushing the thought aside, and left the room. Instead of joining Becca outside, I wandered through the main floor, taking in my surroundings. The kitchen appeared as though it had been prepared for a *Better Homes & Gardens* photo shoot, complete with granite countertops and gleaming appliances. The view from the window was stunning. A seemingly endless expanse of mountains stretched out before me. October's foliage had burst into full autumnal splendor, vibrant oranges, fiery reds, and golden yellows painting the landscape.

I leaned closer to the window, pressing my hand against the cool glass. The colors were so vivid they looked like something out of a painting. My fingers twitched with the urge to grab my camera.

This is exactly the kind of thing Casey would roll his eyes at, I thought, smiling to myself. But I could already imagine the shots I'd take. Framing the radiating trees against the blue sky, capturing the way the sunlight filtered through the leaves like stained glass.

The sound of laughter echoed from upstairs. I froze. That laugh.

Twisting around, I looked up and spotted him on the landing. Matt. My stomach tightened, and a lump formed in my throat. He looked so carefree, as if our breakup was nothing but a distant memory. My heart sank further when I saw the dark-skinned girl clinging to his side. She kissed him lightly on the cheek, and his laugh deepened, the sound cutting through me like a knife.

I ducked into the main room, pretending to admire the colorful mountains beyond the windows. My hands gripped the edge of the sill, knuckles white.

Memories I had tried to bury came rushing back. I thought of the day Matt officially ended things with me.

I'd barely been home for two days after leaving the hospital. Everything still felt raw, like I was trying to piece myself back together with trembling hands. When his car pulled into the driveway, I thought maybe—just maybe—he was coming to fix things, to say he understood, that we'd get through this together.

But the Matt who walked up the steps wasn't the Matt I knew. His smile was forced, the usual warmth in his eyes replaced by something distant and cold.

"I wanted to see how you were doing," he'd said, shoving his hands into his pockets. "Becca told me you got out a couple of days ago."

"Yeah, I escaped through a window," I'd said, trying to make him laugh.

He sighed and rolled his eyes, his gaze skimming over me but never meeting mine. "I'm sorry I didn't visit."

"You wouldn't have wanted to see me in a straitjacket."

"Can you be serious?" he snapped. "Look, I came by to talk."

"That's never good."

"I can't do this anymore, Hazel."

The words had hit like a punch, knocking the air from my lungs. "Do what?"

"Us. I just think our paths are going in two different directions."

"Wait—you haven't said a word to me in two weeks, and now when you do, you're breaking up with me?"

"I figured you didn't want to be with me since you made out with Oliver—"

"I did not make out with him!" My voice rose, anger cutting through the hurt. "He kissed me all of a sudden. But you wouldn't know that because you never asked. You just assumed and ignored me."

"Haze, you're ... a lot. The ups and downs, the unpredictability. I just can't handle it anymore."

"You said you liked my unpredictability." Tears blurred my vision, but I refused to let them fall. "So what? You're just giving up? I'm working on it, Matt. You said—"

"I know what I said," he snapped, finally looking at me. His eyes were filled with guilt but also something harder, colder. "But it's not enough."

And then he was gone.

He left with his empty apologies, while I sat in that room for hours, his words echoing in my mind, crushing me under their weight.

You're a lot. You're too much.

Now, Matt's voice broke through the fog of memories, dragging me back to the cabin.

"Incredible, isn't it?" he said from behind me.

His voice used to have the power to melt me, but now it made my skin crawl.

"Yeah, it's great," I replied, forcing the words out. My lips felt stiff, and I couldn't bring myself to turn around.

"I wasn't expecting you here," he said, his tone light, as if we were nothing more than old acquaintances.

"Well, I'm here," I said flatly, keeping my gaze on the mountains.

"You look well. It's good to see you."

The words made me freeze. Confused, I turned to face him, my throat tight. "What?"

His messy light brown hair fell across his forehead. I imagined myself sweeping it back so I could see his warm hazel eyes.

Matt's expression softened, almost hesitant. "I just ... it's good you're not sitting at home this week."

I clenched my teeth, his audacity testing my patience. The nerve of him. He *knew* why I'd been sitting at home, why I'd been hospitalized, and now he had the gall to act like he was being supportive?

"Why would I be sitting at home?" I asked sharply.

"I mean ... given recent situations..." he started, but his words faltered as he realized his mistake.

"Seriously?" I spat, narrowing my eyes.

"I didn't mean you being locked—uh, getting care," he stammered, his face reddening as he stumbled over his words.

"Then what did you mean?"

"I just meant ... with us."

The anger bubbled up, mixing with sadness and confusion, forming a knot in my chest. "Don't worry, Matt," I said, my voice cold. "I'm over it."

"Hazel—"

"No. We didn't mean anything to each other. Isn't that what you wanted me to think?"

"That's not what I said."

"You didn't really say much of anything. Anyway, have fun." With a sense of newfound strength, I turned and walked away, leaving him standing there.

Chapter Five

Forcing a smile, I joined Logan, Marcus, and Becca in a game of cornhole. My laughter felt hollow as I tried to pretend everything was fine, but the image of Aniyah and Matt kissing clung to my thoughts like a burr. A reminder of how little I had meant to him, and how my best friends had hung out here all summer without me.

I blinked hard, willing the sting behind my eyes to fade. *Did I ever mean anything to anyone?*

I cried out after my third toss landed several inches from the board, missing the target completely. "I suck at this!"

"Just takes practice," Logan said, his voice calm and reassuring.

"Says the guy who can clearly throw with precise accuracy."

He laughed, a rich, easy sound that made something flutter in my chest. "Relax." He stepped closer. "Can I show you?"

I hesitated for a moment, acutely aware of Matt and Aniyah watching from the sidelines. Then I nodded. "Sure. Why not?"

Logan moved behind me, his presence both grounding and disarming. He gently took hold of my arm, his fingers grazing my skin with a lightness that sent a ripple of heat through me.

"Okay, like this," he murmured, guiding my arm through the motion. His voice was low, soothing, and I couldn't help but notice the warmth radiating off him.

The bag left my hand, sailing through the air and landing with a satisfying thunk right in the hole.

I turned to him, narrowing my eyes in mock suspicion. "See what I mean? That was all you."

Logan raised his hands in defense, his grin wide and teasing. "That was all you, girl. I just gave you a little nudge."

I rolled my eyes, but a smile tugged at the corners of my lips. The way he said "girl," so effortlessly charming, made me feel oddly giddy.

Becca groaned dramatically from across the lawn. "Oh, come *on*! Logan, stop being all smooth and let her mess up so Marcus and I can actually win."

Logan shrugged, feigning innocence. "I'm just being a good teammate. Can't help it if she's got natural talent."

I shook my head, laughing softly. His words felt too easy, like he'd said them a hundred times before to a hundred different girls.

When I glanced at Matt, I swore I saw something flicker in his eyes. Jealousy, maybe? He shifted in his seat, his jaw tight as he watched us.

The sight of him sitting there, arms draped casually around Aniyah, made something snap in me. If he wanted to look jealous, then fine, I'd give him a reason.

I stepped closer to Logan, brushing my hair back with a deliberately casual gesture. "So," I said, tilting my head up at him. "Any more expert tips, or was that the secret sauce?"

Logan smirked, his gaze steady on mine. "Depends. You think you can handle another lesson, or are you afraid you'll beat Marcus and Becca too badly?"

"Excuse me!" Becca called out, hands on her hips. "We're still very much in this game, thank you."

"Oh, I'm not afraid of beating them," I said, my voice lighter now, playful. "But I might need another nudge."

Logan chuckled, his eyes glinting with mischief. "Anytime, partner."

I smiled, though a small voice in the back of my head whispered doubts. *Becca probably asked him to be nice to you because of Matt. He doesn't actually like you. He's just playing along.*

But as Logan handed me another bag, his fingers brushing mine ever so slightly, I let myself ignore that voice. Even if it was just for the week, I decided I didn't mind playing along too.

When a Jeep pulled up behind Becca's car, I noticed Logan tense. His posture stiffened, and his jaw tightened as his gaze locked on the vehicle.

But my heart flipped. *Jax.*

The driver's door opened, and Jax stepped out, his auburn hair longer than I remembered, brushing the collar of his shirt. His defined jawline and five o'clock shadow gave him a rugged charm, but his green eyes still held that familiar glint of mischief. Jax's smile lit up his face, radiating warmth and tugging at something deep inside me, a reminder of how easy things had felt when we were kids.

Then the passenger door opened, and a pretty girl slid out. Her honey-blonde hair cascaded in loose waves nearly to her waist, and her blue eyes, bright and sharp, matched the dark button-down shirt she wore over a low-cut white top.

Becca froze, the bag she was holding slipped from her hands, and without a word, she turned on her heel and walked inside.

Marcus sighed loudly. "Why did he bring a girl?"

Logan crossed his arms over his chest, his lips pressing into a thin line. "Guess he couldn't help himself." His tone was clipped, the warmth I'd seen earlier replaced by something colder, sharper.

I glanced between Marcus and Logan, confused by their reactions. Was this about Becca? They had to be upset for her.

Jax and the girl made their way toward us, Jax's grin widening as he spotted me.

"Hazel!" he said, extending his arms as he reached me. "So good to see you. Miss me?"

"More than you know," I replied, stepping into his hug. His familiar warmth wrapped around me, a welcome reminder of home.

"We go way back," Jax said, pulling back and gesturing toward me with pride. "Since kindergarten." He turned to the girl beside him. "Everybody, this is Candace."

Candace gave a small wave, her smile polite but reserved. "Wow," she said, her voice light. "I've moved so many times I don't have any friends from that long ago."

I forced a smile, but my attention drifted back to Logan. His gaze remained locked on Jax, his expression charged with something I couldn't quite name.

"Nice to meet you," Marcus said flatly to Candace, with none of the warmth he'd shown me.

"Same here," Candace replied, glancing around, clearly picking up on the tension in the group.

Jax draped an arm casually around Candace's shoulders, his carefree demeanor in stark contrast to Logan's stiff posture. "So, what's the plan for the evening? Becca already running off to plot her victory in cornhole?"

Logan's lips twitched, but it wasn't quite a smile. "Something like that."

I couldn't ignore the weight in his voice, the way his eyes flicked back to Candace before returning to Jax. There was something going on here. Something I didn't understand.

"She just had to step inside for a bit," I said, trying to sound casual.

"Ah," Jax replied, his smile faltering for a split second before returning.

I forced a laugh and swatted Jax's arm. "You haven't texted me in ages." *Or told me about Candace.* But I bit that last part back, the thought landing heavier than I wanted to admit. It was another reminder that we weren't as close as we used to be. Maybe none of my friends wanted to be around me anymore. Had I scared them off with my breakdown? The thought dug into my chest, sharp and unrelenting.

I swallowed hard and tried to push the sadness away. I was there now with them. They'd invited me. That had to mean something, didn't it?

"I know, I'm sorry," Jax said. "School."

"Looks like college is treating you well," I said, glancing at Candace, and she blushed.

We laughed, and the worry I'd been carrying melted away. Jax's presence was a breath of fresh air, injecting a burst of energy into this week, except for how his bringing another girl hurt Becca.

We all started toward the cabin door. The sun was setting, casting long shadows, and the chill of evening crept into the air. The porch was lit with tall lamps and hanging bulbs, bathing the space in a warm, inviting glow.

"You're the last ones so you get to choose top or bottom floor," Logan told Jax and Candace.

Knowing Becca would be moody the whole trip, I had a strong hunch I'd be spending the week babysitting her. Again. With a sigh, I made my way to her room, the weight of it already settling on my shoulders. Inside, she was sprawled on the bed, scrolling through her phone with the kind of intense focus that screamed she was trying not to think.

"You okay?" I asked gently.

She rolled her eyes but lowered the phone, and I caught the shimmer of unshed tears clinging to her lashes. "Can you believe him? He led me on. Kept telling me how excited he was to see me," she said, her voice breaking slightly.

I eased onto the edge of the bed. "Maybe he *is* excited to see you. Aren't y'all friends?"

Her glare could have cut glass. "Friends?" she scoffed, as if the word tasted bitter.

"He didn't mention Candace?" I asked cautiously, already knowing the answer.

"No!" she snapped, sitting up abruptly and jerking her bag onto the bed.

"We aren't leaving," I said firmly, leaning back on my elbows. If I had to endure Matt and Aniyah, Becca could handle Jax and Candace.

"No, we aren't." She yanked out tops and tossed them into a haphazard pile. Her energy crackled, a storm brewing just beneath her skin.

"What are you doing?"

She glanced at me with a fire in her eyes. "I'm gonna make sure he sees what he's missing."

I arched an eyebrow. "Really?"

"Did you see her? She even looks like me." She rolled her eyes.

I hesitated. Besides their hair color, I didn't think they looked anything alike but pointing that out would only stoke the flames. Becca didn't want logic, she wanted validation.

She ripped off her T-shirt and swapped it for a crop top that left her midsection bare, then turned to her reflection in the mirror, reaching for her makeup bag.

"Maybe you should heed your own advice," I said, watching her apply mascara with precision born of determination. "Move on."

She froze, the mascara wand hovering mid-air. Her eyes flicked to mine in the mirror, dark and defiant. "I love him. He's my person."

There it was. The line she clung to like a lifeline, even as it dragged her under. I bit back a retort and forced myself to nod. "Okay."

I gave up. No matter what I said, Becca would never listen. She thrived on the chase, on the drama, on the illusion that she could make Jax love her the way she wanted him to. She'd had other boyfriends, sure, but they'd all been props in the same tired play. None of them mattered. Only Jax did.

Pushing myself off the bed, I glanced at her one last time. "I'm gonna go back outside."

"I'll be there soon."

As I turned to leave Becca's room, a faint sound caught my ear. A whisper. I froze in the doorway, my breath hitching as I strained to hear it again. It was so faint I almost convinced myself it was nothing, just the wind or a creak of the old cabin. But then, there it was again—soft, urgent, like someone calling my name.

"Hazel..."

I spun around, my eyes scanning the room. Becca was still by the mirror, oblivious, brushing her hair. I forced a laugh to shake off the prickling unease. "Did you say something?"

She glanced at me through the mirror. "No. Why?"

"Nothing," I mumbled, retreating quickly. My heart thudded in my chest as I moved down the hall, glancing over my shoulder. I told myself it was all in my head, but the faint whisper lingered in my ears as I stepped outside.

I walked out onto the deck, where laughter rippled through the crisp night air. Jax must've been telling one of his stories. Everyone's expressions lit with amusement, their voices blending with the soft crackle of the fire. The scent of charred marshmallows and woodsmoke hung in the air.

I settled into a chair, leaning back just enough to catch a glimpse of the darkened sky above me. Countless stars scattered across the vast expanse, like shards of broken glass flung across black velvet. I'd never seen so many, each one twinkling in quiet defiance of the shadows that surrounded them. The moon hung high and proud, its face mostly illuminated but still clutching a sliver of shadow, reluctant to bare itself completely. A waxing gibbous, only a few days from full glory. I chuckled softly, shaking my head as Casey's absurd fear of the full moon drifted through my mind.

The sound of Becca's arrival pulled me back to the present. She stepped onto the deck, radiating the kind of confidence she wore like armor. I didn't miss the way Jax's gaze followed her, a flicker of longing in his expression. Even Candace noticed, her smile faltering just enough to make me wince. Poor girl.

Logan handed me a skewer and passed a marshmallow to me.

I carefully speared the marshmallow, holding it just above the flames. Within seconds, it was ablaze, a tiny fireball of sugar and shame.

Logan burst out laughing and handed me another one. "Try again," he teased. "This time, aim for toasted not torched."

I shot him a playful glare as I blew out the flaming marshmallow and swapped it for a new one. But, true to form, the second marshmallow met the same fiery demise.

"Maybe I'm just too hot to handle," I joked, nudging him with my elbow.

"Or maybe you need a little help from a marshmallow expert. Have you done this before?"

"Nope."

"What? Never?"

I shrugged, a little embarrassed but mostly amused by his reaction.

Logan shook his head dramatically. "I'm gonna need more marshmallows." He stood and headed inside.

"I'll come with you," I said, standing. I needed a drink if I was going to survive the night.

The warmth of the fire faded as we stepped into the cool, dimly lit kitchen. The hum of the refrigerator and the faint creak of the wooden floors were the only sounds as Logan rifled through the pantry.

"I bought a ton of marshmallows. Where the hell did they go?" he muttered, shifting boxes around with increasing frustration.

While he searched, I moved to the counter, grabbing a plastic cup and reaching for the cider. As I poured myself a drink, I heard someone enter the kitchen.

Looking up, I was face-to-face with Matt's girlfriend. She was my age, with long black dreads, warm brown eyes, and flawless skin that made me instinctively touch my own face. Of course she'd have perfect skin. Of course.

She smiled, her presence radiating confidence. "Hey, I'm Aniyah. You must be Hazel."

There was a split-second pause before I forced a polite smile. "That's me."

Aniyah stepped farther into the room, her gaze sweeping over the kitchen before landing back on me. "Matt's told me a lot about you."

My chest tightened at his name. I kept my expression neutral, gripping my cup a little tighter. "Has he?"

"Yeah. He told me you're a great photographer. That must be fun."

"It can be."

"Are you going to take photography classes when you get to college? Matt told me you'd gotten held back."

I clenched my teeth, trying not to react. *Thanks for announcing it to the world.*

"It's a beautiful cabin, Logan," Aniyah continued, glancing toward him with an easy smile. "I didn't know your dad was a baseball player. How cool is that?"

"Super cool. We got free peanuts at games, so, you know, perks."

I snorted, unable to help myself. Logan grinned at me over his shoulder.

"Finally." He pulled a bag from the pantry. "Found them. Might be expired, though. Think they're still safe to eat?"

"Let me know how that works out for you." I smirked.

He shrugged. "Good enough for me. Come on. Let's go make s'mores without setting anything else on fire."

I giggled, falling into step behind him, but as we reached the door, Aniyah stopped me with a light touch on my arm.

Logan, oblivious, kept walking leaving me alone with her.

Our eyes locked, and I gripped my cup tighter. "Can I help you?"

Aniyah smiled, leaning casually against the counter. "Look, I'm sorry things didn't work out with you and Matt. But you need to move on. It's been six months."

The words hit like a slap. My grip tightened, my knuckles whitening. "Six months?" I echoed, my voice faltering. The math churned in my head. He'd told me he needed space, but he didn't break up with me until after I got out of the hospital which was only four months ago. My stomach twisted as the jagged pieces fell into place. When Matt said he needed space, it wasn't about us. It was about her. I'd spent two months clinging to hope, blaming myself, thinking I was too much, too broken. Two months of waiting, while he'd already moved on.

Aniyah's syrupy smile didn't waver. "Time flies when you're with the right person. He told me about the messages you've been sending him. I can't stop you, but we love each other. He's not in love with you."

Messages? My chest tightened. "What messages?" I managed. I hadn't sent him any. Had I?

She tilted her head, her expression soft and condescending. "It's okay. I know you still love him. Breakups are rough, but things don't have to be weird between us."

"Sure," I forced out, the word scraping against my throat.

Aniyah studied me a moment longer before pushing off the counter. "Well, I'm sure we'll get to know each other better this week," she said lightly, as if she hadn't just shattered my world.

"Yeah, I guess we will," I murmured.

With one last smile, she walked out, leaving the room steeped in silence.

The timeline replayed in my mind, cruel and precise. *Six months.* He'd already been with her when he told me he needed space. And when my life fell apart, when everything crumbled, he'd been with her.

My stomach churned as I rushed to my room, my breath shallow and ragged. I barely managed to shut the door before the emotions spilled over. Gripping the sink in the bathroom, I squeezed my eyes shut, trying to steady the chaos in my chest.

I pulled out my phone and scrolled to Matt's name. The last text I'd sent him was June 18. Four months ago. My hands trembled as I stared at the screen. Had he lied to Aniyah? Or had I somehow sent messages I couldn't remember and deleted them?

I took a long sip of my drink, the bitterness biting as hard as the betrayal. Matt had been lying to me. For months, I'd carried the weight of blame, thinking the breakup was my fault, that I was too erratic before my diagnosis.

Maybe I was still the problem. Maybe … maybe it still was my fault.

I swallowed hard, forcing the tears back. I wouldn't let this break me. Not here. Not now. Staring at my reflection, I willed the redness in my cheeks to fade. My fingers raked through my chestnut-brown hair, yanking at the knots in frustration. My amber eyes caught the light, their warmth now sharp against my flushed skin.

I turned on the faucet and splashed cold water onto my face, grounding myself in the sensation. As I reached for the towel, I glanced up at the mirror and froze.

There was a girl behind me, her dark hair falling across her face.

My heart jumped, and I spun around with a gasp. "Sorry—"

But the girl was gone.

My breath caught as I scanned the bathroom, then my room. Nothing. No one. But I knew what I'd seen. A girl, clear as day.

Fuck. Had I imagined that? *It's just stress.* Or was it?

Chapter Six

"Where have you been?" Becca asked when I spotted her in the kitchen. Her sharp eyes scanned my face. "Have you been crying?"

Leave it to Becca to notice. I ducked my head, hoping no one else had overheard her. "You were so right about Matt."

"Ugh. What did he say now?" She refilled her drink.

"Apparently, he and Aniyah have been together since April."

Becca's eyes widened. "What?"

"Yeah." I tried to sound detached, but the bitterness crept into my voice. "I just need to get through this week. Then I can avoid them forever."

"What a dick." She leaned against the counter, her lips pressing into a thin line.

"She also said Matt told her I'd been sending him messages."

"Have you?" She gave me a knowing look.

"No, Becca," I snapped, annoyed at the implication. "I haven't."

"Okay, okay." She held her hands up. "Just had to make sure. Do you think he lied to her?"

"Who knows? He's lied about a lot of things, apparently."

Becca stepped closer, looping an arm around my neck in a loose hug. "Don't let them win." Her voice carried a firmness that reminded me of why she was my friend, even when she drove me insane. The words hung in the air, grounding me, reminding me that I *was* strong. I could get through this.

Once outside, I settled into the empty chair next to Logan.

"There you are." He flashed me a grin that somehow made the tension in my chest ease just a little. He reached for a skewer, sliding a marshmallow onto it before handing it to me. "Here. Try not to burn it this time."

I took the skewer with a small smile, settling the marshmallow over the flames. The fire crackled and danced in the pit, throwing flickering shadows across the group and painting their faces in shades of amber and gold.

Jax was mid-story, his voice dipping low as he built tension in his scary tale.

For a brief moment, I focused on the fire, the way its heat brushed against my skin, the way the flames consumed the wood with a quiet ferocity. It felt oddly grounding.

But then my gaze wandered across the circle and landed on Matt. He was completely engrossed in Jax's story, his hand intertwined with Aniyah's. The sight of them together sent a fresh wave of anger surging through me, hot and unrelenting.

I tore my eyes away, focusing instead on the marshmallow that was just beginning to brown. I could feel Logan's gaze on me, and when I looked up, he raised an eyebrow.

"Want me to handle that before you set it on fire?" he teased.

I managed a weak laugh and shook my head. "I've got it."

Though Logan didn't push, a fleeting worry crossed his face before he returned his gaze to the fire.

"And then she screamed, and the ghost slashed her throat," Jax finished, his voice low and dramatic.

Candace and Aniyah squealed, their faces twisting in mock disgust. Candace clung to Jax's arm, while Becca silently refilled her drink, her expression unimpressed.

"Why so gory?" Candace asked, wrinkling her nose.

"Scared?" Becca teased, leaning forward with a sly grin. "All kinds of weird stuff happens in these mountains. Hope you survive the night." Her smile was as fake as her innocence, and I nudged her, catching Candace's frown.

"I have a story," I quickly said.

Marcus raised his eyebrows. "Alright. Let's hear it."

I leaned forward, letting the firelight flicker across my face. "It happened on a night just like this—drinks, marshmallows, friends. There was a howl that started it. Everyone jumped, but Henry assured them it was just a wolf. Still, as they fell asleep, a scream pierced the night, followed by another howl. Drew went to check it out. Then another scream. One by one, they vanished, leaving Diana alone. She knew she had to kill the wolf to survive. She grabbed a gun and a lantern from the cabin, heading into the cold, dark woods.

"No sound but the pounding of her heart. Then, a growl behind her. She spun, gun ready, but it wasn't a wolf. It was Henry. Hair began sprouting across his skin, bones snapping and reshaping as his face morphed into a wolf's: sharp ears, long fangs, glowing yellow eyes. And then ... he licked her cheek and panted."

A burst of laughter erupted.

"Ugh!" Becca threw a marshmallow at me. "You read too many of those stupid werewolf romances."

I laughed, dodging the marshmallow. "Had you all going, though."

"Not as good as when Casey and I got you earlier," Becca quipped.

I rolled my eyes.

"Ah! I missed a prank on Hazel?" Jax leaned back, feigning outrage. "Damn. We used to prank her all the time. She's super easy to scare. One time, Becca hid in a trashcan and jumped out.

Hazel screamed so loud I thought the neighbors would call the cops."

Becca let out a bellowed laugh. "I forgot about that!"

"Remember when we'd go hang out in the woods by our houses?" Jax asked.

I narrowed my eyes. "And Becca and I caught you and Aaron with *Playboy* magazines and beer out there."

Becca doubled over laughing. "Oh my god, I forgot about that. You were, what, ten or eleven?"

"I have no idea what they're talking about," Jax said, grinning at Candace.

"Please." Candace rolled her eyes. "I'm sure you were just as much of a playboy as all the boys at that age."

"All boys are innocent," Marcus claimed.

A barrage of marshmallows pelted him in response, drawing laughter all around.

Logan shook his head, leaning forward. "Alright, I've got a story to top all yours."

"We're listening," Becca said.

Logan nodded toward the cabin, his face lit by the fire's glow. "My dad told me this one about our cabin. Years ago, a young woman named Eleanor lived in a nearby village. She was engaged to a man she loved deeply, but on the eve of their wedding, he vanished. Heartbroken, Eleanor searched everywhere for him, convinced he'd been taken by something supernatural. One night, she came to this cabin ... and never returned.

"A search party found her wedding dress floating in the lake, but her body was never recovered. They say her ghost, still in her tattered wedding dress, wanders the lake, knocking on cabin doors and whispering her fiancé's name. If you hear her, it means she's chosen you to help her. But anyone who tries to help ... disappears. My dad heard her knock on our door one time, but he refused to answer."

A sharp knock echoed through the night. The sound startled me, Candace, and Becca into gasps, while Aniyah let out a full-blown shriek.

Logan's laughter filled the air as Matt walked out from the cabin, grinning mischievously. "Just me."

"Man. Your freaking cabin is haunted?" Jax asked.

Matt chuckled, pulling Aniyah closer. "You scared?"

Becca grinned at Jax. "Don't worry, I'll protect you."

I didn't miss the glare Candace shot Becca.

Logan's smirk was quick, but there was a flicker of something colder in his eyes as he glanced at Jax. "You might need it. Who knows what's lurking out here. Some things go missing and never come back." His voice was light, almost casual, but the weight of his words settled heavily in the air.

Jax's jaw clenched briefly before he forced a grin. "Maybe. But at least I'm not going to jump at every knock on the door."

The group laughed, but a silent tension hung between Logan and Jax.

"Whelp, I'm not getting any sleep tonight," Marcus said, trying to lighten the mood.

"You guys are such babies," Becca said.

"Babies?" Jax shot back. "I remember when you cried the day you left for Paris."

The group erupted into laughter, the lighthearted banter continuing. But as the others started sharing stories, I couldn't help noticing Logan. He was staring at the fire, his jaw tight, his usual playful demeanor replaced by something more guarded.

I leaned toward him, lowering my voice. "You okay?"

Logan blinked, his focus snapping back to me. For a second, I thought he might actually say something, but then his lips curled into a small, practiced smile. "Yeah, I'm good," he said, his tone light, though it didn't match the tension in his shoulders. "Just tired of Jax's stories. They get worse every time."

I gave him a look, letting him know I wasn't buying it, but I didn't push. "Sure."

He shifted in his seat, then skewered another marshmallow and held it over the flames. He grabbed some graham crackers and chocolate, quickly assembling a s'more before handing it to me. "Here. Since you keep annihilating my marshmallows."

Rolling my eyes, I took the s'more, our fingers briefly brushing. "Thanks." I bit into it, but my attention lingered on him. Our eyes locked, and my stomach fluttered, warmth spreading to my cheeks. I quickly looked away, focusing on the s'more.

"So, Hazel," he said. "What's your story? How'd you end up here?"

I met his gaze, a playful spark in his eyes putting me at ease. For a moment, I hesitated, wondering how much he already knew. Becca said she hadn't told him about me. "It's a long story," I said, offering a faint smile. "Life got all messed up, so now I'm chilling in the woods." I took another bite to avoid elaborating. "What about you? What's it like being the son of a pro baseball player?"

"It's fine." He shrugged. "Normal for me. Going to home games as a kid and watching him play was fun. It's nice having my dad home now."

"Does anyone ever give you crap about it?"

"Nah. People are decent about it, mostly."

"Lucky you." I sipped my cider. "You play too, right?"

"I do."

"Let me guess, pitcher?"

"Catcher."

"Damn. So, you're on your knees a lot. Doesn't that hurt?"

He chuckled, shaking his head. "You get used to it."

"I bet." I smirked, enjoying the way his grin widened.

"Becca told me you like photography. How'd you get into that?"

"Oh." I hesitated, caught off guard by his interest. "I kinda stumbled into it. When my mom and my brother's dad, Gary, were still together, we went to this coastal town once. My grandma gave me a camera, and I started taking pictures of sunsets, seashells, random locals. It was the first time I realized how photos could tell stories or capture moments you don't want to forget. I think I knew even then that their marriage wouldn't last, and I wanted to hold onto something real. Like fragments of time, you know? Memories suspended."

Logan stared at me. "Wow."

My cheeks flushed. "I sound like such a nerd." *More like an idiot.* I sipped my cider, trying to hide the embarrassment.

"No, it's cool." He leaned closer, his tone lowering slightly. "You sound passionate. That's rare."

My cheeks warmed, and I looked down at my drink. "Thanks."

"Have you ever taken pictures of sports?" he asked.

"Not really. Maybe I could take some of you."

"Me?" He chuckled. "I'm not exactly photogenic."

"Somehow I doubt that." I studied his face, the firelight casting shadows and highlights across his features. The sharp angles of his jaw, the warmth in his eyes—it was the kind of face a photographer dreamed of capturing.

He caught my look, and his lips curled into a slow smile. "You've got a great smile."

Another blush. "So do you."

"You know what could be cool for photos? Catching the sunrise from one of the mountain peaks. There's this spot—a bit of a drive and a hike, but it's totally worth it."

I perked up, my interest piqued. "Really? I love photographing the first light. It's like the world wakes up differently each time."

He grinned. "I've done it before. The view is incredible. Watching the world come alive... It's like nothing else. I could take you."

My excitement surged, but a flicker of caution crept in. I barely knew Logan. The idea of heading to a secluded mountain with him gave me pause. "Um ... I don't know."

He nodded, his expression remained relaxed. "I get it. But it's not just us. It's a group thing. Kind of a tradition."

Becca groaned. "Are you seriously talking about your sunrise adventure again?"

"Yep."

"Yeah, hard pass. I'm not waking up that early."

"We'll go," Jax said, glancing at me. "You'll love it."

Becca shot him a look. "Since when do you go?"

Jax smirked. "I've been before."

Relieved by the idea of others joining, I smiled. "Okay, count me in."

"Awesome." Logan's smile widened, his gaze lingering on me for a moment longer. "You'll love it. I promise."

As the night continued, the crisp scent of pine mingled with the anticipation of the sunrise excursion, heightening the excitement around the firepit. I couldn't tell if it was the alcohol or if I genuinely began to feel a connection with Logan. I already imagined the photographs I could capture and the memories we would share under the canvas of a mountain sunrise. Or maybe I was getting too far ahead of myself. Wouldn't be the first time.

"I'm getting another drink. Any takers?" In a blissful haze, I gracefully stood up, my body tingling with delight as the warmth of the alcohol enveloped me, filling me with pure happiness.

"Ooh, yeah!" Becca handed me an empty cup. "This cider is seriously good."

As I stepped into the kitchen, the soft glow of the refrigerator illuminated Matt, who was probably scouring the fridge for a late-night snack. I used to find his perpetual hunger endearing.

"I talked to your girlfriend," I blurted out, the alcohol fueling my courage.

Matt straightened up, closing the fridge door. "Okay?"

"She's ... interesting." I crossed my arms. "Said you two were in love. So ... how long has it really been going on?" I already knew, but I needed to hear him say it. Maybe just to punish myself.

His jaw tightened. "Don't act like the victim. You're not exactly innocent."

That hurt. "I was sick, Matt."

"You know that's not what I mean."

"Then what? How is it my fault?"

He ran a hand through his hair. "You know damn well what I'm talking about. Oliver."

I clenched my teeth. "I didn't make out with him. He kissed me. You *saw* it."

"You didn't push him away. What was I supposed to think?"

"Maybe believe me?" I shot back, anger tightening my chest. "But no, you had to twist it around. Meanwhile, you were already sneaking around with Aniyah. She told me everything, Matt."

His expression flickered. "That's not true. Aniyah and I didn't start anything until after we broke up. We were done, Hazel."

"Were we?" I snapped. "Because we didn't break up in April, and she said you two have been together since then. You lied to me."

He glanced away, the silence heavy. "It's complicated."

"Whatever." I grabbed a bottle of liquor from the counter and turned toward the exit.

"You always leave when things get tough."

I halted and turned around. "*I* leave? *You* left the second things got tough. You let me believe everything was my fault—my diagnosis, Oliver—when you were already with her. You never even tried to understand. And what messages have I supposedly been sending you?"

His head snapped up. "What?"

"She told me *you* said I'd been texting you, begging for you back."

"I never said that."

"Oh, so now *she's* lying?" I let out a sharp, humorless laugh.

He scrubbed a hand over his face. "Hazel, I don't want to fight with you."

"No, of course not. Because that would mean admitting what you did." My grip tightened around the bottle of liquor, fury burning through me. "You *cheated*. And instead of owning up to it, you let me believe I was the one who ruined everything."

"That's not what happened."

I shook my head, disgust twisting in my gut. "Keep telling yourself that."

Without waiting for his response, I turned and walked out, slamming the door to my bedroom behind me. My hands trembled with leftover rage.

Matt had seen Oliver kiss me, yet he still blamed me. He had been with Aniyah for months, but I was the one who had to answer for something I never did.

And the worst part?

For months, I had let him blame me.

I hated how easily he could get under my skin.

Starting a conversation with Matt had been a mistake. I'd wanted him to feel uneasy, to carry even a fraction of the pain he'd caused me. Instead, I was left grappling with doubt. Had I remembered it wrong? My head spun, the alcohol dulling the ache but not the weight of the past year pressing down on me.

Coming this week had been a mistake. I should've listened to Casey. I unscrewed the bottle and took a sip.

There was a knock at the bedroom door, then Jax appeared. "You okay?"

I shrugged. "You heard all that?"

"Yeah." He frowned, lowering himself onto the bed beside me. "I thought those two were a bit chummy before you broke up, but he kept denying anything was going on. Also, Oliver ... that dude from the graduation party? That was true?"

I rolled my eyes. "We didn't make out. He kissed me."

"Well, he seems to like you."

I smacked his arm. "So, Candace. How long?"

A smile tugged at his lips. "A couple of months. I like her."

"Hate to do this, but ... what about Becca?" I passed him the bottle.

He took a swig, then let out a long breath. "We don't work. We always fight."

"I just meant why bring Candace if you kept telling Becca you were excited to see her?"

"I *was* excited to see her. As a friend."

I couldn't blame him, but Becca wouldn't see it that way. "She really thought you two were getting back together. You should talk to her."

"I will." He draped an arm around my shoulders and gave them a squeeze. "Look, Matt's a jackass. You're better off without him. I know that sounds cliché, but it's true."

"If I'd known he and Aniyah were here, I wouldn't have come."

"But then you wouldn't have gotten to see me." He grinned.

I returned the smile. "True."

"It's really good seeing you," he said. "How ... have you been since. . .."

My breakdown.

"I've been okay. Going back to school was a little tough."

"Yeah, Becca told me a little."

I narrowed my eyes. "Why didn't you just ask me instead of getting it from Becca?"

"I suck. I know. College has been hectic, but that's not an excuse. I should've made time. I'm sorry."

"Even before you left, you seemed distant." I hesitated. "Or maybe it was me. The months leading up to everything are ... fuzzy."

"No, you're right. I was distant. There was a girl. Not Candace."

"Oh? Who?"

He shook his head. "Doesn't matter."

"You can still talk to me."

He took another sip of liquor. "Noticed you and Logan flirting."

My lips curled into a small smile. "Yeah. He seems nice."

Jax exhaled, rubbing a hand over his jaw. "Just ... be careful."

I studied him. "Why?"

"He's messed up. Got a lot of personal issues. I don't trust him." Jax turned to face me.

"Then why are you here?"

"To see you."

I arched an eyebrow. "Bullshit."

His jaw tensed. "It's nothing. I'm probably being overprotective. Just ... if anything feels off, trust your instincts."

The way he said it, the way he *wouldn't* meet my eyes made my stomach knot.

I watched him carefully. "Did something happen between you two?"

Jax hesitated, then shook his head. "It's not like that."

"But there *is* something."

His jaw tightened, and I could see the struggle behind his eyes, the war between what he *wanted* to say and what he *could* say.

"I just don't trust him," he finally said. "That's all."

I didn't buy it. "Does Becca know? Because she's the one who wanted me to meet Logan."

Jax frowned. "Why?"

"She thought he'd be good for me."

He sighed. "I don't know why Becca brought you."

The words landed like a gut punch. *No one wants me here.* Were they afraid I'd lose control again? "Maybe because she thought I needed some fun, Jax."

"No, Haze, I didn't—"

"You should go."

"I didn't mean it like that."

"Then what *did* you mean?"

His mouth opened, but nothing came out.

Realizing that my buzz was wearing off, I handed him the bottle. "Here, just go. I'm gonna shower."

He let out a sigh and stood. "I'm sorry. We'll have fun tomorrow morning. I promise."

I gave a short nod, focusing on that instead of everything else gnawing at me. When he left, I grabbed my toiletries bag and pajamas.

I waited for the water to warm, steam curling through the air, fogging the mirror. As I started the shower, the soft patter of water filled the bathroom, its rhythmic sound lulling me into a brief moment of peace. I stepped inside, letting the warmth cascade over me, washing away the tension coiled in my muscles. The water wrapped around me like a comforting hug, the only thing that didn't feel complicated.

But as my body relaxed, my mind did the opposite.

Matt's words replayed, sharp and bitter. Jax's cryptic warning about Logan. His disappointment that Becca invited me at all.

How could he be so protective when he'd barely spoken to me all year? And what girl was he talking about? I hadn't known Jax to date anyone this year. Or last. Becca would've told me. *Or maybe not.* Maybe I had been so lost in my own world that I had become unreliable. Maybe that's why they hadn't wanted me here.

The thought made my throat tighten.

"Leave."

I froze.

The voice was faint, distant, almost drowned beneath the rushing water. My stomach clenched.

Slowly, I reached for the fogged-up glass door and peeked out.

The bathroom was empty. Steam coiled in thick tendrils, distorting the shadows, but nothing was there.

"...Becca?" My voice was barely above a whisper.

Silence.

Swallowing hard, I shut the door and turned back into the spray, shoving the unease aside. *Just my imagination.* The alcohol was messing with me. I submerged my head, and the water coursed down my skin. My muscles loosened, the warmth seeping into me, and I forced my thoughts to drift. I was over Matt. *I am over him.* Yet...

A long sigh slipped from my lips, the steam wrapping around me like a second skin.

Get through the week. That was the goal. *Survive Becca's drama. Survive Matt.*

Another deep breath. Another attempt at peace. I opened my eyes.

And choked back a scream.

The water had darkened, swirling into a deep, sickening red. Blood.

I stumbled back, my breath coming in quick, shallow bursts. My gaze darted down—no wounds, no cuts. I twisted, scanning my arms, legs, stomach. *Nothing.*

The showerhead sputtered. A harsh, wet gurgle.

Then the water exploded into thick, crimson streams.

It coated the shower walls. Splattered against my skin.

A strangled cry escaped my throat. I lurched for the handle, slipping against the slick tile, barely catching myself. My lungs heaved, panic clawing up my throat. I blinked against the steam, trying to force my brain to make sense of what I was seeing.

Then, as suddenly as it had come it was gone.

Water poured from the showerhead. Clear. Harmless.

My pulse thundered in my ears. I pressed a trembling hand to my chest, my breath shallow and unsteady. Not real. *Not real.* But it *felt* real.

I stumbled out of the shower, nearly collapsing against the counter. My shaking fingers fumbled with the cap of my prescription bottle. I forced it open, tapping a pill onto my palm before dry swallowing it.

Had I been drinking too much? Or ... was I losing my mind again?

I gripped the edge of the sink, my damp hair clinging to my face, my breath still uneven.

I wasn't hallucinating. I *wasn't*. I repeated the thought, but the doubt gnawed at me, deep and insidious. Because if it wasn't real...

Then what the hell had I just seen?

Chapter Seven

Muffled explosions filtered through the walls from the main room. Someone was playing a video game. I walked to the window, glancing outside at Becca, Marcus, Matt, and Aniyah laughing around the fire pit. Becca threw her head back, smiling, but I knew her well enough to see through it.

At least she was trying.

I wanted to join them, but the thought of seeing Matt again made my stomach twist. My emotions were stretched too thin tonight. Instead, I leaned against the window, letting the cold glass press against my skin. The air outside looked damp, clinging to the night in a way that sent goosebumps rippling over my arms. I wanted to build a fire, but I didn't know how.

Instead, I pulled on my hoodie and grabbed my book from my bag. Reading had always been my most reliable escape. I grabbed a blanket from the closet and eased into the comfortable chair next to the window, cradling the book in my hands, the soft glow of my bedside lamp casting long shadows against the walls.

The world inside the book wrapped around me, its words pulling me far from the tension lingering in this cabin. I traced the rough edges of the pages, each turn a quiet comfort. Outside, stars dotted the night sky, glinting like distant fireflies, while the moon cast a pale glow over the landscape. The play of light and shadow had a strange comfort to it.

I could get used to these cabin retreats. Without all the drama.

A loud crash shattered the silence.

I flinched, and my heart lurched. The sound came from the kitchen. Glass breaking. I rolled my eyes. Someone must've knocked over a cup.

But then I realized something.

The sounds of the video game were gone. No chatter. Just silence. I glanced at my phone. 2:37 AM. I hadn't realized it was so late.

Pulling my hoodie tighter around me, I opened the door. A thick, inky darkness stretched before me, swallowing the hallway. The air felt heavier, colder. My thumb hovered over my phone screen before I flicked on the flashlight. A narrow beam cut through the dark as I stepped forward.

As I reached the kitchen, my foot kicked something, and I looked down. Shattered glass.

What the hell? Someone broke something and didn't even clean it up?

Shaking my head, I switched on the kitchen light, its glow flooding the space. The room was empty. The air held a chill, seeping through the cracks of the cabin.

I moved toward the closet, pulling out the broom. It was too quiet. I shivered, blaming the lack of heat. My fingers gripped the handle tighter.

As I swept up the glass, a whisper of cold traced down my nape, light as spider legs.

I froze.

Slowly, I glanced over my shoulder. No one.

But the sensation didn't fade. And that feeling like being watched.

My breath hitched. The broken glass gleamed, catching the light in jagged, unnatural patterns. The floor creaked beneath me as I swept, each feeling unbearably loud against the silence pressing in.

I forced myself to finish, dumping the shards into the trash. Closing the broom closet. Turning off the light.

The darkness folded in again.

I quickened my steps down the hall, pulse hammering in my throat. Once I reached my room, I shut the door with more force than necessary. My heart pounded against my ribs.

It was just my imagination.

Wasn't it?

Saturday

Chapter Eight

The alarm pierced through the quiet of the room, and I groaned, burying my face in the pillow for a moment. I dragged myself out of bed. The morning air bit at my skin, a stark contrast to the warmth of the blankets. 5:30 AM. Too early for most things. But the thought of capturing the sunrise from a mountain peak sent a flicker of anticipation through me.

Rubbing sleep from my eyes, I grabbed my camera and gear. Logan, Jax, and Candace were already in the kitchen filling thermoses with coffee and packing snacks. Their faces wore the familiar mix of determination and sleepiness that came with an adventure at dawn.

My eyes landed on Logan. For a second, my pulse stuttered, catching on the way the dim kitchen light framed his sharp features, his tousled hair still slightly messy from sleep. The easy way he moved, like he belonged anywhere he stood. The warmth that settled in my chest was unexpected but not unwelcome.

"I made some tea for you." Logan handed me a thermos, his fingers briefly brushing mine.

I furrowed my eyebrows. "Thanks. How did you know I liked tea?"

"Becca."

Candace yawned. "It's so dark outside."

Jax smiled, pressing a kiss on her forehead. "Won't be for long."

I had to admit, they were cute together. And so far, one night and no fights. Quite the opposite of him and Becca.

I hesitated for a moment before speaking. "Someone broke a glass last night."

Logan's brow furrowed. "I was wondering why there was glass in the trash."

"Yeah, I heard it and cleaned it up."

Candace frowned. "They just left it?"

Jax clicked his tongue. "Some of us were pretty drunk last night."

Logan and Candace headed toward the door, but Jax lingered, catching my arm lightly.

"I'm really sorry about what I said last night," he said. "I was drunk and didn't mean you shouldn't be here. I *am* glad you're here. I just don't know why Becca would want to set you up with Logan."

"Why?"

Jax hesitated, as if debating how much to say. Then, finally, "You deserve someone better, Haze."

I frowned. Was Logan really the issue or was it me?

Jax nudged me toward the door. "Come on."

We stepped outside into the pre-dawn darkness, the crisp mountain air striking my face. As we approached Logan's truck, he opened the door for me, waiting until I climbed in before shutting it behind me. The small gesture sent another unexpected flutter through me.

Sleepy banter and the occasional yawn filled the truck as we drove, the rhythmic hum of the road lulling us into a comfortable silence. I stole glances at Logan, watching the way the dashboard lights cast soft shadows along his profile. His hands gripped the steering wheel with an ease that made it seem like second nature.

I wanted to capture it. That quiet focus. The way the dim light made him look almost unreal.

But I didn't want to distract him.

Logan skillfully parked in a designated spot, with the truck engine humming its last note. As I climbed out, my breath curled in the cold morning air, visible against the thick fog that still clung to the mountains. The darkness stretched around us, but the first hints of dawn were already painting the horizon.

Something about the moment—the chill, the quiet, the slow shift from night to morning—felt like the beginning of something.

I just wasn't sure what.

Led by Logan, we began our hike. The forest canopy enveloped us as we started our ascent. Tall trees, their leaves a vibrant palette of autumn hues, formed a natural cathedral above the trail. The morning mist, a delicate veil draped over the forest, carried subtle hints of pine and Fraser firs from the nearby woods.

I inhaled deeply, letting the crisp air fill my lungs. "Smells like Christmas," I murmured.

"Oh gosh, it does." Candace smiled.

Up ahead, Logan came to an abrupt stop and pivoted, his gaze scanning the surroundings. A peculiar smile played across his face. "Do you guys hear that?"

I stilled, straining my ears. Nothing.

Not the rustle of leaves. Not the distant call of a bird. Just an eerie absence of sound, thick and absolute, pressing in from all sides.

"I don't hear anything," I said.

Logan's smile deepened. "Exactly. It's incredible."

I'd never thought silence could be so beautiful.

Distracted by the quiet, I barely noticed the uneven terrain beneath me until my foot caught on a hidden root. My body lurched forward, the ground rushing toward me.

A strong hand wrapped around my wrist, steadying me just before I could fall.

I blinked up at Logan.

His fingers were firm but gentle, his grip unwavering. "Careful," he said, amusement flickering in his eyes. "I'd hate to lose my best photographer before we even get to the view."

Heat crept up my neck. "I was just testing your reflexes."

"Good to know I passed." He held onto me for a second longer before finally letting go, and I swore I could still feel the warmth of his touch as we continued our climb.

With each step, the world gradually revealed itself, the mist thinning, unveiling the magic that awaited at the mountain's crest.

The trail led us to a meadow bathed in the soft glow of the emerging sunrise. The world stretched before us in quiet splendor, the morning sky shifting from indigo and violet to soft pinks and fiery oranges. The mist melted away like a dream, revealing golden grasses swaying in the crisp breeze, their tips catching the first light.

I exhaled, awestruck.

The mountains, once dark silhouettes against the night, slowly revealed their rugged details, bathed in warm, golden hues. It was the kind of beauty that felt almost untouchable, like a moment you could step into but never fully hold onto.

With my camera in hand, I lifted it, the quiet *click* of the shutter breaking the stillness. I took photo after photo, knowing full well that no image could ever truly capture the way this felt.

We found a perfect vantage point in the meadow, settling onto a patch of soft grass.

I continued snapping pictures, lost in my own world, until I felt eyes on me. When I turned, Logan was watching me.

His coffee rested loosely in his grip, his expression unreadable, yet there was something in his gaze that made my stomach flutter. A slow grin tugged at his lips, as if he was studying me, amused.

"What?" I asked, self-conscious under his stare.

"Nothing." He took a sip of coffee, his smirk lingering. "Do I get to see these photos, or do you just hoard them in a collection?"

"You wish you could be in my collection."

His low chuckle sent a small shiver down my spine. "You don't even know."

I glanced at him through the lens, my heart doing a little flip when I caught the teasing look in his eyes. The way the sunrise softened his features, the golden glow catching in his tousled hair, made me wish I *could* capture this moment. I snapped a few photos.

Jax cleared his throat loudly.

I flinched, breaking eye contact with Logan as Jax flopped down next to me, slinging an arm lazily over my shoulder. "Come on, Haze. If you're gonna take pictures, at least get my good side."

I snorted. "You don't have a good side."

"Rude." He dramatically clutched his chest. "Candace, defend my honor."

She giggled. "She's kinda right, though."

Jax dropped his arm from around me, turning his attention to his girlfriend. "What the hell?"

Candace leaned into him, kissing his cheek. "I'm just keeping you humble."

Logan smirked, his gaze flickering to me, before taking a slow sip of his coffee. I wasn't sure what to do with the heat simmering in my chest—whether it was from the sunrise or the way Logan had been looking at me before Jax cut in.

"This place is incredible," I said, trying to steady myself.

Candace nodded. "Yeah, it really is."

Jax leaned back on his elbows. "It's pretty in the winter, too."

Logan's smile vanished. His entire body tensed, his grip tightening around his cup. His jaw twitched. A fleeting expression of anger or pain crossed his face before he regained his composure, but I'd already seen it.

Jax caught it, too, because he held Logan's gaze, his own expression calm but pointed.

The tension between them pressed into the air, sharp and unspoken.

I shifted my weight, suddenly hyperaware of the space between them. The pieces weren't fitting together. Jax's warnings, Logan's reactions, the quiet friction neither of them fully acknowledged.

What had happened between them?

I turned away, my fingers tightening around my camera as I snapped a few more shots of the sunrise, pretending I didn't feel the weight of the silence that had settled over us.

I wished I could share this moment with Casey.

I lowered my camera. "Thanks for bringing me here," I said to Logan.

He glanced at me, his posture relaxing slightly, like he was letting go of something. "Yeah, no problem. I've had a good time."

A small smile played at my lips as I looked away, focusing on the beauty before us instead of the mystery between Jax and Logan.

For now.

When I entered my room, the faint sound of running water reached my ears. The shower?

A chill crawled down my spine as I stepped into the bathroom. The sink faucet was on, water streaming steadily into the basin, swirling before disappearing down the drain.

Had I left it running all day?

I shook my head as a wave of shame settled in. *I can't believe I did that. I'm such an idiot.*

With a sigh, I twisted the faucet, shutting the water off.

I needed a shower. The hike had left me sweaty and gross, and the day's emotions clung to me like grime I couldn't scrub away. But as I reached for the shower handle, I hesitated.

The memory of blood pouring from the spout flashed in my mind.

It wasn't real. I was drunk.

I inhaled deeply and turned on the water.

The pipes groaned, but when the water gushed out, it was clear.

Normal.

The knot in my stomach loosened slightly. I stepped in and let the warm water wash away the dirt and exhaustion. But it couldn't completely rinse away the unease prickling at the edges of my mind.

I tried to focus on something else. Something good. The morning. The way the colors bled into each other as the sun rose. The scent of pine and damp earth. The easy laughter. The way Logan had looked in the golden light, his tousled hair, the way his lips had curved when he teased me.

My heart did a little flip. I shut my eyes, exhaling, letting the moment sink in.

After I got out of the shower and dried my hair, I reached for the doorknob. It wouldn't turn. I frowned and tried again, twisting harder. It wouldn't budge. My stomach dropped.

I yanked the handle, but the door didn't move. My pulse quickened. It wasn't locked. I was *sure* I hadn't locked it. Then, a shadow shifted in the crack at the bottom of the door.

Someone was standing on the other side.

I swallowed. "Becca?"

No answer.

My breath hitched, and suddenly, the small bathroom felt suffocating. I pulled on the knob, harder this time, frustration turning to panic.

"This isn't funny! Let me out."

No response.

I pounded on the door. The TV was blasting in the main room. They couldn't hear me.

I pressed my ear to the wood, listening. The air beyond the door was thick with silence, yet the unsettling feeling of someone *waiting* on the other side slithered through me.

In a last attempt, I clenched the doorknob once more, bracing myself for the familiar resistance. But this time, it turned effortlessly. The door swung open, and I stumbled into the room, my breath ragged, my hands shaking.

My head snapped up, ready to confront Becca.

But the room was empty.

No one was there.

Chapter Nine

The bathroom door must have been old, or maybe Becca really was trying to prank me. I wasn't sure. Either way, I didn't feel like questioning it anymore.

Sitting cross-legged on the bed, I scrolled through the pictures I'd taken earlier. Each image brought back the crisp morning air, the scent of fir trees, the way the sunrise melted across the mountains. Logan had been right. It *was* beautiful.

A small smile tugged at my lips as I stopped at a picture of Jax and Candace. Jax was kissing her temple, and her eyes were closed, a peaceful smile stretching across her face. It was the kind of photo that *felt* like a memory, one they'd look back on years from now.

Then I swiped to another picture—Logan.

His profile was cast against the fading stars, the sun's orange light bleeding into the sky behind him like a melting candle. His eyes, though, were what held me captive. There was something in them. Lost? Pensive? Sad? I wasn't sure, but it sent a shiver down my back.

My heart thumped.

I stared for a second longer than I should have before voices from the living room pulled me back. I turned off the camera and stood.

I wanted to show Jax and Candace the picture, but I knew Becca would get upset.

Shaking the thought away, I made my way into the main room, where everyone except Logan, Matt, and Aniyah was gathered around the TV, taking turns playing *Mario Kart*.

"Hey, you've missed me kicking everyone's ass," Jax said, leaning back with a smug grin.

I shook my head. "I was just looking at my pictures."

"Oh, can I see them?" Candace asked.

"Yeah." I handed her the camera and sat beside her on the couch.

"Boom!" Marcus yelled. Large ink blots covered Becca's side of the TV thanks to Blooper.

"Oh! You are *so* dead, Marcus!" Becca said.

"I need a better car," he groaned, gripping his controller.

"Dude, you've changed cars *four* times now," Jax said.

I watched Candace flip through the photos while Jax and Becca argued about the game. "Where's Logan?" I asked, only half-expecting an answer.

Jax's gaze flicked to mine for half a second before Marcus replied, "He went for a walk."

My stomach dipped. "Did he go with Matt and Aniyah?"

"Nah, he went by himself," Marcus said, eyes glued to the screen.

By himself? I frowned but let it go. "Oh. I wanted to tell him that I think the bathroom door is broken or something. It wouldn't open earlier."

"Doors are tricky sometimes," Jax teased.

"Or maybe Becca was pranking me."

"Hey!" She spun toward me, her character flying off the track. "I've been out here the whole time. Besides, that'd be a *weak* prank."

Marcus let out a triumphant yell as his player crossed the finish line. "*Boom!* Two in a row, baby. Ready for round three?"

Becca shoved his shoulder, muttering something about pure luck.

"These are amazing pictures, Hazel," Candace said, handing the camera back to me.

I shrugged. "Thanks."

"What do you look for when taking pictures?"

I hesitated, surprised by the question. "Well ... I try to capture moments that make me feel something. That tell a story. I love finding beauty in things that people don't always notice—expressions, angles. Interesting shots that capture the true soul of the subject."

Candace smiled. "Wow. That's amazing. I wish I had a hobby like that."

I ran my fingers along the camera strap. "I think I just like freezing time. Preserving memories. I dunno, it's comforting."

"Hazel's always had a camera," Jax said. "She takes great pictures."

I rolled my eyes. "I *enjoy* it. That doesn't mean I'm great at it."

"Do you want to be a photographer?" Candace asked.

"Yeah, maybe."

The conversation drifted into easier topics, and the afternoon melted into night. The glow of the TV bathed the room as Jax, Becca, and Marcus continued playing, their voices rising in playful banter. Eventually, Jax switched over to a football game, settling in comfortably with Candace curled against him. I let myself relax, sinking into the couch. But even as I laughed along with the others, my mind drifted back to Logan. Where had he gone? Did it have something to do with Jax?

The door creaked open, and Logan walked in, his face etched with fatigue and his clothes coated in dirt.

I stilled.

His hair was damp with sweat, and his jacket was dusted with dried leaves. Like he'd fallen. Or run into something.

I raised an eyebrow, my curiosity sparking. "Are you okay?"

Logan paused mid-step, surprised. His eyes flickered with a moment of hesitation before he offered a tired smile. "Yeah. Just needed some fresh air."

Jax scoffed. "Didn't get enough this morning?"

Logan met Jax's gaze.

I frowned. The tension between them was palpable, no longer a lingering feeling, but a thick, heavy presence.

"What happened?" I asked, studying Logan's face.

He exhaled, shrugging off his coat. There was a faint scrape on his forearm. "Got a bit carried away exploring in the woods. Tripped and fell, you know how it goes."

Something in the way he avoided my gaze sent a warning bell through me.

His explanation was too casual. Too rehearsed.

Jax leaned back on the couch, stretching his arms behind his head, but his eyes never left Logan. "Yeah," he said slowly. "Happens all the time."

Logan didn't reply. Instead, he disappeared into his room, closing the door behind him.

A few minutes later, he emerged, freshly showered, his damp hair curling slightly at the ends. His clothes were clean, the evidence of whatever had happened in the woods rinsed away, but the tension remained.

The comforting crackle of the fire filled the air, mixing with the soft hum of laughter from the others. The heat licked at my skin, but a different kind of warmth settled beside me. Logan.

He sat rigidly, staring into the flames, his fingers curled tightly around his beer bottle. The firelight danced in his eyes, but instead of flickering with amusement or relaxation, they reflected something else. Something heavier.

I followed his gaze directly to Jax. A sharp pang of unease tightened in my chest. "You okay?"

Logan blinked, like I'd yanked him from deep thought. His grip on the bottle loosened slightly as he turned toward me, forcing a small smile. "Yeah, just got a lot on my mind, you know?"

"Oh." I hesitated. "You can talk to me if you want."

His smile softened, genuine but distant. "Thanks. I just need some time to figure things out."

I nodded, but a strange awkwardness settled between us. Had I said something? Done something? Or ... had someone else?

I glanced toward Matt, wondering if he'd made some offhand remark, but Logan's focus remained on Jax. The same weirdness I'd picked up on that morning crept in again, more obvious now. Logan's jaw was tight, his posture stiff, his beer untouched.

Why had he disappeared after the hike?

I didn't understand the shift in Logan, how yesterday he'd been flirty, teasing, relaxed, and now, he sat there like a rubber band pulled too tight.

The others chatted and laughed, oblivious, but Logan's silence stood out like a shadow against the fire's glow. Then, without a word, he downed the rest of his beer, set the empty bottle down, and stood. A chill crawled up my arms as he walked away.

I swallowed, fiddling with my cup.

Jax and Candace curled into each other, their quiet laughter a contrast to the silent weight Logan left behind. Across from me, Matt and Aniyah were deep in conversation. I didn't know where Marcus had gone.

And suddenly, I felt alone.

I glanced toward the empty spot where Logan had been, my chest tightening with something I couldn't name. Maybe the spark I'd thought I felt wasn't really a spark. Or maybe it had burned out before it even had a chance to catch fire.

When I glanced at Becca, I cursed internally. Her eyes were glazed over, her skin pale. She'd had too much to drink and was going to be sick.

I stood and wrapped an arm around her shoulders, pulling her up.

Jax jumped to his feet. "Is she okay?"

"She'll be fine." *No thanks to you,* I wanted to add.

I guided Becca to her room, barely making it to the bathroom before she collapsed to her knees, vomiting into the toilet. I knelt beside her, holding her hair back.

When she finally stopped, she slumped against the tub, sweat beading along her forehead, her mascara smudged into a watery mess. Tears streamed down her cheeks. "I can't believe he brought her," she whispered.

"I know," I murmured. "Have you told him how you feel?"

She wiped at her eyes with the back of her hand. "It doesn't matter. It's clear how he feels."

"You don't know that. He could've brought her to make you jealous."

"That's dumb."

"Yeah. Well, boys are dumb. But if you don't say anything, you'll regret it."

Her expression wavered, and she exhaled shakily. "Thanks for coming. I needed you."

I offered a small smile. "Anytime."

A beat of silence stretched between us before I hesitated. "What's up with Logan? Did you see him when he got back from his walk?"

She shrugged. "We've all learned not to ask questions when it comes to Logan. I told you, he keeps to himself."

"Are none of y'all concerned? He came back filthy, and tonight he was super distant."

She gave me a pointed look. "Sorry, I wasn't paying attention to your *new boyfriend*. I was dealing with my *ex*."

I flinched. "Becca?"

But she groaned and turned back to the toilet, heaving again.

I sighed, standing up. "I'll see if there's any ginger ale or something for you."

I left, her sharpness still stinging. It was so frustrating the way she let Jax dictate her emotions.

When I entered the kitchen, I stopped short, my breath hitching. The room was silent and empty. But every cabinet and drawer was open. I blinked, my pulse quickening.

Then, I let out a slow breath, rolling my eyes even as my stomach twisted. *Casey.* It reminded me of how he'd always leave cabinets open, like I was playing a perpetual game of closing doors—a real-life version of being Vanna White. Casey insisted he just forgot to look around before leaving the kitchen. His brain worked faster than his body. Maybe somebody here was the same way.

"Dude. Looking for something?"

I jumped slightly as Jax entered the kitchen.

"Wasn't me," I muttered, shaking off the unease.

Jax grabbed a bottle of water and leaned against the counter. "How's Becca?"

I busied myself closing the cabinets, avoiding his gaze. "A mess." I slammed one shut a little harder than necessary. "Who do you think you are bringing Candace this weekend?"

He sighed. "I don't need your judgments."

I turned, leveling him with a glare. "Fine. But maybe next time, *think* before you do something that's gonna wreck her."

"Did she say something?"

"You are so daft."

Jax frowned. "What?"

I found a can of ginger ale in the fridge, then plucked a couple of ice cubes from the freezer and dropped them in a glass. I shook my head, frustrated by both of them. They were locked in this stupid, destructive cycle and expected *me* to pick up the pieces. I had enough to deal with already.

"Just—" I exhaled sharply. "You two should talk. *Stop hurting each other.*"

His jaw tensed, but he didn't argue.

When I returned, Becca was curled in a ball on top of the bed, her tear-streaked face buried in the pillow. My stomach sank.

I set the ginger ale on the nightstand and climbed onto the bed beside her.

She shifted, resting her head in my lap. "Why doesn't he like me?" she whispered, her voice trembling.

I swallowed hard. "He likes you, Becca. He just ... needs to mature."

"He doesn't love her. He *can't.*"

I didn't have an answer for that.

Instead, I gently ran my fingers through her damp hair, slowly, rhythmically, offering comfort in the only way I could. Eventually, her breathing evened out, the quiet of the room settling like a weighted blanket over us both.

I lingered for a little while, watching over her with a mixture of sympathy and concern. Becca had always been reckless with her emotions. But Jax had been reckless with her heart.

And I was stuck in the middle.

The night settled over the cabin in an eerie hush. I curled up in the chair, book in hand, trying to lose myself in its pages, but a sudden chill prickled my skin.

I pulled my hoodie tighter, then paused mid-turn of a page as a distant, mournful cry reached my ears.

I stiffened.

At first, it was a soft, barely audible sound, but Becca's distinctive weeping was unmistakable. A sound I'd heard too many times before. A twinge of sympathy tugged at me, but beneath it, frustration simmered.

This trip was supposed to be a break. Instead, I was dealing with my ex flaunting his new girlfriend, Becca unraveling over Jax, and whatever weirdness was going on between Logan and me.

Sighing, I set my book aside and pushed out of the chair. As I crossed the room and opened the bedroom door, the hinges let out a loud squeak, making me wince and freeze.

Did anyone hear that?

Probably not. They were either too drunk, asleep, or preoccupied.

The hardwood floor was cold beneath my socks as I padded to Becca's room. The door swung open with a soft creak, revealing the moonlit space.

"Becca?"

No response.

I stepped closer and spotted her curled beneath the blankets, her sleeping face peaceful in the dim glow.

Okay, so she isn't crying.

Relief washed over me. Maybe I'd imagined it.

I returned to my room, slipping back into my chair, book in hand.

And then—

The crying returned.

My fingers clenched around the book. A shiver crept down my spine as I darted a glance around the room. The sound was unmistakable now, and closer.

I sucked in a slow breath, my mind scrambling for logic. Maybe someone had left a window open, and it was the wind ... or a fox? Foxes could sound like crying women, right?

Then, a long, heart-wrenching wail tore through the cabin.

I inhaled sharply and jerked upright, my pulse slamming against my ribs. The lamp beside me flickered, casting erratic shadows across the walls.

It had to be something outside, right?

Slowly, I got to my feet and peered through the window. The yard was empty, the trees swaying in the breeze.

"Hello?" I called out hesitantly. The second the word left my lips, I felt incredibly stupid.

The sobbing grew louder. Closer.

My throat tightened. A primal fear gripped me, and I stepped into the hallway again. The darkness stretched ahead like a tunnel, the wooden floor groaning beneath my hesitant steps. The cry grew louder with every inch I moved forward.

Shadows clung to the corners, morphing into shapes my mind didn't want to name.

Then, I saw her.

A faint figure stood at the end of the hall. A girl. She wasn't solid. Her form wavered, translucent, glowing with an unnatural light. Tiny droplets of water dripped from her onto the floor, pooling at her bare feet.

Her eyes met mine. Hollow. Drenched in sorrow.

"Help me," the girl wept.

Terror gripped me like icy tendrils. I wanted to scream, to move, to run, but I couldn't.

I was frozen.

She took a step forward. The glow around her flickered and vanished. Her face was too pale. Too wet. Too real. "You can see me."

A gasp caught in my throat, stealing my breath. I recoiled. "No, no, no," I gasped, stumbling back. "You're not real."

She took another step and started sobbing again. The sound was louder this time, surrounding me, filling my ears. Drowning me.

I spun, bolting back into the living room, my heartbeat a wild, frantic rhythm against my ribs. I slammed the bedroom door behind me, barricading myself inside, my hands trembling.

I grabbed my pills and counted them. I'd taken them today.

Then why was I seeing things? Was I hallucinating?

Or had I really just seen a ghost?

Sunday

Chapter Ten

The early morning sunlight stabbed through my closed eyelids like shards of glass. A groan slipped from my lips as I shifted, a dull, throbbing ache radiating through my skull. The room tilted for a moment, forcing me to grip the edge of the bed for balance.

Too bright. Too loud. Too much.

A queasiness settled in the pit of my stomach, the stale taste in my mouth a bitter reminder of last night. My head pulsed in time with my heartbeat, every movement a fresh wave of discomfort. I didn't think I'd drunk that much, but maybe the exhaustion, the stress, the weight of everything, had made it worse.

And the dream.

The memory of it clung to me, blurry around the edges but still unnerving. I wasn't sure why I'd dreamed of a ghost, but I'd dreamed of worse things before. Maybe it was just Logan's story creeping into my subconscious.

A door clicked shut, and I peered out the window in time to catch a glimpse of Logan disappearing into the woods.

Again?

My brows furrowed as I watched him move, his gait steadier, more determined than it had been last night. Logan seemed to prefer solitude, but I couldn't shake the feeling that he wasn't just out for fresh air.

I sat there for a moment longer before finally forcing myself to move.

Big mistake.

The groaning floorboards beneath me sounded like gunshots in my skull, and I winced at the sharp pang behind my eyes.

Shuffling toward the shower, I left the door open this time. I wasn't taking any chances. Hoping I wouldn't see any blood or whatever, I turned on the water and sighed when the water ran clear. It was all in my head. Maybe I needed to adjust my medication. The thought made me groan.

Ever since my diagnosis back in February, it felt like I was stuck playing this never-ending game of medication roulette. Every new pill was like flipping a coin. Would this one help me sleep through the night without the nightmares? Would it stop the random bursts of energy where I felt like I was vibrating inside my skin? Would it quiet the voices enough to hear myself think?

Some days, I'd think, *Okay, maybe this is the one.* But then, boom—side effects would hit. Hands shaking so bad I couldn't even text. A fog so thick in my brain that focusing on anything felt impossible. And even if there were no side effects, eventually the symptoms would creep back in, like they were mocking me. It was exhausting, like chasing something I wasn't even sure existed.

In the shower, I closed my eyes and let the steam envelop me, filling my lungs with heat, as if I could breathe out last night's fear.

It was just a dream.

I turned off the water. Stepping out of the shower, I reached for a towel and draped it over my body.

The bathroom was thick with steam, a dense fog curling along the walls. I turned, expecting to see the open doorway.

The door was shut.

My stomach dropped.

I knew I'd I left it open. I hadn't closed it. The hair on my arms lifted as a faint high-pitched squeak broke the silence. Like the sound of a finger ... dragging across glass.

A chill coiled around my spine as letters began to form on the fogged mirror. The condensation trickled down, carving paths through the mist, revealing a single name: "Hannah."

I gasped, paralyzed in place.

No. No, no, no.

My pulse roared in my ears, drowning out reason. The uneasy sensation of being watched slithered over my skin, tightening around my throat.

I wasn't alone.

I lurched for the doorknob and wrenched it open, stumbling into the cooler air beyond. My lungs seized as I gulped down breaths. My mind scrambled for an explanation.

A prank. This had to be a prank. Jax. Or Becca. They were always messing with me.

But the name... Hannah. They wouldn't write that. Would they?

I turned back toward the bathroom. As I crept closer, my heartbeat quickened. I swallowed, forcing my feet forward.

One more step.

I finally mustered the courage to glance inside at the mirror. The letters were gone. Vanished. Like they'd never been there at all.

A shudder tore through me.

My head throbbed, a relentless ache pounding in sync with my pulse. The pressure built behind my eyes, like a storm brewing inside my skull.

I needed to hydrate. I needed to calm down. I needed ... to get the hell out of this cabin.

Once dressed, I made my way to the kitchen in search of relief. The house was still, the kind of early morning silence that made everything feel fragile. I poured myself some water, the clink of my glass against the countertop echoing too loudly in the empty space, and gulped it down, as if I could wash away the unease still clinging to me.

"Didn't peg you as an early riser."

I nearly dropped the glass. Turning, I saw Logan, his bare chest glistening with water droplets from his shower, stretching languidly as he ambled into the kitchen. The smell of his soap lingered in the air.

Heat flashed up my neck, and I quickly looked away, focusing on anything but the lean definition of his torso. *Get it together, Hazel.*

"How'd you sleep?" he asked, his voice warm with amusement.

Now he was talking to me again? I hesitated. "Good. The bed is comfortable." A half-truth. The dream still lingered, clawing at the edges of my mind. I turned to leave. "Sorry, I'll go back to my room."

"No, it's okay." He sighed.

I hesitated, facing him again.

Logan ran a hand through his hair, shifting on his feet. "I'm sorry about last night. Sometimes I just ... get stuck inside my head. Thinking about things."

I studied him for a moment, sensing there was so much more behind those words. "I understand that more than you know."

His gaze flickered to mine, something unreadable in his expression. "I just don't like talking about things sometimes."

I nodded. "I get it."

Because I did.

There were a lot of things about me I didn't like talking about either.

A pause hung between us, neither awkward nor tense. Just ... there.

Logan took a step closer, his voice softer. "Maybe we don't have to talk. Maybe we can just be here. Together. No pressure."

Something warm bloomed in my chest. I swallowed. "I'd like that."

A slow, easy smile curved his lips. The tension between us dissolved like steam off the coffee maker.

"Speaking of 'no pressure,' want some tea?" he asked.

"Sure," I murmured. My head throbbed as I moved toward the counter. "But I need to get rid of my headache first."

Logan plucked the empty water glass from my hands, refilled it, and grabbed a small packet from the cabinet. With practiced ease, he tore it open, stirred the powder inside into the water. "This will fix you up. Promise."

I arched a brow. "You seem like a professional."

"You could say that." He grabbed two tea bags and placed them into two mugs. As the coffee maker spit hot water into a mug, Logan leaned against the counter, his gaze meeting mine. "So, why are you up so early?"

I shrugged. "Just couldn't sleep. I wake up a lot when I'm in new places." The image of the mirror flashed in my mind. The name. The squeaking sound of invisible fingers tracing letters. I suppressed a shiver.

"Yeah, I get that. I'm sorry."

Why was he apologizing?

"It's okay." I felt a strange solace in our shared silence. I hardly knew him, but I felt comfortable around him. But I couldn't get carried away. I still didn't understand Jax's warnings.

Once the coffee maker finished pouring the steaming water, he handed me a cup.

Our fingers brushed. It was barely a touch, but something hot and electric jolted through me, setting my pulse racing.

Logan's eyes flicked to mine.

I pulled back first, wrapping my hands around the cup, desperate for something to hold onto.

"To early mornings," Logan toasted, lifting his mug with a small, knowing smile.

"To early mornings." I brought the cup to my lips. The warmth settled in my chest, but I wasn't sure if it was from the tea or from him.

"Hazel." A voice pulled me from the depths of sleep.

I groaned, rolling over, blinking against the morning light, only to find Becca's face inches from mine.

"Good morning, sunshine." She smiled. "Did you fall asleep on the couch?"

Confused, I sat up, taking in my surroundings. The blanket pooled in my lap. Had I fallen asleep after talking to Logan?

Becca studied me. "Are you okay?"

I swallowed the dryness in my throat. "I'm fine. How are you?"

Becca shrugged, her tone breezy, as if she hadn't been puking and crying her eyes out last night. "I'm good. Logan made pancakes, bacon, and eggs." She said it like she hadn't just spent the night drowning in heartbreak.

Her words barely registered. *How did I end up on the couch?*

I got to my feet, following Becca into the kitchen, where everyone was already at the table with empty plates and easy smiles. They looked like a family. I was the outsider.

None of them seemed remotely hungover.

So why did I feel like I'd been hit by a truck?

Logan stood. "Are you feeling better?"

My gaze flicked to him, something gnawing at my gut. "A little. What—what did you give me?" I barely remembered drinking what he gave me. I hadn't even asked what it was before downing it. Had he drugged me?

Logan blinked. "Oh, just a supplement for dehydration. I take it when I train. Or if I drink too much. It helps." He flashed an easy smile. "I figured you could use it."

I hesitated. "Does it make you sleepy?"

"No," he said, tilting his head. "But you looked exhausted. You laid down on the couch and passed out."

I exhaled slowly. I was overthinking this. Jax's warning about Logan had wormed into my brain, twisting everything.

"Are you hungry?" Logan asked.

"A little."

"I can make some more eggs and bacon or—"

"I'll just have a bagel."

"You got it." He moved through the kitchen with an ease that should have felt comforting but didn't.

I watched him, the way he toasted the bagel, how he prepared my tea like he'd done it a hundred times before. It was unsettling how attentive he was.

"We're all going to town for Oktoberfest if you want to come," Marcus said.

I rubbed my temples. "I think I'll stay here for a bit. I have the worst headache."

Becca frowned. "Maybe when we get back, we can slip into the hot tub."

"Yeah, sounds good."

As the others got ready, I forced myself to eat, though every bite felt heavy in my mouth. When the door finally shut behind them, a suffocating silence wrapped around the cabin. I was alone. A prickle of unease crawled up my spine. I wasn't sure if I wanted to be.

As I made my way toward my room, Logan walked out of his room. My heart flipped. Would it just be the two of us? "You're not going with them?"

He shook his head, slipping into his jacket. "Nah, I've been to Oktoberfest too many times. I'm going for a walk."

A strained, heavy look was on his face as he walked outside. Was he really just going for a walk? It was weird that this was his second walk of the day and his third in like two days. Not that I was counting.

The image of the mirror flashed in my mind. The crying. The name. I couldn't stay in the cabin alone. Prank or not. Before I could second-guess myself, I yanked on my shoes and hurried to the front door. I couldn't ignore the nagging feeling that Logan needed me, even if he hadn't asked explicitly.

Stepping outside, I was met by the crisp morning air and the sound of dew-kissed grass crunching under my feet. I scanned the surroundings, spotting Logan in the distance. With a purposeful stride, I closed the gap, catching up to him just as he reached the edge of the woods.

"Logan!" I called.

He turned, surprise flickering across his face as I caught up to him at the edge of the woods.

I offered a small smile, hoping I didn't seem too eager. "I thought I'd join you. Sometimes, it helps to have company."

For a moment, he looked at me like he wanted to say yes, like the words were right there. But something held him back. I saw it in the flicker of his eyes, the quiet war playing out behind them.

"Thanks, but ... I need some time alone today." Oh.

My stomach dipped. I swallowed down the sharp pang of embarrassment. "Oh. Yeah. Of course."

Stupid. I was so stupid.

I forced a weak laugh. "Well, if you change your mind or need someone to talk to, I'm here."

He gave me a small, tired smile. "I know."

And then he turned away.

I stood there, watching his figure disappear into the trees, the wind biting at my skin.

Logan was only nice to me around other people. Why had I let myself think there was something more?

I let out a slow breath, shoving my hands into my pockets.

What was he hiding? What had Jax meant?

Closing the door to the cabin, I stood listening to the utter silence. I really should've gone with Becca. I didn't want to be there alone.

Shrugging off my coat, I moved into the kitchen. The air felt colder now, as if the warmth from earlier had been sucked out the moment the others left.

I turned on the coffee maker and absently scrolled on my phone. The screen blurred beneath my tired eyes. It didn't help my headache, but it kept my mind off the dream. The name on the mirror. Matt. Everything.

I needed something to ground me.

Grabbing a mug, I made a cup of herbal tea and leaned against the counter, watching steam curl into the air. The soft glow of morning sunlight filtered through the curtains, casting long shadows across the floor.

Suddenly, I felt a touch. Faint, featherlight. Fingertips sliding through my hair.

I froze.

My breath hitched as an icy chill danced along my scalp. My hands clenched around the mug, heat pressing against my palms.

Someone was touching me.

My heart slammed against my ribs as I scanned the room, every nerve in my body locked in place. And then my gaze caught on the vent above me.

A slow exhale escaped as my muscles loosened. The heater. That's was all it was.

But ... the vent wasn't blowing any air.

A sharp, splintering throb pierced through my skull, making me wince. *God, my head.*

I shut my eyes, willing the tension away. Jax and Becca's pranks were messing with me. That was all. I was on edge, reading into things that weren't there.

I sighed and pushed off the counter, my tea sloshing slightly as I moved toward my room.

Then, I halted, spilling the scalding tea across my hand. The mug slipped from my grasp and shattered against the floor.

I sucked in a sharp breath, my feet rooted to the spot.

The girl from my dream stood before me.

Chapter Eleven

Again, water dripped onto the wooden floor from the girl, pooling around her bare feet. Panic clamped around my chest, yet, oddly, a strange calm settled over me a moment later, as if some part of me knew she wasn't here to hurt me.

The figure stood eerily still, staring at me, her damp T-shirt and jeans clinging to her body. Not Victorian lace or a tattered wedding dress. Just ordinary clothes, ordinary features. Yet everything about her felt wrong.

The pounding in my skull eased, fading into a dull hum as I stared back at her. I knew that face. But from where? I squeezed my eyes shut. Just a hallucination. *It's in my head. It's all in my—*

"Help me."

I opened my eyes. She was still there. Hollow eyes. No smile. No flicker of emotion. Just ... watching me. A cold sweat prickled along my spine.

"Who are you?" I whispered.

She said nothing. The room felt frozen in time, the air thick, charged with something beyond my comprehension.

I swallowed hard, remembering Logan's ghost story. "Are you ... Eleanor?"

She shook her head. Her lips barely moved, but I heard the words. "I never meant to hurt him."

A sharp inhale lodged in my throat. "Hurt who?"

She didn't answer. Time seemed to slow to an unbearable crawl before she vanished as quickly as she'd come. Not like a candle blown out. More like water dissolving into mist. The warmth of the sun crept back into the room, golden light spilling across the floorboards, but it felt ... hollow.

My headache was gone. But my body was locked in place, my heart battering against my ribs.

That was real. Wasn't it?

I stared at the spot where she had stood, but all that remained was the faint glimmer of moisture on the floor. The tea in my trembling hands had grown cold.

I turned, half-expecting to see her again. But the cabin was still, its creaks now sounding like distant whispers from another realm.

Had it been real? Had I truly seen her? Or was this just another sign that I was losing my mind again?

A knot of unease twisted in my stomach. If she was real, that meant ghosts existed. But if she wasn't... That meant I was slipping. Again.

My fingers clenched the mug tighter. Jax. Becca. They wouldn't prank me like this. Would they? And how could they? How could they have faked the girl's voice or the chilling weight of her presence.

The frustration burned in my chest. I hated this. Hated how I couldn't even trust my own senses. I just wanted to be normal.

I squeezed my eyes shut, inhaling deeply, forcing the fear down. But the ghost—or whatever she was—was burned into my mind. Hollow eyes. A familiar face I couldn't quite place. And the name written on the mirror.

Hannah.

Chapter Twelve

The cabin door swung open, startling me. Laughter and the crisp scent of the autumn air flooded in as everyone returned, their energy buzzing like static in the air. I forced a smile, attempting to conceal the unease that lingered beneath the surface. I had never been happier to see them.

"Hey, hey!" Jax called, his voice carrying the excitement of the day. "You feeling better?"

I nodded, my eyes scanning each familiar face, searching for any sign of the ghost. "Yeah. Did y'all have fun?"

Candace plopped down beside me, her cheeks flushed from the cool air. "We rode the aerial tram and saw miles of mountains and the town stretched below us. It was insane."

"Jax almost cried like a baby on that sky lift." With a hearty laugh, Marcus playfully smacked Jax's back.

"Whatever," Jax said. "At least I didn't wuss out like you did when we went bungee jumping this summer."

Marcus grinned. "Man, I had my reasons for not jumping off a bridge."

Becca rolled her eyes, sinking into a chair beside the couch. "Always a pissing contest with you two."

I managed a weak smile, but their excitement felt distant, muffled, like a conversation happening underwater. My thoughts kept dragging me back to the ghost. To Hannah.

Jax arched an eyebrow, studying me. "You good? You seem a little ... off."

I hesitated, my fingers tightening around the fabric of my sleeves. Should I say anything? Would they laugh at me? Would Becca? "Yeah, I ... I think I saw something," I finally said.

"Like what? A bear?" he asked.

I swallowed. "Can I talk to you, Becca?"

Becca's brows lifted slightly before she shrugged. "Sure."

I followed her into her room, shutting the door behind us.

The moment it clicked shut, I turned to her, crossing my arms. "I know you're messing with me."

Becca blinked. "Huh?"

"Trapping me in the bathroom, the sink always on, the name on the mirror. You can stop."

Her brows furrowed. "What name?"

I huffed. "Hannah."

I swore I saw a flicker of something in her eyes.

But then she tilted her head and asked, "Who's Hannah?"

I let out a short, humorless laugh. "I don't know. You tell me."

Becca exhaled and looked at me like she thought I was spiraling. "Hazel, I have no idea what you're talking about."

The sincerity in her voice threw me off. I studied her, waiting for some kind of smirk or telltale shift that would reveal she was lying. But there was nothing.

A small knot of unease twisted in my stomach. "Something strange is happening."

"Like what?"

I swallowed hard. "I know you're going to think I'm batshit, but I'm not." I inhaled a shaky breath. "The other night ... I saw ... or I thought I saw blood coming out of the shower."

Becca sat up straighter, her face softening. "Hazel."

I continued before she could stop me. "And last night, I thought I heard you crying, but when I checked, you were asleep, and then I saw her. And this morning, I saw her again."

Becca watched me carefully, her concern deepening. "Who?"

"The girl. Hannah ... or whoever. She was just ... standing there. She kept saying 'help me.'"

My words just hung there, filling the room with an uncomfortable silence. Becca's expression was a mix of disbelief and curiosity. The residual fear clung to me like a shadow. But no matter how scared I was, I couldn't tell if I should've kept my mouth shut.

Becca reached for my hand, squeezing it. "Hazel, you've been through so much. Maybe with everything going on. Matt, this trip, the stress. You're just on edge."

I shook my head. "I know what I saw."

She smiled at me, but it wasn't patronizing. Just calm, steady, empathetic. The way she was when I fell apart before. "I believe that you *believe* you saw something."

I opened my mouth to argue, but she continued, her voice soothing. "Think about it. Logan's story freaked you out, right?"

I hesitated. "I mean ... yeah, but—"

"Your mind could be playing tricks on you. It happens to everyone. You know how stress can make things feel more ... intense. I mean, you're taking your meds, right?"

The words hit me like a slap. I deflated. "Yes."

"And you've been doing great lately. But maybe the alcohol is messing with them?"

I chewed my lip. That ... was possible. "But why 'Hannah'?" I whispered. "Who is she?"

"No one wrote on your mirror." Becca focused on each word as if to make sure I understood.

I sighed. "I hate this. I never know what's real or not." I blinked rapidly, trying to hold back the tears that welled up in my eyes. Deep breaths filled my lungs as I fought against the overwhelming emotions that threatened to consume me. "I should go home."

She placed her hands on my shoulders. "You're okay. I promise."

"If I'm having delusions, I don't need to be here. I can just call an Uber or something."

"You aren't having delusions. Messed up dreams, maybe. Why don't you not drink tonight and see how you feel?"

"Okay." I nodded. "I'll give it another day."

"Good." She smiled. "We're going to Coyote Hollow for dinner. Wear the white skirt and jean jacket. Oh, and those boots I packed for you."

I snorted. "Cowboy bar?"

She winked. "Damn right."

I rolled my eyes. "Okay." I closed Becca's door behind me and went to my room.

Despite Becca's reassurance, I couldn't stop thinking about the weird things going on in the cabin. Maybe Logan would know, but I didn't want to ask him. He'd think I was losing it. Still, I wondered if I was right. Was the girl's name Hannah? Who was she?

Chapter Thirteen

The dim glow of restaurant lights blended with the golden haze of whiskey, perfume, and laughter. A live band played from the small stage near the back, their music thumping through the worn wooden floors, vibrating beneath my boots as Becca tugged me through the crowd.

People spilled from the bar to the tables and back again, drinks sloshing, hips swaying, voices rising over the beat. I adjusted my skirt, feeling exposed in a way I didn't like. The fabric was too short. The place was too loud, too alive. But at least it wasn't the cabin.

At a table in the back, Logan stood out effortlessly. His relaxed posture, the way he took in the room like he owned it. That quiet confidence I envied.

A waitress approached, all curls and familiarity. "Well, hey there, Logan." She pulled him into a hug.

He let her, but his smile was tight. "Hey, Stacey."

"Been a few months. How are you holdin' up?" She looked at him with pity.

My brows furrowed. Holding up? From what?

"I'm fine," Logan said, brushing it off. "Can we get a round?"

She raised an eyebrow. "You know I can't."

A knowing look passed between them, and Logan huffed a quiet laugh. "Fine. Round of Cokes, then."

"You got it. I'll get you some menus."

As the waitress walked away, Becca grabbed my arm. "I need to use the bathroom," she said.

I followed her, curious as to what she wanted to talk about. Once we were in the bathroom, she turned to me. "I need you to dance with Jax."

I snorted. "Excuse me?"

"Dance with him. Candace won't suspect anything. Then I'll cut in."

I sighed. "Why don't you just ask him yourself?"

She gave me a knowing look. "Come on. Please?"

"Fine." *The things I do for her.*

We walked out and as I passed Stacey, I caught snippets of her speaking to another waitress.

"Logan looks good. Better than last time I saw him."

"That boy was such a mess."

"Can you blame him?" Stacey asked.

My stomach tightened. What had happened to Logan? Why did everyone talk about him like he was a tragedy?

The hum of conversation dimmed as the soft notes of a piano floated through the air. A slow, aching melody curled through the air, low and rich, wrapping around my ribs. The kind of song that made the rest of the world feel too far away.

I didn't know the song, but something about it tugged at me. The rough sincerity of the lyrics, the way the singer poured raw emotion into each word, settled in my chest like a stone.

Logan slid off his chair and held out his hand. I blinked. "What?"

"Want to give it a try?"

I stared at his outstretched palm. My heartbeat tripped over itself. "Dancing? To this?"

"Why not?" His lips curled, but his eyes held something else.

I hesitated, but the calm, patient, sure way he waited made it impossible to say no. Slowly, I slid my fingers into his.

He led me to the open floor, one hand on my waist, the other curling around mine. My heart was trying to escape my chest. I'd never slow-danced with a boy before. I rested my hand on his shoulder. His touch was gentle but firm, guiding me with effortless ease.

I took a hesitant step, stumbling slightly.

"You're fine," he murmured, his voice a quiet rumble close to my ear. "Just relax."

Yeah. Sure. Like that's possible.

I tried, but my body was stiff, uncertain, like I was moving underwater.

His hand at my waist tightened slightly, pulling me closer.

The song wrapped around us, slow and electric, and I became hyper-aware of everything. The rough callouses on his fingers. The warmth radiating from him. The way his thumb brushed absently against my side, like he wasn't even aware he was doing it.

I wanted to ask him so many questions. Why had he been a mess? Why had Jax warned me about him at the same time that Becca wanted me to meet him so badly?

"What's on your mind?" he asked.

I snapped my gaze up to his. "Huh?"

"You're thinking really hard about something."

"Maybe I just don't want to step on your feet."

He huffed a quiet laugh. "I think you're giving me too much credit. I might step on *your* feet."

His small, crooked, almost lazy smile made something strange stir in my stomach.

I searched his expression, looking for the same flicker of distraction, of distance I'd caught before.

"I'm sorry about this morning," he said. "I used to hike here with my family. I'm not used to having anyone else there."

"You don't have to explain. It's okay."

He tilted his head, like he wasn't expecting that answer. "I guess I still should've asked you to come with me. It was a dick move."

I smiled slightly. "I think I might know something about closing people off too."

His grip tightened briefly, like he understood that more than I meant him to. "I know it's gotta be hard to see your ex here."

I shrugged. "A little, but I'm okay."

Truthfully, Matt wasn't even on my mind. Logan was.

His fingers flexed against my waist. "Maybe you need a night off from thinking. I know I do."

Before I could process his words, he spun me.

A startled laugh escaped my lips as I landed back in his arms.

He was closer now.

Too close. Not close enough.

His breath was warm when he murmured, "See? You're good at this."

My cheeks burned. "I think you're just a good dancer."

His smirk deepened. He liked flustering me. His hand rested just a little heavier on my waist.

My pulse stuttered, tripped.

Maybe it was the intimacy of the moment or the way he held me like I was something delicate but unshakable. Or maybe it was the fact that I knew nothing about him, but I felt drawn to him anyway. I looked up and caught a flicker of something tired and vulnerable in his gray eyes, and for a moment, I forgot how to breathe.

Whatever haunted him, I wanted to take his mind off it. "What's your favorite thing about baseball?"

He blinked at the shift in conversation, but then his lips twitched. "Playing. I love it. I'm good at it. The strategy, the unpredictability. Anything can happen."

I smiled. "Are you going to the majors?"

"I hope to."

"Wow." He had a future. A plan. A dream. Me? I didn't even know if I could make it through the week.

"What about you?" he asked. "Are you studying photography?"

The moment shattered. Heat rushed to my cheeks, and I shook my head. "No, I'm ... still in high school." I looked away.

His movements slowed for half a beat. "Wait, how old are you?"

I hesitated, not wanting him to know that I was old and still in high school. "Um, eighteen," I mumbled.

The slightest tension in his shoulders eased. "Okay, good. I was scared you were younger."

My stomach flipped. So, he had thought about it. Me.

Before I could process that realization, Jax's voice cut through the air. "Mind if I steal her?"

Logan's jaw ticked. His grip on me lingered for a breath longer, but he let go. "Sure."

I took Jax's hand, but my mind was still on Logan.

Jax spun me, too dramatic, too playful, forcing my focus back. "Careful, Haze," he said, lowering his voice. "You're playing with fire."

I shot him a look. "What's that supposed to mean?"

"Just ... don't get too close," he said, his voice tight. "Not until you know more."

A cold weight settled in my stomach. What the hell did that mean?

Jax spun me too suddenly, forcing a laugh out of me like he was trying to shift the mood. Like he was trying to distract me.

But it was too late. Because now, I was wondering what he wasn't telling me.

And more importantly, what Logan was hiding.

Back at the cabin, Logan disappeared downstairs to set up the home theatre, leaving me to wander into the kitchen. I stopped in my tracks. All the cabinets hung open again.

A sharp chill ran down my spine. This had been happening since we got here. Silent little disturbances no one else seemed to notice.

"Seriously?" I muttered, closing each one.

Maybe someone here just had terrible kitchen habits. Or maybe it was ... Nope. I wasn't going there.

I reached into the fridge for a soda, letting the cool air wash over my face. But when I shut the fridge door, my breath caught in my throat.

The cabinets were open again.

A cold knot twisted in my stomach. I glared at the doors, willing them shut, yet they remained open and silent. I blinked, rubbed my eyes. Still open. Every single one.

A shadow moved in the doorway.

"What the hell?" Matt's voice made me jump.

I spun around, my pulse hammering.

Matt and Aniyah stood there, watching me.

"Just ... getting a drink," I said.

Aniyah tilted her head. "Why are all the cabinets open? Looking for something?"

I swallowed hard. "No. They were like that when I walked in."

Matt chuckled under his breath. "Reminds you of Casey's old habit, huh?"

The mention of Casey hit me like a slap. My jaw tightened. How dare he bring him up?

Aniyah began shutting the cabinets one by one. I watched her as a thought prickled at the back of my mind. Was someone messing with me?

The cabinets. The bathroom door. The running water. The mirror.

It all felt too deliberate. Too pointed. Like someone wanted me to question myself.

And who else would do that besides Matt and Aniyah?

The thought burned in my chest. They'd already made me feel small just by showing up here together, parading their relationship in front of me. It wasn't enough that Matt had moved on. He had to bring her here to rub it in my face. Maybe this was their idea of a twisted joke, trying to make me look unstable in front of everyone. Matt would do anything to protect his perfect image, wouldn't he?

And Aniyah's sweet, innocent act wasn't fooling me. She'd probably love to humiliate me.

My frustration boiled over. "Are you enjoying this? Messing with me?"

Matt frowned. "What?"

"You planned this, didn't you? Bringing her here, making me look insane." My voice sounded more confident than I felt. "The bathroom lock, the running water, messages on my mirror. It's you, isn't it, Aniyah?"

Genuine surprise registered on Aniyah's face. Or perhaps she was just a skilled actress. "What are you talking about? Why would I do that to you?"

Matt's brows furrowed. "Are you serious right now?"

"Who else would do this?" I demanded.

Aniyah's demeanor softened, a trace of concern in her voice. "I promise I haven't done anything to you. I know things are awkward between us, but I would never mess with you." She hesitated. "Are ... are you okay? I mean are you having ... seeing things?"

My stomach dropped. *Seeing things.*

Matt looked away.

I turned to him, my breath catching in my throat. That single moment of silence told me everything. He'd told her. Matt had told Aniyah about me.

The betrayal hit like a punch to the chest. Heat burned behind my eyes. My soul felt stripped bare in front of them. Like Matt had taken the most broken pieces of me, my worst, darkest moments, and handed them over to someone else. Someone who would never understand.

"You *told* her?"

Aniyah spoke quickly, hands raised. "Please don't be upset—"

"I don't want your pity," I snapped. I turned my glare to Matt. "I can't believe you."

He opened his mouth, but I didn't wait for an excuse.

Leaving the kitchen, a heavy, painful knot settled in my stomach. And now, I wasn't sure what was worse—the possibility that ghosts were real ... or that the people I once trusted were capable of something even crueler. I just knew I wanted to escape.

Some horror movie played on the enormous TV screen in the theatre room, but my mind was elsewhere. I shouldn't have joined them. I felt out of place. Again.

Jax and Becca kept sneaking glances at me, their expressions a mix of concern and subtle judgment. Becca had probably told Jax everything I'd said earlier. They thought I was losing it.

And Aniyah knew my secret now. That meant she could use it against me. The water. The mirror. The cabinets. Had she been behind them all?

The cabin, meant to be an escape, had twisted into a trap.

I finished my third cider and pushed off the couch, ignoring Becca's warning about drinking. Why did it matter? I wasn't imagining things. I couldn't be.

I wound my way upstairs toward the kitchen, pushing my thoughts to the only good thing I'd experienced this week, the sunrise hike. The scent of Fraser firs. Crisp mountain air. The sun cresting over the hills, painting the world in fire.

I stopped short.

The cabinets were open. Again.

My pulse hammered. Jaw tight, I exhaled sharply and started slamming them shut.

A low chuckle broke through the silence. "Damn. What did the cabinets do to you?"

I turned, startled, to find Logan leaning against the doorway, watching me with amusement flickering in his gray eyes. I rolled my eyes and chuckled. "Someone keeps leaving all the drawers and cabinets open."

He tossed his empty beer bottle into the trash. "Could be Eleanor."

I froze. My eyes snapped to his, searching for some hint that he was kidding. "That's not funny."

But he chuckled and brushed past me. He smelled like oak and secrets and a hint of lemon. My heart raced like a wild stallion, galloping uncontrollably in my chest. Pulling open the fridge, he grabbed a beer, then held up a cider in silent offer.

I nodded, and he handed it to me.

For a moment, neither of us moved.

The firelight flickered, casting golden shadows against the walls. The tension in the air thickened, unspoken thoughts crackling between us like static before a storm.

Logan took a slow sip of his beer, his Adam's apple bobbing with the movement. I shouldn't have been watching him, but I was.

"Enjoying yourself?" he asked.

I looked away. Was he asking about the cabin? Or about him? "Yeah. Are you?"

He gave me a pointed look and leaned against the island across from me. "Politeness only gets you so far."

A breath of laughter escaped me. "It's fine. Just ... some things." I stopped myself before mentioning the cabinets. Before mentioning Aniyah.

His gaze dipped to my lips.

A shiver rolled down my spine.

Logan closed the distance. Tentatively, his fingers brushed my cheek before his warm, steady hand fully cupped my face. My breath caught.

He waited, watching me.

Then his lips met mine in a tender, prolonged kiss, sending warmth throughout my body. Time seemed to halt, the world outside the cabin fading into oblivion. The kiss was soft yet intense, a blend of curiosity and desire. I was taken aback at first, but I reciprocated, our lips moving in unison. It was a dance of vulnerability and yearning.

My fingers curled against his shirt, fisting the fabric. His other hand gripped my waist, pulling me closer, like he wanted to know exactly how we fit together.

Everything outside this moment ceased to exist No Matt. No Aniyah. No ghosts. Just Logan.

When we finally broke apart, my lips felt bruised in the best way.

He didn't step back, didn't let me go. His forehead nearly brushed mine.

A soft chuckle rumbled from his chest. "I've been wanting to do that since you got here."

A dizzy warmth spread through me. Maybe this was just a cabin thing. Maybe it would mean nothing outside these walls.

But that kiss hadn't felt like nothing.

"Really?" I whispered.

His thumb swept against my hip. "Yeah. I know it's probably complicated with Matt here and..." He trailed off. "But I can't ignore this. Whatever this is." Something real, a raw emotion, flickered in his eyes, like a hidden flame.

I hesitated. I didn't want to hurt anyone. But I also wanted this.

"Unless I'm reading into this wrong?" he said.

"No. I just—I don't want to hurt anyone."

His fingers threaded through mine, sending a pulse of warmth straight to my stomach. "I don't want that either," he said quietly. "I like you, Hazel, but I understand if you're not ready."

My chest tightened. Because I liked him too. But he didn't know me. Not really. When he found out the truth about my breakdown, about my meds, about how utterly broken I was, he wouldn't look at me like this anymore.

Still, I wanted to be reckless for once. I wanted to kiss him again.

But I knew being daring always got me in trouble. Maybe that was the real reason Jax had warned me. He was worried that I'd end up hurting Logan.

"What are y'all doing?" Marcus's voice cut through the moment like a blade.

I jumped back.

Marcus strolled in, oblivious to the electric tension still crackling in the air. "Y'all are missing the craziest damn movie." He grabbed a drink from the fridge.

Logan exhaled sharply and stepped away. He didn't look at me as he followed Marcus downstairs.

The absence of his touch left a hollow ache in its place.

I let out a breath and rubbed my arms, kicking myself for my actions, and for not saying anything before Marcus ruined it.

I wasn't sure what had just happened.

But I wanted more of it.

Making my way to my room, a rare sense of calm settled over me. The kiss had shifted something inside me, grounding me in a way I hadn't felt in a long time. For the first time in days, my thoughts weren't consumed by shadows or unanswered questions. The fear of ghosts, the eerie happenings, suddenly felt distant, almost irrelevant. Maybe Becca was right. Maybe I really had been imagining things.

But the faucet was running again.

Frustrated, I turned it off with a sharp twist of the handle. They needed to stop messing with me.

I exhaled, shaking off the tension as I stepped back into the familiar comfort of my room. Just four walls, a bed, my scattered belongings. No ghosts, no eerie whispers. Just me.

And Logan.

A gentle blush warmed my cheeks as I sank beneath the covers, the memory of his lips lingering like a spark still dancing along my skin. My heart fluttered, an unfamiliar but welcome sensation after weeks of unease. I could still feel the soft press of his hand on my waist, the way he'd looked at me—not through me, not past me, but at me. A quiet thrill ran through me, like a flicker of warmth in the cold.

With a contented sigh, I switched off the light, welcoming the darkness not with fear, but with the rare feeling that maybe tomorrow wouldn't be so bad.

A whisper stirred me from sleep.

"Hazel."

It floated through the room, faint and eerie, barely louder than a breath.

I stirred, shifting under the covers. "Becca, what do you want?"

Silence.

The bed sank near my feet. A prickle of unease crept up my spine. Someone was sitting there.

Blinking against the dim moonlight seeping through the curtains, I saw a figure perched at the foot of my bed. My pulse stuttered. "Becca?"

No.

As my eyes adjusted, dread chilled my veins. It was *her*.

The girl from the hallway. From the living room. And, I suddenly realized the same girl from the missing poster I'd seen at the grocery store.

Water dripped from her in slow, deliberate drops, soaking into the bed. A damp, rotten smell curled in my nose, and goosebumps rose along my skin. The room felt wrong. Too cold, too quiet, too still.

I scrambled backward, my fingertips pressing into the carved wood of the headboard. This wasn't real. It *couldn't* be real. I squeezed my eyes shut, taking a shaky breath. Just a dream. Just—

"Hazel."

My eyes snapped open. She was closer.

Her hollow, sorrowful gaze locked onto mine, something unreadable flickering in their dark depths. It was as if she could see straight through me, past every wall I'd ever built, every secret I had buried.

The air grew heavy, suffocating. My breaths came fast and shallow. *Please leave.* But I couldn't tear my eyes away. There was something about her that drew me in, a magnetic pull I couldn't resist.

I forced myself to speak. "Hannah?"

"Yes."

My stomach twisted. *It really is her.* "What do you want?" I asked, trying to sound brave.

Hannah's eyes flickered, as if the question hurt. The shadows around her thickened, stretching unnaturally along the walls. The temperature plummeted.

"I didn't mean to hurt him."

A cold dread curled in my stomach. "Who?"

She didn't answer.

The air turned sharp, biting against my skin. "Help me."

"I ... I can't."

Hannah lifted a translucent hand, fingers trembling as she reached for me.

A strangled gasp caught in my throat. *No.*

Panic clamped around my chest as I yanked the blankets over my head, praying she wouldn't touch me. The air rippled, an invisible force pressing against me, sending a fresh wave of frigid air curling under the covers.

I held my breath.

Waited.

Silence.

Slowly, I peeled the blanket away, my heart hammering.

She was gone. But the room still felt wrong. The stench of decay clung to the air. It was a mix of musty books and damp earth, like something long buried just beneath the floorboards.

My body ached with cold, the chill sinking into my bones, making my muscles stiff and unyielding. I swallowed hard, forcing breath into my lungs.

She was gone.

But I wasn't alone. Not really.

Hannah was still there. Waiting.

Monday

Chapter Fourteen

Sitting by the window in the main room, my breath fogged the glass as I watched the rain cascade down in steady streams. The mountains, usually so sharp and vivid against the sky, blurred under the October drizzle, their peaks swallowed in mist.

The rhythmic tapping of raindrops against the windowpane should have been soothing, but my thoughts churned, unsettled. The rain could wash away a lot of things, but not the nightmares. Not the hallucinations. Not the doubts clawing at my mind.

The sudden slam of a door made me jump.

Logan stepped inside, drenched, a small bag of groceries clutched in his grip. Water dripped from his soaked hoodie, puddling onto the wooden floor, and for a second, the image of Hannah, dripping wet and sitting at the foot of my bed, flashed through my mind. My stomach twisted.

"Oh my god, you're totally soaked," I said.

Logan shook his head, sending droplets flying in every direction, a lazy grin tugging at his lips. "Just a little water."

I grabbed a towel from the half-bath and tossed it to him. He caught it easily, running it through his damp hair with a shrug.

"It's just rain," he said, but his eyes lingered on me, something unreadable flickering behind them before he looked away. "Nothing a hot shower won't fix."

A wave of heat rushed to my face at the unintentional image his words sent through my head. *Pull yourself together, Hazel.* I cleared my throat. "What did you need so badly that you had to trek through a storm?"

He smirked. "A few essentials." He stepped into the kitchen and placed a carton of coffee creamer on the counter. "And maybe a little surprise."

I raised my eyebrow. "Surprise?"

His smirk deepened, and he winked. "You'll have to wait and see." Logan pulled out a neatly wrapped package and set it in front of me on the counter before heading toward the bathroom, his footsteps leaving wet prints on the wooden floor. As he disappeared down the hall, my heart thumped way too fast.

What did he get me?

I studied the package, but didn't open it.

A few minutes later, Logan returned smelling like oak and lemon and soap. He handed me the package. "For you."

I carefully unwrapped it, revealing a small jar of locally made honey. The label was hand-drawn, with tiny bees buzzing around the name. Beneath the jar, there was a delicate ceramic mug painted with a mountain scene, the kind of mug that felt like it was made for cozy mornings.

"I remembered you said you loved tea, especially when it's raining," he said. "Figured it might be a good time for this."

I ran my fingers over the smooth surface of the mug, my throat tightening. "Logan, this is ... really sweet."

He shrugged, though his eyes shone with a quiet satisfaction. "Just thought you could use something nice."

I wanted to tell him how much I liked him, how much the kiss last night had shaken me in the best way possible, but the words stuck in my throat.

"Are you cold?" he asked.

"Yeah. It's really cold in my room, too. Do you have space heaters?"

His brow furrowed. "You know we have fireplaces and central heating, right?"

I flushed. "I don't know how to start a fire."

He smirked. "You definitely did with those marshmallows."

I rolled my eyes. "That was an accident."

"Uh-huh." Logan shook his head, laughing under his breath. "I'll check your vent."

He disappeared down the hall, and I took a shaky breath, staring down at my new mug. I was trembling again, but I wasn't sure if it was from the cold or the way Logan made me feel like I could actually let my guard down.

A few minutes later, he returned. "Damn, sorry. Looks like your vent was closed."

"Oh." My fingers tightened around the mug. "It's okay."

Kneeling on the hearth, Logan gave me a lopsided smile. "Want to learn how to start a fire?"

"Sure, but I'm not fancy. I don't have a fireplace at home."

"Well, maybe you'll be able to next time you come here."

I blushed and kneeled beside him. He showed me how to arrange the logs and kindling properly. His hands moved with ease, his smile never faltering as he explained each step. The fire crackled to life, and he handed me the metal poker.

"Now, this is the fun part," he said mischievously. He showed me how to stir the logs.

I took the poker from him, nudging the logs carefully. The warmth of the flames wasn't the only heat I felt.

The silence stretched, comfortable but charged. My pulse pounded in my throat, my thoughts tangled.

I liked Logan. Maybe too much already. Maybe in a way that meant trouble. Maybe in a way that went against Jax's warnings, against my own self-preservation. But I liked the way he paid attention to details. The way he didn't push, just waited. The way his presence felt steady when everything else in my head was chaos.

Logan wasn't just a passing crush. He felt ... different.

But what if I told him how I felt, and he changed his mind? What if he realized I wasn't worth the trouble?

He turned, his gray eyes catching the fire's reflection. "You okay?"

I nodded, but my throat was tight. It was my chance to say something, to be brave for once instead of overthinking everything until the moment passed. The words sat on the tip of my tongue, warring with my fear.

"I like you," I blurted out.

Silence settled between us, thick and uncertain.

Logan didn't move at first. He just looked at me, really looked at me, as if searching for something in my face. His expression was unreadable, and for a terrifying second, I thought I'd made a mistake.

Then, slowly, he reached out and tucked a strand of hair behind my ear, his fingers lingering just slightly at my temple. My skin burned where he touched it, heat spreading down my spine.

"I was hoping you'd say that," he murmured.

My breath hitched as his thumb brushed along my cheek, so lightly I might have imagined it.

He moved in slowly, deliberately, giving me time to pull away, but I didn't.

His lips met mine in a kiss that was soft but intense, a slow unraveling of tension I hadn't realized I'd been holding. His hand found the small of my back, pressing me just a little closer, and I melted into it. The scent of oak and lemon wrapped around me, grounding me as my fingers curled into the fabric of his shirt.

His thumb grazed my jaw, tilting my face slightly, deepening the kiss just enough to leave me breathless. Every nerve in my body lit up, the warmth of the fire matching the heat between us.

When we finally pulled apart, our foreheads rested together, breathless. Logan smiled, a little shy, his voice barely above a whisper. "That okay?"

I exhaled a shaky laugh. "Yeah," I whispered. "More than okay."

A low chuckle rumbled from his chest, and I realized my fingers were still tangled in the fabric of his shirt. Slowly, he lifted my hand, pried my fingers loose, and interlaced them with his own. His grip was warm, solid, grounding me in a way that made the world feel less uncertain.

Then the fire flickered strangely, like an invisible gust had blown through the room.

I glanced toward the nearest window, expecting it to be cracked open, but it wasn't. A shiver ran down my spine.

The moment of warmth between us shrank, replaced by something cold slithering beneath my skin.

Hazel, a voice whispered in the back of my mind.

I pulled away from Logan, swallowing hard.

"You okay?" he asked.

I forced a smile, shoving the unease aside. "Yeah. Just—"

"Oh my god, y'all made a fire?" Becca's voice rang through the room as she made her way into the room.

Logan sighed, shifting away, and just like that, the warmth of his touch was gone.

Jax and Candace trailed in behind her. Jax's gaze immediately landed on me and Logan, his expression darkening. His jaw ticked, his hands shoving into his pockets as he took in the way we had been sitting so close together.

The tension tripled.

The weight of Jax's stare, the lingering ghost of Logan's kiss, and the strange flicker of the fire all tangled together, leaving me breathless, uncertain, and a little bit haunted.

The trail twisted through a tunnel of trees, golden leaves fluttering down like lazy snowflakes. The air was crisp, carrying the scent of damp earth and pine. A steady wind made the branches creak, but the sounds of the forest were oddly muted, as if the trees were holding their breath.

I tugged my beanie lower over my ears, adjusting my camera strap as I trailed behind the others. The shifting light filtering through the trees created a dreamlike glow, painting the mossy rocks and fallen leaves in hues of amber and green.

"Wow, this is beautiful," I said, lifting my camera for another shot.

Logan slowed his pace to match mine. "I'm glad you like it here."

"How often do you come out here?" I snapped a photo of the sunlight streaming through a break in the trees.

"I used to come a lot, like once a month, but this is the first time I've been back since the summer."

"Oh, wow. How come?"

His hesitation was brief, but I caught it. "Just haven't made the trip."

Not the full truth.

"If I had a cabin out here, I don't think I'd ever leave," I said, but in the back of my mind, a whisper of doubt slithered through me. Would I really be that comfortable isolated in the woods? Especially with what had been happening in *this* cabin?

Logan gave a small smirk. "I used to spend entire summers here. Hiking, swimming."

"Lots of parties?"

He chuckled. "A few. But mostly it was just me, Jax, Marcus, and my family." His expression shifted, revealing the familiar sadness that clouded his eyes.

Without thinking, I slipped my hand into his, and he curled his fingers around mine. A jolt, then a thunderous beat, filled my chest. I hoped he couldn't feel how fast it was racing.

"Maybe we can come back together," he said. "At some point. Or something. Go out on the boat. Maybe swim."

A small smile tugged at my lips as I gazed up at him. "Maybe. Though I don't know how to swim."

His steps faltered slightly. "Really?"

"Yeah."

He squeezed my hand, his thumb brushing against my skin for just a second before he said, "I'll teach you."

I raised an eyebrow. "You will?"

"Yeah, why not?" His lips tilted in a teasing smirk, but there was something softer beneath it.

Before I could say anything else, Becca squeezed herself right between us like a cold gust of wind. "How much longer?" she groaned.

Logan chuckled, slipping his hand from mine. "We've only gone three-tenths of a mile."

She shot him a glare. "I don't know what that means."

"It's not far."

"I'm dying. I need a break." She dramatically plopped onto a rock, her face flushed, strands of hair sticking to her forehead.

Marcus handed her a bottle of water. "Damn, girl. You gonna make it?"

She chugged half the bottle, wiped her mouth with the back of her hand, and pointed at Jax. "I thought you said this was an easy hike."

Jax shrugged. "Logan said 'easy to moderate.'"

"I hate you."

Candace sighed. "We should keep going. We don't want to lose daylight."

"Lead the way, prom queen," Becca muttered.

Candace rolled her eyes and took Jax's hand, the two of them disappearing up the trail with Matt and Aniyah close behind.

Becca sighed dramatically. "We'll catch up," she told Logan and Marcus. "I need a minute."

Logan hesitated. "We can wait."

"I know. I just need to talk to Hazel. You know, girl stuff."

Marcus clapped Logan on the shoulder before heading up the trail. I watched Logan for a second longer, but he didn't look back. My stomach twisted slightly as I turned to Becca.

"I hate this so much." Becca took another sip of water.

I sighed. *Here we go.* "Then why did you come?"

She waved her hand dramatically toward Jax and Candace, clutching each other like they were in a romance movie. "I'm talking about that."

"At least she's not saying weird shit to your face."

Becca snorted. "True." Then she hesitated. Just for a second. "Speaking of weird," she continued, her voice lowering, almost too casual, "are you still … seeing things?"

A small chill crept up my arms, but I shrugged. "No." It wasn't a lie, exactly. I didn't want to talk about it. More importantly, I didn't want to see the look on her face when I did.

Becca sighed, stood up, and looped her arm through mine, dragging me forward. "You know how you get about things, Haze. You latch on and obsess over it for a while. But you got me to keep you grounded."

I stiffened at that, but before I could respond, she grinned. "So, you and Logan, huh?"

The shift in topic was so fast I almost tripped.

A smile tugged at my lips. "Yeah. I had a moment with Logan."

Becca gasped, her eyes lighting up. "What happened?"

I hesitated. My fingers twitched toward my lips as warmth crept up my neck. *Damn it.* "He kissed me."

She let out an actual squeal and smacked my arm. "And?"

"And what?"

"What'd you think? Do you like him?"

"I … yeah. I like him. I just … I don't know. Matt."

Becca rolled her eyes so hard I thought they'd get stuck. "Screw Matt."

I hesitated, lowering my voice. "What if …?" *What if Logan finds out about me? About everything?*

"You can't be afraid forever," Becca said firmly. Then she flashed an innocent grin. "Besides, if he ever hurts you, I'll throttle him."

I laughed.

"You should definitely get to know Logan. Maybe you can get him to open up. Tell you all his deep secrets."

I narrowed my eyes. "What secrets?"

"It's a joke," she said quickly, too quickly. "Logan's a mystery. Maybe you can crack the code."

I studied her for a moment. "Is that why he's been weird sometimes?"

"Logan's just had some adversities," Becca said. "He—"

Marcus cleared his throat loudly as we caught up with him. Logan was still up ahead, walking with Jax and Candace.

Becca fell silent.

Marcus arched an eyebrow. "Adversities. That's what you call it?"

"Well, it's true," she said quickly.

Marcus huffed. "That's an understatement. Logan's been through some serious stuff. It's like he's carrying the weight of the world on his shoulders."

I frowned. "What kind of stuff?"

Becca waved a dismissive hand. "He's just good at hiding things."

Marcus glanced at Logan, then back at us. "He's just afraid to let people in."

I knew that feeling. "What's going on between him and Jax?"

Marcus stiffened, glancing ahead at Logan before looking back at me. "It's ... complicated."

I wanted to ask more. Wanted to press, to dig into this thing that was eating at Logan, but Becca grabbed my wrist and pulled me closer.

"I only wanted to come so I could get alone time with Jax," she whispered. "You should start a conversation with her. Distract her."

"With Candace?" I scoffed. "Give it up."

"Haze, come on. Please? Help a girl out."

I sighed heavily, glancing at Logan. I wanted to walk with him, but Becca wouldn't stop bugging me.

Fine.

I quickened my pace, catching up to Candace. "This trail is amazing."

"Yeah, it really is," she said.

"Do you hike often?" I asked, sneaking a glance at Becca as she grabbed Jax's arm and steered him to the side.

Candace shook her head. "Not really. I think this week has been the most hiking I've ever done in my entire life."

I laughed, relieved. At least she wasn't mad about me talking to her. "Same." My mind raced with topics that could keep Candace engaged. "So how long have you and Jax been together?"

"A couple of months." She glanced back at Jax and Becca. Her expression flickered. "How long were he and Becca together?"

Not the topic I really wanted to discuss. "Uh ... I don't even know. They'd been off and on for a while."

"Sometimes I wonder if they're still on. I guess that's why you came to talk to me."

I froze. "I—"

"It's okay. If she wanted to talk to Jax, I don't know why she needed you to distract me."

I flushed. Candace was sharper than I thought.

Scrambling for another topic, I blurted, "Do you believe in ghosts?"

"Ghosts?"

"Yeah."

"I don't know. Haven't exactly given it much thought."

I hesitated. A cold gust of wind snaked through the trees, and for just a second, I swore I heard a whisper. "I think the cabin is haunted," I told her.

Candace stopped walking. "What? Because of Logan's story?"

I hesitated again. I'd replayed the events in my mind so many times, each time trying to convince myself they weren't real. "I've been ... seeing things. And hearing things. At the cabin." The words felt heavy as they left my mouth.

Her expression didn't change. "What kind of things?"

I took a deep breath, the cool, pine-scented air steadying my nerves. "At first, I thought it was stress. But it's more than that. I've seen ... someone. A girl. And I've heard whispers, my name being called when no one's there."

Candace's brows furrowed.

"It sounds wild, I know. But it feels so real."

The path beneath our feet seemed to stretch longer as my confession unfolded, the surrounding forest a silent witness to my turmoil.

She reached out, touching my arm lightly. "That sounds terrifying."

"You haven't experienced anything, right?"

"No, but that doesn't mean it isn't happening to you. Have you told anyone else about this?"

"I tried, but Becca didn't believe me. She thinks Aniyah is playing with me or it's all in my head. But I don't think she believes in ghosts or anything like that."

"Listen, Hazel," Candace said firmly. "Maybe there's a logical explanation for everything. I can try to help figure it out if you want."

"You would do that?"

She shrugged. "Yeah. Why?"

For the first time since I arrived, I felt something small and fragile bloom inside me. Hope.

Maybe I wasn't alone in this after all.

Pausing for a moment, I turned my attention to a break in the trees that unveiled a stunning vista of mountains cloaked in the rich, warm hues of fall. I focused and clicked. Changed the angle and clicked.

"You really do have an eye for shots," Logan said behind me.

I turned to face him, my heart giving a little flutter at how easily he closed the distance between us. "It's all an act. I really have no idea what I'm doing."

"Let me see."

I hesitated before handing him the camera, watching as he tilted his head slightly, studying my photos. His expression was unreadable at first, but then he shook his head with a small smile. "It looks like you know what you're doing. You have a gift."

Warmth bloomed in my chest. No one had ever called it that before. I looked away, biting my lip as a blush crept up my cheeks.

Logan's fingers brushed under my chin, guiding me to look at him again. My breath hitched at the quiet intensity in his gray eyes. The world shrank. All faded—the sounds of the wind through the trees, the distant laughter of our friends—as his thumb traced the edge of my jaw.

And then, he kissed me.

Soft, warm, unhurried. The pressure of his lips against mine was gentle but certain, like he'd been waiting for the right moment. A slow, sweet unraveling of tension, of curiosity turning into something more.

A breath hitched in my throat. The kiss sent warmth trickling down my spine, pooling in my stomach in slow, molten waves. The faint scent of oak and lemon wrapped around me, grounding me. I didn't realize I'd placed my hands on his chest until I felt the steady rhythm of his heartbeat beneath my fingertips.

Then someone cleared their throat.

Logan and I broke apart like we'd been caught doing something scandalous.

"Come on, lovebirds." Becca's teasing voice cut through the quiet.

I wanted to kick her. I shot her a glare, but it was nothing compared to the way Jax stared at Logan.

Jax's usual smirk was gone, replaced with something hard. Not just annoyance, but something sharper. His eyes flickered to mine, then back to Logan, like he was biting back whatever he really wanted to say.

A cold trickle of unease ran down my spine. Why did it feel like I'd done something wrong?

As we trekked farther into the woods, the atmosphere shifted. The dense canopy of trees cast eerie shadows, and an unsettling silence replaced the usual cheerful chirping of birds. We came to a clearing.

I walked cautiously into the open space and noticed a small, abandoned house, barely standing.

Something about it made my stomach drop. Obscured by thick underbrush and gnarled trees, the house gave off an aura of isolation and desolation. It didn't just look old. It looked … wrong.

The windows were long devoid of glass, allowing the elements to infiltrate its interior freely. Jagged shards of broken panes still dangled precariously from rotting frames. The hollow, dark windows looked like empty eyes, watching us.

"Damn, Logan," Marcus muttered, shifting uneasily. "Where did you take us?"

I halted behind Candace, Jax, Matt, and Aniyah.

Logan shrugged, too casual. "It's just an old house. Built in the 1800s or something." Then, with a smirk, he added, "Or maybe it's Eleanor's house." His teasing tone masked a more deliberate, calculating intention.

Jax's entire body tensed. He took a slow step toward Logan, his shoulders squared like he was physically restraining himself from reacting. "Seriously?" His voice was sharp, edged with anger.

Logan turned to him, unfazed. "What?"

Jax let out a breath, running a hand through his hair. His jaw clenched tight. "You could've picked anywhere," he said, his voice low but firm. "Any hike. Any trail. Why this one?"

A charged silence filled the space between them. Logan met Jax's glare but didn't answer immediately. Instead, he rolled his shoulders, as if shrugging off the weight of whatever Jax was implying.

"I don't know, man," Logan said, his tone light. "Seemed like a good spot."

Jax didn't buy it. His fingers curled into a fist at his side before he exhaled, shaking his head. He muttered something under his breath, something I couldn't catch.

I looked between them, confused. What was happening?

"Chill, dude," Marcus said, trying to ease the tension. "It's just an abandoned house."

"Yeah," Logan added, his lips tugging into an easy smirk. "Unless you're scared?"

Jax visibly stiffened, his fingers flexing at his sides. For a second, I thought he might actually swing at Logan. His shoulders tensed, his jaw clenching as if he were holding something back. But instead of reacting, he let out a forced chuckle, shaking his head. "Whatever."

The word came out flat, but his eyes were dark and unsettled. The muscles in his jaw ticked, and his gaze flickered toward the trees, then to the rotting house in the clearing. Like he was bracing for something.

Becca let out a dramatic sigh, rolling her eyes. "Good grief." She crossed her arms, then strode toward the house like she had something to prove. "Eleanor isn't real," she called over her shoulder, flashing a mischievous smile. "I'll prove it."

Her voice held confidence, but her steps slowed as she neared the house.

For just a moment, I saw the slightest hesitation, the way her body tensed, like she'd just walked into ice water. She glanced at Jax, who was still rooted in place, his stare locked onto the house.

Becca straightened her shoulders and disappeared inside.

A knot coiled tight in my stomach. Something was wrong.

I glanced at Logan, but he wasn't watching Becca. He was watching Jax. A crease formed between his brows, his fingers twitching like he was debating whether to say something. But then he just shrugged, shoving his hands in his pockets.

A gust of wind slithered through the trees, carrying with it a musty, sour scent. My stomach twisted as the familiar stench of damp decay settled over me. The same smell from last night. The smell of Hannah.

Goosebumps prickled along my arms as I rubbed them, trying to shake off the unease settling over me like a second skin. The woods, once filled with rustling leaves and distant bird calls, had gone unnervingly silent. Even the wind seemed to hold its breath.

"Is it going to rain again?" I asked.

Logan glanced at the sky, his brow furrowed slightly. "Not that I'm aware," he said, but there was something distant in his tone, as if his thoughts were elsewhere.

I turned back toward the house, my gut twisting.

Then it came.

A scream.

Shrill, raw, and blood-curdling. It ripped through the air like a jagged blade, shattering the silence and sending every nerve in my body into high alert.

Chapter Fifteen

We all sprinted toward the house. My legs felt heavy, as though the very air of this place resisted our intrusion.

The stench of decay grew thicker, curling in my nostrils, clinging to my skin. It wasn't just the smell of rotting wood or mildew. It was deeper, fouler like something long-buried was surfacing.

The scream echoed in my ears, its raw terror still vibrating in my bones. My stomach churned, my pulse hammering so loudly that I could barely hear anything else.

The moment I stepped inside, the air turned icy, thick and heavy, like stepping into a different world. The light outside barely pierced the dust-covered windows, casting warped shadows along the peeling wallpaper.

Something felt wrong.

And then I saw her.

To my left, Becca lay in a crumpled heap, her wild curls sprawled around her, her body unnaturally still.

My breath caught in my throat. "Oh my god! Becca! Becca!" I dropped to my knees beside her, my hands trembling as I reached for her.

The others crowded around, voices overlapping in panic. Logan's hand brushed against my shoulder as he knelt beside me, his voice sharp and commanding. "Is she breathing?"

A shiver ran down my spine as I checked for injuries, my fingers skimming over her cool skin.

And then her eyes snapped open.

A slow, wicked grin spread across her face. "Haha, got you."

For a second, no one moved. The world held its breath.

Then came the groans, the collective exhale of frustration.

But I couldn't move. Couldn't speak.

My pulse still pounded, my breath coming too fast. The fear hadn't left my body yet. I was still caught in that moment where I thought something horrible had happened. "Seriously?" My voice came out hoarse. "I thought you were—" I cut myself off, my jaw clenching.

Becca sat up, dusting herself off like it was no big deal. "It was just a joke."

Logan shot to his feet so fast I felt the air shift beside me. His expression was dark, but his voice cut through the room like a blade. "That's not even remotely funny."

He turned on his heel and strode out of the house, his movements sharp, purposeful. The rest of the group followed without a word.

I was still kneeling beside Becca, my hands clenched into fists.

"It was a joke!" She stood and brushed off her jeans.

I exhaled sharply, pushing to my feet. "What the hell is wrong with you?"

"Me? What's your problem? Why have you been bitchy all day?"

"I haven't. But this place gives me the creeps."

"Why? It's just some old building."

No, it wasn't. Jax knew something, and so did Logan. What had happened here?

I wanted to follow everyone else outside, but something made me want to explore. While I wandered through the rooms, a faint, sweet scent of lavender drifted through the air, mingling with the musty aroma of aged wood. The contrast was unsettling as if something unnatural lingered here, hiding beneath the ordinary scents. Strange, since moments ago it smelled like something was rotting.

In a dimly lit corner, a narrow ladder led up to an attic. My fingers curled around the rungs, the aged wood cool against my skin. My stomach twisted with unease, but curiosity propelled me forward. Just as my hand reached the attic door—

"Hazel."

I froze.

The voice was distant, almost swallowed by the silence of the house.

"What?" I called back, my pulse quickening.

Nothing.

A flicker of irritation shot through me. Becca and her damn tricks.

I let out an exasperated sigh, and the floor above me groaned. A slow, heavy creak echoed through the silence, like the weight of unseen footsteps pressing down on rotted wood. A shadow flickered through the gaps between the attic boards.

Something or someone was up there.

A lump formed in my throat, but my feet moved on their own, my body caught between terror and a sick need to know. I climbed the rest of the ladder, forcing myself not to hesitate.

The attic door yawned open, revealing a space thick with dust and memories. Sunbeams trickled through cracked windows, illuminating the swirling motes in the air.

A faint whisper brushed against my ear.

I spun around, but the attic was empty.

The scent of lavender deepened, cloying now, suffocating.

My gaze landed on an old, dust-caked mirror in the corner, its ornate frame cracked like spiderweb fractures. I took a slow step forward.

The reflection wasn't mine.

A girl stood in the mirror. Her hollow eyes locked onto mine. Water dripped from her hair, pooling at her bare feet.

I gasped.

Hannah.

The mirror trembled. She stepped through it.

A bone-deep cold sliced through me as Hannah moved closer. My breath misted in the frigid air, and the room itself felt like it had drawn in a sharp breath, waiting.

Stepping back, my heart seized in my throat. Despite my fear, I wanted to understand why Hannah was appearing now. We weren't at the cabin. Was Hannah ... *following* me?

"Why are you here?" I whispered.

Hannah's sorrowful gaze never wavered. Her lips parted, but no sound came out.

I shuddered, a primal fear clawing its way up my spine. "Why are you doing this to me?"

"Be careful who you trust." Her voice was distant, echoing, like words carried across water. "Or you'll end up like me."

A chill sank into my bones. "What?" I took a step forward, my heart hammering. "What do you mean?"

But Hannah flickered like a candle about to go out. The shadows swallowed her whole.

And she was gone.

I choked on my breath, my entire body trembling.

The attic's silence was deafening.

I'd had enough. Bravery only lasted so long. I turned and fled down the ladder, moving too fast, and my foot missed the bottom rung. Pain ripped through my palm as I caught myself, a sharp splintered edge driving into my skin.

A cry escaped my lips.

"Hazel?" Becca's voice rang out. Footsteps pounded towards me.

I staggered back, clutching my bleeding hand. The wound stung like fire, warm blood trickling between my fingers.

"What the hell happened?"

"I—" My throat was too dry, my mind still in the attic, still with Hannah. "I fell off the ladder. There was ... a rat."

I knew Becca would press if I told her the truth. Pain pulsed in my palm as I clamped my fingers over the wound.

A bloodcurdling scream echoed through the trees.

Becca and I exchanged wide-eyed looks and bolted out the door.

Outside, Candace stood frozen, her hands clamped over her mouth.

Everyone else had already turned their gaze upward, faces twisted with alarm.

When I followed their line of sight, my heart froze.

Perched on the peak of the roof were six black vultures. Their dark wings stretched, feathers ruffling as they shifted, silent sentinels watching us from above.

A thick wave of unease rolled through me.

Vultures meant death.

And somehow, I knew they weren't there by accident.

Chapter Sixteen

Back at the cabin, I perched on the edge of the bathroom counter, my legs dangling as Logan stood between them, focused intently on my hand. The sharp pinch of tweezers against my skin made me flinch, but his grip was steady, his touch surprisingly gentle.

"Hold still," he muttered, his voice low and even, the kind of tone that made it hard to argue.

The bathroom light buzzed softly above us, casting a warm glow over his furrowed brow and the streak of dirt smudged across his cheek. He'd insisted on taking care of this himself, brushing off my protests like they were nothing.

"Don't you have better things to do than play nurse?" I winced as he dug at another splinter.

"Not really," he said, not looking up.

The moment was quiet, almost too quiet, the hum of the cabin settling around us like a blanket. But beneath the surface, my thoughts churned. The abandoned house, Hannah, the tension I couldn't quite name hung heavy in the back of my mind.

I studied Logan's face as he worked, trying to read him, to understand what he wasn't saying. There was something about him, about the way he carried himself, the way his eyes darkened when he thought no one was looking, that made me think he was keeping secrets of his own.

"Almost done," he said.

The tweezers pricked my skin again, but this time I barely felt it. I wasn't sure if it was the adrenaline wearing off or the fact that Logan was close enough for me to catch the faint scent of pine and something earthy, something that felt distinctly him.

"Are you ... okay?" I asked.

"Yeah."

But I could tell he wasn't. "I'm sorry about Becca."

"It's not your fault." He plucked the last splinter. "Is your camera okay? After your fall?"

"Yeah."

He grabbed a cotton ball and soaked it with alcohol, then dabbed my wounds.

I sucked in a breath through my teeth, feeling the sting. "You know, you don't have to do this."

"I know. I want to," he said as he tore open a Band-Aid and softly placed it on my wound.

His words sent a strange warmth curling through my chest.

"Why are you being so nice to me?" I asked. "Did Becca ask you to?"

He looked up, confused. "No. I like you, but I also try to be nice to everyone."

"You don't know me."

He nodded. "I'm getting to know you."

We were quiet for a moment as he crinkled the trash and tossed it into the waste basket. I wanted to ask him more questions, but I needed to tread lightly.

"What's the deal with you and Jax?"

Logan sighed. "He dated my sister."

"Oh." I hadn't expected that. "Did ... did it end badly or something?"

"I don't really like talking about my sister's love life."

"Fair enough." I exhaled. "Thanks for patching me up."

He shrugged. "It's the least I could do after walking out and leaving you alone in that creepy old house."

"It's not your fault. I was pissed at Becca, too. She's always doing things like that. She and my brother love to play pranks on me."

"Do you scare easily?" he asked, a playful glint in his eyes.

"No," I lied, very aware of his arms gently grazing my legs, his hands braced on the countertop on either side of me. "They try their best to scare me, but I always stay one step ahead."

Logan raised an eyebrow. "Is that so? Maybe I should team up with your brother. We could give you a real scare."

I feigned offense, playfully swatting his arm. "Oh, so now you're plotting against me? I thought you were here to patch me up."

He chuckled. "Got you to smile."

I grinned, but my chest tightened. I wanted to believe I could let my guard down with him, but Jax's warning rang in my head. What was Logan hiding?

Logan's eyes dropped to my lips, and my pulse thudded in response. His warm hand brushed my cheek, his thumb skimming lightly across my skin.

For a split second, I hesitated. We'd only known each other for four days. I shouldn't have wanted this, not this much, not this fast. But the way he looked at me … like I was the only thing keeping him upright, I couldn't pull away.

And when he leaned in, I closed the space between us.

The moment his lips touched mine, a dizzying heat bloomed through me, swirling low in my stomach, setting fire to my nerves. He tasted like something sweet and familiar, citrus and honey.

His fingers drifted from my cheek to my waist, then slipped lower, gripping enough to pull me closer. The kiss deepened, no longer soft or tentative. It was hungry now, full of tension and want, like he was trying to pour every unspoken word into me.

His mouth moved over mine with a slow, aching intensity, and I felt it everywhere—under my skin, in my chest, low in my stomach.

His other hand slid to the small of my back, anchoring me against him. Heat coiled between us, the kind that made it hard to think, to breathe—

Until a chill swept through me. Sudden. Bone-deep.

I stiffened. Something felt … wrong. I opened my eyes and saw her.

Hannah. Dripping wet. Standing behind Logan. Her eyes locked on mine, empty and unblinking.

I gasped and tore away, my fingers trembling as I pressed them to my lips, the warmth of the kiss vanishing beneath the icy flood of fear.

Logan's brow furrowed. "What is it?"

She vanished. But the air still felt damp. Wrong.

I forced myself to breathe, to push away the terror clawing at my throat. "Nothing," I said too quickly.

His gaze searched mine, unsure, like he was waiting for me to give him the real answer.

I slipped off the counter, suddenly too aware of every inch of space between us. "We should … we should go back. Everyone's probably wondering where we are."

He hesitated. "Okay."

As we walked out, I could feel the tension still clinging to the air, like the ghost of a touch, the ghost of her. And beneath it all, I swore I still heard the steady, rhythmic sound of water hitting the floor.

Drip.

Drip.

Drip.

Outside, the firepit crackled. Laughter and conversation floated in the night air. But everything felt different now. Flickering shadows cast by glowing embers, dancing across faces that didn't know what I'd just seen. What I couldn't unsee.

"It was creepy," Candace said as we joined the conversation.

"They were vultures," Becca said. "You screamed like you were being chased by Freddy."

"Hey, six giant vultures suddenly appearing was peculiar," Jax muttered, tossing a twig into the fire.

Marcus shook his head. "Right? They just came flying around and landed on that cabin like it was some kind of omen."

"Omen of what, exactly?" Logan cut in, tone light but too quick, like he didn't want them to keep talking about it.

I could only muster a weak smile. The night was the coldest it had been all week. Logan had brought blankets for everyone, and I wore my hoodie and beanie, but I couldn't shake off a lingering discomfort that had nothing to do with the temperature.

"Be careful who you trust."

Hannah's voice echoed in my mind, and my stomach knotted. What had she meant? My gaze flickered to Logan. Was she warning me about him?

I turned to Candace instead, needing an anchor in something normal.

"Are you okay?" she asked softly.

"Yeah. Just tired." I wasn't about to tell her what I'd seen in the abandoned house or what I'd seen only a minute ago in the bathroom with Logan.

"Logan seems to really like you."

A small smile pulled at my lips. "We kissed," I whispered, suddenly grateful for something else to focus on.

Candace gasped. "That's exciting."

I hesitated, glancing toward Logan, who sat across from us. His fingers absentmindedly traced the lip of his bottle, but his eyes were locked on me. His intense stare was impenetrable, but the moment I looked, his expression changed into a hasty smile. It was small, almost shy, like he wasn't used to people paying attention to him.

Still ... Hannah's warning clung to me.

I turned back to Candace. "What do you know about him?"

"I've only met him a couple of times. He seems nice. Kinda quiet."

My chest tightened. Too quiet. "Has Jax talked about him at all?"

"Not really. Just that they're friends."

I almost told Candace about Jax's warning, but now there was another warning looming. Hannah's.

Be careful who you trust.

"I guess I'm just scared," I admitted.

"That's fair," Candace said. "So am I. I really like Jax, but..." She flicked her gaze toward Becca, who was sitting next to Jax.

Becca was talking, animated as always, but Jax wasn't really listening, his eyes kept darting toward Logan.

Candace sighed. "I thought coming here would make things simpler. It hasn't."

I nodded, swallowing the lump in my throat. "Yeah."

Was Hannah warning me about Logan? Candace? Marcus? They all seemed eager and nice. Almost too nice. Or was it Aniyah?

My mind swirled with confusion. What was happening to me? Was I being haunted ... or was I on the verge of another breakdown?

The night stretched out beyond the window, a vast sea of darkness pierced by sharp pinpricks of starlight. It should have felt calming, but the cold in my room was relentless. My breath fogged against the glass, a thin veil of frost forming at the edges.

I shivered, pulling my hoodie tighter around me. No heat. Again. My fingers were so numb I could barely feel them, and my socks did nothing to stop the ice creeping up my toes.

Was it just me? Or was it getting colder?

Needing a distraction, I grabbed my phone and opened Google.

I wanted to learn more about Hannah, to understand the connection between us, if there was one. What if I didn't find anything? What if I did? Either way, I couldn't just dismiss Hannah's appearances as hallucinations or attribute everything to my mental condition. There was something deeper at play, and I was determined to uncover the truth.

I swallowed hard and entered "Hannah + Blue Ridge."

The first article stopped me cold.

16-year-old teen with mental health issues reported missing by Fannin County Police

By Helen Parker *News Reporter*

Posted 8:45PM | Monday, January 8, 2024

Fannin County Police have reported a missing teen.

16-year-old Hannah Foster was last seen on Wednesday, January 3 in the Blue Ridge area, and police are asking the public for their help to find her.

She has a history of leaving her family's house without permission. She was last seen wearing a white shirt and blue shorts. She is 5'6", 120 pounds.

She is known to suffer from bipolar disorder.

A sharp, electric jolt shot through my chest. My breath hitched. My lungs refused to expand.

Bipolar disorder.

The words sat there on the screen, glaring back at me.

A door I had worked so hard to keep bolted shut cracked open in my mind, and suddenly I was back there.

The racing thoughts. The ones that made the world move too fast, faster than I could catch up.

The scribbled notebooks. Pages and pages of ideas I was convinced would change my life, except I couldn't remember writing them.

The whispers in the middle of the night. Just outside my door. The certainty that they were talking about me, plotting something, until my mother's voice broke through. "Hazel, no one is there."

The crash. The deep, sinking feeling that felt like drowning. Like my bones were made of lead, and my own mind was turning against me. The hospital walls. The clipboard scribbles. The cold judgment in the nurse's eyes.

I gasped and forced myself back into the present.

My hands trembled violently, my knuckles white as I gripped my phone. The screen blurred through the haze of tears. I rubbed at my face, sucking in a shaky breath. This was ridiculous. I couldn't fall down the rabbit hole. Not again.

But my gaze drifted back to the screen.

Hannah Foster. Long, brown hair. A bright smile that matched her eyes. Except for the smile ... she looked just like the girl in my dreams. Like the girl I had seen in the hallway. At the abandoned house. Behind Logan.

A deep, twisting nausea coiled in my stomach.

What if Hannah wasn't just a ghost? What if she was a warning?

I let out a sigh. No. I needed to stop.

Maybe some hot tea would help me sleep. If nothing else, it would at least keep me warm.

The kitchen was dark except for the soft glow of the under-cabinet lights. I stood by the counter, mindlessly scrolling through my phone, sipping my tea.

Hannah's warning echoed in my head. *Be careful who you trust. Or you'll end up like me.*

I clenched my jaw and shook my head. *No. I'm not doing this. Not tonight.*

"Can't sleep?" A voice from behind startled me.

I jumped, nearly dropping my tea. Whipping around, I found Logan standing there, watching me.

"Geez." I exhaled, pressing a hand to my chest. "You scared me."

His lips curved into a smirk. "Sorry," he said, not sounding sorry at all. His hair was a little messy, like he had just run a hand through it. His T-shirt clung to his frame, and his sweatpants hung low on his hips.

Damn.

I turned back to my tea before my brain could go anywhere dangerous.

"You okay?" He stepped closer. "You look like you haven't slept much."

"Yeah. I'm fine," I lied. "I made some tea. Hope that's okay."

"Of course. Why wouldn't it be?"

I shrugged.

Logan leaned against the counter. "I was about to watch some TV. Want to join me?"

"Sure." I needed a distraction from the thoughts clawing at the edges of my mind.

I followed him into the main room and sat on the plush leather sofa, stretching out, my back against the arm. Logan started a fire and turned on the TV, then settled at the opposite end of the couch, handing me a blanket.

"Thanks."

Late-night television was the worst.

The flames crackled, the scent of burning wood mingling with the faint traces of Logan's scent, like oak and lemon and the lingering crispness of night air. As the TV droned on, we found ourselves drawn into a conversation that flowed effortlessly.

"Tell me about one of your favorite baseball memories," I said.

Logan's lips twitched. "That's tough," he said, but I could tell he already had an answer. "Probably would have to be this one game. We were down by two runs in the bottom of the ninth inning. Bases were loaded, and it was my turn to bat. I remember feeling the pressure, but also this rush of excitement. I swung, and the ball, by some miracle, slipped past the first and second basemen. Two guys scored and the outfielder threw the ball and missed. The guy from third base scored and we won the game."

His eyes lit up, and I found myself smiling, caught up in the way he told the story.

"I love that feeling, like I'm making a difference. Like I'm part of something bigger than myself."

"I get that. Photography makes me feel the same way. Capturing a perfect moment, freezing it in time. It's like capturing a piece of someone's soul." I glanced at him, drawn to the intensity in his eyes. The firelight danced within them, casting an almost hypnotic glow that held me captive. Shadows flickered across his face, sharpening the angles of his jaw and hinting at the depth beneath his quiet demeanor.

Logan reached out, gently tucking a strand of my hair behind my ear. Goosebumps prickled across my arms. My heart fluttered in my chest as a rush of warmth flooded my cheeks. His touch sent a wave of desire coursing through every nerve ending in my body. Our eyes locked, and in that moment, the room seemed to shrink, leaving only the two of us.

Logan leaned in, closing the gap between us. His lips pressed to mine, hesitant at first. But as the seconds passed, the kiss deepened. The warmth that I sought in tea and blankets paled compared to the heat that now enveloped us.

He pulled me closer, our bodies pressed against each other. The room seemed to fade away, our desire for each other growing with each passing moment.

His lips found my neck, caressing the sensitive skin with feather-light kisses. The warmth of his breath sent shivers down my spine. I leaned into his touch, craving more of his intoxicating presence. A soft sigh escaped my lips, betraying the pleasure that coursed through my veins.

With a gentle touch, my hands ventured beneath his shirt, discovering the velvety softness of his back. My heart drummed in my chest as his kisses grew more intense, sending waves of pleasure through my body. The heat between us built, heady and all-consuming, until reality tugged at the edges of my mind.

The weight of this moment, this shift, pressed against my chest. *What are we doing?*

I slowed the kiss first, easing back enough to catch my breath. Logan hesitated, his lips still lingering close, as if waiting to see if I'd pull away completely.

The kiss ended, but our eyes lingered, the space between us charged with an unspoken question neither of us was ready to answer.

Logan's smile was soft, almost breathless. "I didn't expect my night to take this turn."

I let out a nervous laugh, my fingers still grazing the fabric of his shirt before I slowly withdrew them. "Neither did I."

Just as he was about to get off me, I pulled him back, nuzzling into his chest. A slow, contented sigh escaped him as he settled back down, his arms wrapping securely around me. His heartbeat was steady beneath my ear, a quiet rhythm that somehow eased the whirlwind inside me. I let myself melt into him, my fingers absently tracing small patterns along his arm.

He let out a chuckle, and I could feel the gentle rumble in his chest. "Who knew not being able to sleep could lead to this?"

I rolled my eyes, but a smile tugged at my lips. The glow of the fire, the hum of the TV, the warmth of his embrace was all so easy. Too easy.

We stayed like that for a while, listening to each other's breathing and whatever meaningless show was playing in the background. I should've let myself enjoy it, let the moment linger. But the questions that had been gnawing at me refused to stay buried.

He shifted slightly, tilting his head toward me, his hand slipping into my hair, the gesture so gentle it sent a shiver down my spine. His eyes held mine, and the weight behind them made my throat tighten.

"Why do you look so sad? Or haunted?" I whispered. "Does it have to do with Jax?"

The warmth between us vanished in an instant, like a candle snuffed out. His body, which had been so relaxed against mine, tensed just enough that I felt it.

Slowly, he sat up, untangling himself from me.

I braved a look at him, and something dark and guarded flickered in his expression. His jaw flexed, his fingers briefly clenching before he willed them to relax. If I hadn't been paying attention, I might've missed the subtle hitch in his breath, the way he forced himself to stay composed.

"I'm sorry," I said, regretting asking him anything.

"It's okay." But his voice was tight, his shoulders rigid. The room felt smaller now, the cozy firelight suddenly casting too many shadows.

I wanted to take it back, to smooth over the cracks I'd just exposed. But the silence between us felt thick, heavy with things unsaid. "I'm sorry," I whispered again. "I don't mean to pry. It's just ... the other day when you went out, and you came back completely dirty ... you looked angry or sad. And I've noticed that look a lot."

Logan exhaled through his nose, running a hand through his hair. When he finally met my eyes, there was no anger. Just raw pain. "Some things are just hard to talk about."

Studying him, I saw the storm beneath the surface. The traces of frustration, the weight of something unspoken. Logan looked tortured. But why didn't Jax trust him?

I understood the need to keep things buried. Slowly, I reached out, my hand hovering for a second before finally intertwining with his. His grip tightened slightly, grounding us both.

The tension between us didn't disappear completely, but it softened.

"There are things that I'm not ready to share," he finally said.

I swallowed hard. "It's okay," I replied, even though a dozen questions screamed inside me.

Becca had said he had secrets. Jax had warned me about him. And now Hannah's voice echoed in my mind.

Be careful who you trust.

I wanted to trust Logan. I wanted to believe that whatever he carried wasn't something I had to fear. But hadn't I thought that about Matt, too?

The thought sent an uncomfortable chill down my spine.

Instead of digging deeper, I forced a smile. "Wanna see if you can beat me at *Mario Kart*?" Distraction was easier than doubt.

Logan turned to face me, his eyes searching mine for a second longer than necessary. Then, the corner of his lip curled into something resembling his usual smirk. "You're on."

The atmosphere lightened, and I was glad of the change.

Except for a single loss, I triumphed in every *Mario Kart* race.

Logan groaned dramatically, tossing his controller aside. "I think you cheated." He narrowed his eyes at me.

I smirked. "Oh? And how exactly did I cheat?"

"I don't know yet, but I'll figure it out." He leaned back, running a hand through his hair. "No one beats me that many times."

"Guess I'm just better than you."

He scoffed. "You got lucky. Rematch tomorrow."

I grinned, stretching my arms over my head. The weight of exhaustion started pressing down on me, but the warmth of Logan's presence was hard to walk away from.

He yawned. "Damn. It's four AM."

My eyes widened. "Oh wow, I'm so sorry I kept you up."

"Don't apologize. I enjoy being with you. But we should probably head to bed." He stood from the couch, his eyes flickering to mine. "Aren't you tired?"

And just like that, my fear returned. I didn't want to go back to my room.

I hesitated, glancing toward the hallway leading to the bedrooms. The idea of facing the unknown in my room overwhelmed me, and an irrational fear of encountering the ghost gnawed at my thoughts. I didn't want to be alone. "I may stay here for a little longer."

Logan furrowed his eyebrows but nodded. "You sure? You gonna be okay?"

"Yeah, I'll be fine."

His hesitation lingered for a second longer than necessary, as if he wasn't convinced. But then he leaned down, pressing a lingering kiss against my forehead. "Sweet dreams."

I forced a smile and bid him goodnight, watching as he disappeared down the dimly lit hallway. Alone in the living room, I wrapped the blanket tighter around me, contemplating whether to brave the journey to my room or find refuge on the sofa.

I settled on the sofa. It was warmer here. Safer. I pulled the blanket over my shoulders, staring into the dying embers of the fireplace. I tried to push thoughts and images of Hannah from my mind.

A few minutes later, soft footsteps creaked across the floor. I jumped slightly, twisting to find Logan standing there with his arms crossed.

"What are you doing back out here?" I asked, my pulse still unsteady.

He plopped down beside me. "I don't really feel like going to bed just yet. Mind if I crash out here too?"

Relief washed over me, but I tried to play it cool. "Yeah, sure. The sofa is pretty comfy."

"Great." He shot me a lopsided grin. "Plus, you'd probably get scared without me."

"I was *not* scared."

"Mmhmm." He disappeared briefly and returned with an extra blanket, making himself comfortable on the sofa next to me. He invited me to cuddle next to him, and I gave in without hesitation.

As I curled into his warmth, his arm settled around me, the steady rise and fall of his chest lulling me into a sense of ease. My fears began to wane, the presence of Hannah fading. At least for tonight.

My eyes fluttered open as a feather-light touch brushed against my face. Warmth pressed against my side. Logan was still fast asleep. The slow, steady rise and fall of his chest should have comforted me, but something was off.

A presence. The unmistakable sensation of being watched.

A chill crept up my spine. Had Matt gotten up? I turned my head slightly, careful not to wake Logan. The only light came from the muted flicker of the TV, casting faint, distorted shadows across the room.

Nothing.

I exhaled, settling back against the couch, closing my eyes. *Relax. You're just imagining it.*

But I felt the weight of eyes on me. Inches away.

My heartbeat hammered, a rhythmic thudding in my ears. *Don't look. Don't look.* My body screamed for me to flee, to run, to shake Logan awake, but I couldn't move.

A slow, deliberate breath ghosted across my cheek. Cold. Icy. Wrong.

The hair rose on my arms. The air thickened, dense with something unseen. My fingers curled into the blanket. The silence stretched, suffocating, pressing down on me like a heavy fog.

A soft whisper, barely audible, slithered into my ears. "Don't be afraid, Hazel." The voice was familiar. "Help me."

A sharp inhale tore through my lungs.

I clenched my fists, forcing every muscle in my body to obey. *Move. Look. Face it.* With a surge of courage, I snapped my eyes open.

Hannah.

Draped in shadows, a flickering, half-formed shape in the dim light, her presence warped the air around her. Her hollow, pleading eyes bored into mine, anchoring me in place.

A silent scream clawed its way up my throat.

Then, she was gone.

The room remained still. Silent. Too silent.

I swallowed hard, my breath shaky, as I clutched the blanket to my chest. My heart pounded so loudly I was sure it would wake Logan. But he didn't stir.

Tuesday

Chapter Seventeen

The rich scent of coffee wafted toward me, pulling me from sleep. My eyelids felt heavy, my limbs sluggish as I shifted beneath the blanket.

I blinked, disoriented for a moment, before I remembered. Logan and I had slept on the couch. He'd stayed with me. Not that I'd asked him to, but maybe he'd seen something on my face. Maybe he knew I didn't want to be alone.

As I rubbed the sleep from my eyes, the image of Hannah's stare seared through the grogginess. The hollow intensity, the silent warning. *Be careful who you trust.*

How much longer did we have at the cabin?

It was Tuesday. So it would be three more days. Three more days of pretending I wasn't seeing things. Three more days of Logan.

I wanted to leave. But I also wanted to stay.

Before I could untangle the mess in my head, Logan walked in, handing me a cup of coffee with an easy smile. "Morning." He settled onto the couch beside me.

The memory of our kiss from last night rushed back all at once. His hands on me, the heat, the way I'd melted into him. I swallowed hard, gripping the coffee a little tighter than necessary.

"Thanks," I murmured, taking a sip.

Logan studied me over the rim of his mug. "Did you sleep okay? You tossed and turned a lot. Bad dreams?"

I frowned. *Did I?* "Oh. Maybe. I don't remember."

A lie. I remembered every second. The whisper, the cold breath against my cheek, the way Hannah had looked through me. But I wasn't about to tell Logan that.

Instead, I forced my focus on something else like Candace's offer. If I was going to make sense of any of this, I needed to figure out who Hannah was. Maybe Candace and I could go into town.

But I knew it wouldn't be good to leave Jax alone with Becca. I could go by myself.

Footsteps thudded down the stairs.

Matt.

His hair was a mess, sticking up at odd angles, and he looked like he hadn't fully woken up yet. But when he saw Logan and me on the couch together, something changed.

His furrowed brows hinted at underlying annoyance or jealousy. "You slept out here?" he asked, his tone carefully neutral.

I nodded, sipping my coffee. "Yeah. My room was cold. Logan built a fire, and we hung out." And made out.

Matt's jaw tensed, his lips pressing into a firm line.

Logan stood up and stretched. "I'm making breakfast. Want some?"

"Sure," I said.

Logan disappeared into the kitchen.

The second he was out of sight, Matt plopped down next to me, his body radiating tension. "What do you think you're doing?" His voice was low, sharp with disbelief.

I turned to him, brows knitting together. "What?"

He shook his head, exhaling through his nose. "Logan?"

My spine went rigid. "What about him?"

"Hazel, he's not good for you. He's ... bad."

I blinked, caught between anger and outright laughter. Was he serious? Matt, of all people, was warning me about someone? "You're kidding, right?"

His jaw tightened. "I'm serious."

I scoffed. "You are the last person I would ever take advice from."

His expression darkened.

"I mean, do you even hear yourself? You cheated on me. You told Aniyah about my diagnosis. You ruined any trust we had."

Matt's gaze dropped to the floor, shame creeping across his features.

Good. He should feel ashamed.

"I know," he muttered. "I just thought you should know about him. That's all."

My pulse hammered. I folded my arms, the anger swelling in my chest. "Know what about him?"

Matt hesitated. Just long enough to make my stomach turn. He opened his mouth but closed it once he saw Aniyah making her way down.

I stared at him, rage simmering just beneath my skin. He knew something. But he wouldn't say it.

With a frustrated sigh, I pushed off the couch. I needed air.

Storming off to my room, I shut the door behind me. I pressed my back against it, chest rising and falling in uneven breaths. My mind spun, the weight of too many unanswered questions crushing down on me.

What the hell was going on? Jax had warned me. Then Hannah. Now Matt? And yet none of them would actually tell me why.

If Logan was so dangerous, so bad, then why did they all act like his secret was some unspeakable thing? Like they couldn't be the one to say it?

I clenched my fists. It didn't make sense.

Logan had been nothing but good to me. He'd stayed up with me. He kissed me like I mattered. He made me feel safe, something I hadn't felt in a long time. And yet, the people who should have cared about me most—the people who had actually hurt me—were the ones warning me away.

I squeezed my eyes shut, trying to process it all. Was I falling into the same kind of trap I had with Matt?

My stomach twisted painfully at the thought. Matt had seemed perfect, too. He'd held my hand, made me laugh, told me everything I wanted to hear, until one day, he didn't. Until I found out he had been playing me all along.

I had promised myself I would never fall for another illusion. But what if that was what Logan was?

I gritted my teeth, pacing the small room as my own thoughts circled like vultures waiting for me to collapse.

If Logan was lying, if he had some dark secret they were too afraid to say, then why didn't I feel unsafe around him? Why was I drawn to him even now? Why did I feel like the one thing I wanted most in the world was to be near him?

I shook my head, swallowing down the lump in my throat. Maybe the scariest part wasn't what Logan was hiding. Maybe it was how much I wanted to believe he was good.

I changed out of my pajamas and got ready for the day, the delicious aroma of bacon, eggs, and syrup pulling me toward the kitchen like a lifeline. The easy chatter of my friends filled the hallway, grounding me in the moment, but beneath the warmth of it all, my thoughts remained tangled. Hannah's eyes. Her warning. The creeping dread that wouldn't let go.

I needed answers.

As I stepped into the kitchen, I found Logan at the stove, plating eggs with a practiced ease, a small smirk tugging at his lips. The table was already set, coffee steaming in mugs, syrup and butter waiting in the center. He had thought of everything.

It wasn't just for me. It was for all of us.

He had welcomed us into his home, shared his space without hesitation. No one else had opened their doors like that. Not Jax. Not Matt. Just Logan.

And if he was so dangerous, why were they all here?

"Morning," Becca said, her voice groggy as she sipped her coffee, her hair a messy ponytail of controlled chaos.

I cleared my throat, forcing myself to focus. "Morning. Thanks for breakfast." I slid into the chair beside Logan.

He smirked. "Since you kicked my ass at *Mario Kart*, I thought I'd butter you up, so you'll take it easy on me next time."

Becca raised her eyebrows while piling bacon on her plate. "When did you two play *Mario Kart*?"

"Last night. You never told me she was good." Logan nudged me playfully.

"Probably because she and her brother play all the time," Matt said. "He and I used to play a lot."

My stomach twisted. There it was. The reminder. The same little territorial maneuver Becca had pulled yesterday with Candace and Jax, except Matt was doing it with Logan.

I clenched my jaw. I didn't understand him. What was he trying to prove? That he still knew me better? That he had some claim over me? After everything?

But then I froze. What if Matt had told Logan about me? About the hospital.

My eyes flicked to Becca in silent question, but she didn't seem to notice.

"Well, now you can play with Aniyah's brother," Becca quipped to Matt, taking another bite of bacon.

"What's everyone up to today?" Logan asked.

Jax stuffed a forkful of eggs in his mouth. "We were thinking of hitting the trails again, maybe a different route this time."

The thought of wandering through the woods again after yesterday made my pulse stutter. The vultures. The smell of decay. Hannah appearing in the mirror. My hands tightened around my coffee cup.

I needed to do something. Something real.

"I think there's an arts and crafts fest in town, too," Candace offered.

Becca groaned. "Boring. What about the snow park? We could ski or skate."

I barely registered their debate. My mind was already spinning, formulating a plan. I needed to know who Hannah was, where she had lived, and why she was appearing to me. There had to be records. More news articles, locals who knew her. If I could get into town, I could start piecing it all together.

I swallowed my last sip of coffee, my decision made. "You guys go ahead. Last time I went skiing, I ended up with a bruised head."

Becca frowned. "What are you gonna do?" Her concern felt like a spotlight. "Why do you keep avoiding us?"

"I'm not. Just don't want to go skiing."

"Sure you're okay?"

I forced a reassuring smile. "Yeah, I'm fine. Think I may check out the arts festival. Explore the town a bit."

Logan leaned back in his chair. "Maybe I could be your tour guide. Show you around town. I know an amazing place to eat."

I hadn't expected that.

Jax stiffened. Matt barely hid the way his jaw clenched.

A flicker of excitement stirred in my chest, but also panic. If Logan went with me, how could I investigate Hannah? Would I be able to sneak in research without him noticing? Would he ask why I was so curious about a dead girl?

And wasn't he part of the mystery, too?

"Oh. Um ... Are you sure? Wouldn't you have more fun skiing?" I stumbled over my words, cursing myself for the awkwardness.

"I ski a lot." He shrugged. "Unless you'd rather be alone?"

Would I?

Before I could answer, Jax said, "Sure you wanna spend your day doing that, Hazel?" His voice was too casual. He took a slow sip of his coffee. "There's not much to see."

"Yeah," Matt added, picking at his eggs. "Small town. But it's easy to end up in the wrong place if you're not paying attention."

Logan smirked. "I think Hazel can handle a little sightseeing."

Marcus clapped Logan on the back. "And who better to show her around than someone who actually knows this town?" He looked between Matt and Jax, his voice easy, but there was a clear warning beneath it. "Unless you think Hazel can't handle herself?"

I straightened in my seat. "Actually, I can handle myself just fine," I said, my voice even. "I don't need permission to go anywhere."

Matt exhaled sharply through his nose. "That's not what we're saying."

"Then what are you saying?" I challenged. I was tired of everyone dancing around things but never saying anything outright.

Jax's expression hardened. "Just ... be careful."

Marcus let out a low chuckle and leaned back in his chair. "Man, you guys are really dramatic." He turned to me with an easy grin. "Ignore them, Hazel. They just don't like when they're not in control."

Becca let out a scoff. "Exactly."

I hesitated, my heart hammering. Was this about control? Or was this about Logan?

I went back to my room, attempting to soothe my racing heart. My mind was a whirlwind of conflicting emotions. Excitement fluttered in my chest at the thought of spending time with Logan, but I couldn't shake off the haunting image of Hannah's ghost. Or the unresolved mysteries that lurked in the background. And the warnings.

I would be okay. Just as I made my way to the bathroom, the door to the bedroom flew open.

Becca stormed in, arms crossed, her eyes sharp with suspicion. "What's going on?"

"What?"

She stared at me like it was obvious. "Why aren't you coming with us?"

"I don't feel like skiing. Plus, I can't afford it."

"You know I'd spot you."

"I know, but I don't really feel like watching Matt and Aniyah."

She groaned. "Really? Also, what was that at breakfast with Matt?"

I shrugged and grabbed my camera, checking for debris under the lens. "I don't know. Apparently, he doesn't like Logan."

"Why? Did he say anything?" Her voice sharpened, her body going still.

I frowned. "Just said he was bad."

Becca's mouth twitched. She recovered quickly, but I caught it.

"Like, who is he to warn me?" I continued. "And what's the deal with Jax and Logan? Jax warned me about him, too."

Becca furrowed her eyebrows. "He did?"

"Yeah. All Logan would say is that Jax dated his sister." I searched her expression. "Did you know that?"

She looked away. Just for a second. But long enough. "No. I've never met his sister. I didn't know Jax dated her."

A flicker of unease curled in my stomach. Was I imagining things, or was Becca in on this, too?

"There's so much weird tension with everyone," I muttered, shaking my head. "Even Casey warned me about coming here during a full moon." I rolled my eyes. Maybe full moons really did make people act strange.

"Other than Matt, what else is going on?" Becca asked.

I exhaled sharply. "I know Aniyah's been messing with me."

"She admitted it?"

"No, but it has to be her."

Becca groaned. "Then you have to come with me. We can mess with her. Besides, I need you to distract Candace so I can spend time with Jax."

I let out a frustrated sigh. "Stop. Jax likes Candace."

Becca's jaw dropped. "I thought you were *my* friend."

"I am. Why don't you just talk to Jax? Stop playing games."

She scoffed. "I have to tread lightly with him. We've both hurt each other, but I have to make him realize that I'm the better choice."

"So why do you need me?"

"Because you and Candace have clearly gotten chummy."

I stiffened. Was she … jealous? Becca could get intense when Jax had another girl in the picture. Then, something clicked. Jax had mentioned a girlfriend before Candace, someone he was with at the same time Matt and I were together. And Becca had been like this last fall, too—hovering, tense.

Had Jax been dating Logan's sister then? Had Becca Known?

The thought lingered for a moment, fuzzy and incomplete, like a thread I wasn't sure I wanted to pull. If Becca had known about Logan's sister back then, why wouldn't she have told me that when I asked?

I shook it off. Becca could be weird about Jax, sure, but it wasn't worth overthinking. Not when there were bigger things to worry about.

Becca narrowed her eyes. "I know something's going on, and it's not about you wanting to be alone with Logan." She leaned in. "You made up your mind to go into town before Logan even agreed to go with you. So, what is it?"

I hesitated.

Taking a leap of faith, I pulled out my phone. "Look at this." I thrust it toward her.

Becca squinted at the screen, reading. She barely reacted. "Okay?"

"She's the one I've been seeing." My voice came out stronger than I expected. "I'm not imagining it. I saw her yesterday at that house. It's why I fell down the ladder. She keeps popping up everywhere. I need to figure out who she is."

A flicker of worry flashed in Becca's eyes.

I knew that look. My entire body tensed. "What?"

"Hazel…" Becca let out a slow breath. "There's no such thing as ghosts."

I flinched.

"This is the girl whose poster was on the grocery store missing board," Becca continued. "You're hooked, and your mind has made up this whole story."

"No," I said, my voice rising. "I saw her. She spoke to me."

Becca sighed like I was exhausting her. "Hazel, think about it. You saw the poster first, right? So, your brain just—"

"I never said I saw the poster." My pulse pounded.

She smirked. "You told me." She rolled her eyes. "We had an entire conversation about it."

"No, we didn't."

"Yes, we did, Hazel." Becca let out a soft, almost patronizing laugh. "In the car after the store."

I shook my head. No. I would've remembered that.

Wouldn't I?

Becca's voice turned gentle. "We talked about it. Don't you remember?" Her eyes searched mine, full of sympathy. Like she was waiting for me to catch up to what she already knew.

My mouth went dry. I tried to remember the conversation. But nothing came to mind.

Becca's hand landed lightly on my shoulder. "It's okay to feel overwhelmed. You've been through a lot, and sometimes ... it's hard to tell what's real and what's not."

Her words sank in, pulling me deeper into doubt. The events replayed in my mind. The eerie sight of blood flowing from the shower faucet, the unsettling image of Hannah's face, the sound of her name etched onto the mirror, her voice.

I'd been so sure it was real. But what if it wasn't?

Becca leaned closer, her voice gentle but firm. "It's not your fault, Hazel. It's just ... the way your mind works sometimes. You've been doing so well, but these things happen. You'll get through it."

Her smile was meant to be comforting, but it only made my stomach churn.

I swallowed hard, but my throat still felt tight. My skin prickled with a cold sweat, and suddenly, the room felt too small. I tried to steady my breathing, but each inhale only tightened the coil of anxiety in my chest.

Maybe she's right. Maybe I'm slipping again.

I sank onto the edge of the bed, my hands gripping the fabric of my jeans, fingers trembling slightly. My vision blurred, and for a moment, I wasn't in the cabin anymore.

It was June. The hallway was dark, but I could feel something there, lingering just beyond my bedroom door. The whispers were soft at first, blending with the sound of the air conditioning kicking on, the rustling of trees outside. But then they grew sharper. Closer.

I held my breath, straining to listen.

I wasn't imagining them. They were *real*. Someone was in the house.

Barefoot, I stepped into the hallway, my pulse hammering. The wooden floor was ice-cold against my feet, the air thick and stale. Every shadow stretched long in the dim glow of the nightlight, shifting as I moved.

I inched toward my mother's room, my fingertips grazing the wall. The house creaked and settled, but beneath that, I could still hear low, whispering voices.

They were right behind me, right outside my bedroom.

A sharp jolt of fear shot through me. I turned too quickly, my vision tunneling as I gasped for breath. My chest ached like it was being crushed.

You're not crazy. You're not crazy. You're not crazy.

A light flicked on.

I flinched as my mother's voice broke through the fog, her silhouette filling the hallway.

"Hazel?"

She found me frozen there, hands clenched into fists, my nails digging into my palms so hard they nearly broke the skin. She asked me what was wrong, but I barely heard her. I couldn't breathe. The whispers were everywhere, pressing into my skull, twisting around my thoughts like vines.

But then she opened the door. Turned on the lights. Nothing.

The air was empty. The house was silent.

I had cried then. In front of her. In front of a nurse. In a hospital room that smelled like antiseptic and lemon cleaner, the walls too white, the bed too stiff.

I had tried so hard to explain. But all they did was write things down, nod, tell me I was under a lot of stress. That I had imagined it.

A shiver rolled through me as I snapped back to the present, still perched on the bed. My chest felt tight, the weight of that memory pressing down like a lead blanket.

Is this the same thing? Am I doing it again?

A sharp sting bloomed in my palm. I glanced down and realized I had been digging my nails into my skin, leaving behind little crescent-shaped marks.

Becca sat beside me, watching carefully, like she was waiting for the realization to set in. She reached out, squeezing my hand gently.

"I don't want to be like this," I whispered, hating how weak I sounded.

Becca squeezed me. "I know," she whispered. "It's okay. It's just a momentary setback. We'll figure it out together."

I sniffled, wiping away my tears with the back of my hand. "It felt so real."

She gave me a reassuring smile. "Maybe it's just stress."

I nodded slowly, my mind still buzzing, my heartbeat unsteady. "But what if it happens again? What if I can't trust my own thoughts?"

"Then we'll tackle it again. But maybe now that you're aware, you won't see anything else. Or you'll know it's not real."

I took a deep breath, allowing Becca's words to sink in. I knew I wasn't alone, that I had someone by my side who believed in me even when I doubted myself.

And with that thought, a glimmer of hope sparked within me. I didn't want my vacation to end so early. If I did, I'd probably end up in the hospital again.

"I don't want to go home."

"Okay. You don't have to. What do you want to do?"

"I'll still go to the arts festival with Logan."

Becca tilted her head. "Are you sure?"

"Yeah. Maybe I can find out more about him and Jax."

Becca shook her head, letting out a breathy laugh. "I wouldn't. Boys have their own drama. You don't need to get mixed in with that. And I wouldn't tell Logan what's been going on this week."

"Why?"

"It's a lot. Don't stress about this. Just go and have a good time." Becca squeezed my hand.

I swallowed my unease, trying to convince myself Becca was right. Maybe I was just stressed. Maybe once I stopped thinking about it, the visions would fade. Maybe if I ignored it, I wouldn't see Hannah again.

Still, doubt curled at the edges of my mind, whispering just beneath the surface.

"Have fun skiing," I murmured, my voice quieter than I intended.

Becca gave me a bright, reassuring smile, but something about it felt too smooth, too practiced. Like she had already decided what the truth was, and my only job was to go along with it. Before she left the room, she turned back. "I will."

The door clicked shut behind her, and suddenly, the space felt suffocating. The silence too thick.

I exhaled shakily and ran my hand through my hair. The pressure behind my eyes was pounding, a dull ache that pulsed in time with my heartbeat.

I needed to focus.

On Logan. On the festival. On anything that made me feel like I wasn't about to spiral.

Still, as I pulled my jacket on and prepared to leave, a single thought wormed its way in, burrowing deep.

What if Becca's wrong?

What if I wasn't losing my grip on reality? What if Hannah was real?

Chapter Eighteen

The engine hummed steadily as Logan guided his truck along the winding mountain road, the forested landscape blurring into a sea of green outside the windows. The late afternoon sun filtered through the trees, casting dappled shadows that flickered across the dashboard.

I sat in the passenger seat, hands folded tightly in my lap. My gaze was fixed on the road ahead, but my thoughts spiraled elsewhere. Logan had tried to make conversation a few times, mentioning the festival, throwing out little details about past years, but I only responded with nods and murmured agreements.

I knew he noticed.

Every few moments, his eyes flicked toward me, assessing, his fingers drumming absently on the steering wheel. His concern was a quiet weight pressing between us, unspoken but heavy.

"You look like I'm dragging you to your doom," he finally said, his voice light. "Blink twice if you need rescuing."

I blinked once.

He smirked. "Cute. You still want to go?"

"Yes." A small smile tugged at my lips, but it faded quickly. I was grateful for his attempt, but no amount of teasing could shake the feeling coiling inside me—a whispering, insidious thing I couldn't ignore.

The shadow I kept seeing at the edge of my vision. The soft breath against my cheek last night. The voice that shouldn't exist.

I squeezed my eyes shut for a moment, willing the thoughts away. *It's nothing. Stress. Sleep deprivation.* Not a relapse. Not that.

"Almost there," Logan said, breaking the silence. His voice was gentle. "You okay?"

I forced a smile and nodded. "Yeah, just tired."

He didn't push, but the quiet stretched between us, thick with the words I couldn't bring myself to say.

As we wound closer to town, the festival came into view. Colorful tents lined the streets, crowds swelled the sidewalks, and bright banners waved in the crisp autumn air. The hum of conversation and distant music bled into the truck's cab, a stark contrast to the storm still raging inside me.

Logan found a parking spot and cut the engine. "Alright, Hazel the Hostage. Ready to face your captors?" His easy grin almost made me laugh. Almost.

I took a deep breath and nodded. "Yeah."

The festival was a blur of movement and sound. Handmade crafts filled the booths. Delicate beaded jewelry, hand-poured candles, rustic quilts, jars of homemade jams. Laughter and chatter mingled with the scent of warm cinnamon bread and freshly brewed coffee.

I should have been distracted. I should have been able to lose myself in that moment.

But every time I glanced toward the edge of a stall or past the crowd, I expected to see Hannah standing there.

Logan noticed my distraction, though he didn't comment on it. Instead, he gently slipped his hand into mine, his thumb brushing against my skin as he led me toward a booth selling metal sculptures.

I let him.

He made me laugh a few times by making witty observations about the more ridiculous art, poking fun at a statue of an owl with eyes way too big. For a little while, it helped.

We eventually wandered toward a small coffee shop, the warm scent luring us inside. We ordered, and as we sat at a corner table, I felt almost normal again.

But then I glanced at the mural on the cafe wall and froze. It wasn't a familiar place. I had never seen that landscape before. But something about it sent a chill through me.

A painting of a girl standing near the edge of dark water. The artist had used deep blues and grays, the strokes hauntingly soft, the girl's reflection distorted as if the water had swallowed parts of her whole.

It wasn't Hannah. But it could have been.

A ghost of a shiver ran down my spine.

Logan must have noticed my change in expression because he set his cup down and leaned in slightly. "You sure you're okay?"

I hesitated. The urge to tell him nearly won. The words balanced at the edge of my tongue, ready to tumble out.

But I thought about what Becca said. *Don't stress about this. Don't tell him.*

I swallowed hard and forced myself to smile. "Yeah."

Logan didn't push, but his eyes lingered on me for a moment longer before he took another sip of coffee.

I tried to focus on the warmth of the cup in my hands, the easy conversation between us.

But no matter how hard I tried, I couldn't shake the feeling that no matter where I went, the shadows would follow.

After the café, we continued browsing the festival, weaving through the booths as I admired the intricate crafts and artwork.

"Hey, check this out." Logan caught my wrist, gently pulling me toward a vendor's stand lined with vintage cameras and old photography equipment.

A delighted laugh slipped from my lips before I could stop it. Rows of aged film cameras sat neatly on display, each one a relic of a different time, leather casings worn soft, brass dials gleaming under the golden evening light.

"These are amazing," I murmured, tracing my fingers lightly over a polished Nikon with an old-school strap.

I felt Logan watching me.

"I thought you might like this. You have a great eye for photography."

Warmth curled in my chest. "Thanks."

He stayed patient while I browsed, never rushing me, even when I lingered over a camera I couldn't afford.

"Are you hungry?" he asked once we walked away from the booth.

The sky had deepened into a soft indigo, the first hints of twilight creeping over the mountain town. The festival's string lights flickered on, casting a warm glow over the bustling streets.

"Yeah."

"I know a great restaurant up the street. We can walk there."

"Okay."

The restaurant stood out with its cozy, cabin-like exterior, adorned with hanging flower baskets and twinkling lights woven through the wooden beams. Inside, the low hum of conversation blended with the soft strumming of a live acoustic guitarist, and a fireplace crackled near the corner, casting flickering shadows against the rustic decor.

I was in awe. "This is amazing."

"I thought you'd like this place." Logan guided me to a table near the fire, the heat a welcome contrast to the evening's crisp air. "It's got great food. And it's quiet."

A tall man with a goatee brought us water, taking our order with an easy familiarity that told me Logan had been here plenty of times before.

I watched as Logan casually unwrapped his straw, but something about the way he fidgeted with the paper, rolling it between his fingers, made me wonder if he was nervous.

"I really like this town," I said, testing the waters. "My brother, Casey, would love it. I think. I don't know. He didn't want me to come."

Logan arched a brow. "Why not?"

I shrugged. "He kept talking about the full moon." I smirked. "You're not a werewolf, are you?"

Logan bit out a laugh. "Last time I checked, no."

"I'll let him know. What about your sister? What's she like?"

The smile faded from his lips. His fingers stopped fiddling with the straw wrapper. The shift was small, but immediate. "She's ... complicated," he said, gaze lowering to the table. "Not really something I want to get into right now."

A tight silence stretched between us, the air heavier than before. I caught the way his shoulders tensed, the way he kept his expression neutral, but his hands curled slightly against the wood, like he was bracing for something.

"Okay," I said softly, giving him an out. But for the first time, I noticed something flicker in his eyes, like a door had almost cracked open, only to slam shut again.

I let the subject drop, pivoting back to safer ground. "Well, if you like video games and an energetic ten-year-old, feel free to come hang out with Casey anytime."

Logan huffed a small laugh. "I'd like that. It's really quiet at home. Could use some excitement."

"Casey's energy could power an army."

"You sound like you spend a lot of time with him."

"I do." The words came without thought, but my chest tightened. "My mom's busy a lot." I left out the part where she spent more time hunting for her next husband than paying attention to us.

"What about your dad?"

I hesitated, my fingers tightening around my water glass. "No idea. But Casey's dad is the only father I've ever known. I never met mine. I think I saw him once, though," I admitted. "A man came to our house and gave me money when I was little.

My mom flipped. Told him to leave and never come back. I don't really remember his face."

"Damn. I'm sorry."

I shrugged like it didn't matter, like I hadn't spent years wondering if I'd imagined it, if he ever thought about me after that day. "I'm used to it." It was a knee-jerk response, the kind I gave without thinking.

Logan studied me for a beat, like he wanted to say something else, but instead, he exhaled and leaned back in his chair. "I think my parents are getting a divorce."

"What?"

"Yeah. I don't know." He let out a tired laugh, but there was no humor in it. "They just don't talk like they used to. It sucks."

His fingers went back to fidgeting with the straw wrapper, twisting it into a small coil. "It was too easy to convince them to let me come here this week. Usually, I have to beg both of them, especially after what happened this summer. But this time, they didn't care."

I frowned. "What happened this summer?"

He hesitated. A shadow flickered across his face. "I'd been dealing with some ... stuff for a few months, and I kind of ... went off the rails for a bit. Drinking too much, staying out too late. Picking fights with random people I shouldn't have. Cops got involved. More than once."

I blinked, surprised. "Seriously?"

"Yeah." He let out a hollow chuckle, shaking his head. "The whole town was talking about it. Probably still is." He looked down at his hands, fingers still tangled in the shredded straw wrapper. "Logan Foster, the local screw-up. That's me."

I opened my mouth, but the words felt inadequate. I wanted to say something to make it better, but what do you say to someone who believes they've already been judged? "You're not a screw-up," I said, but the words felt weak.

He shrugged. "I'm a work in progress. But back then? I didn't care what happened to me."

Before I could respond, the waiter arrived with our food, the conversation fading into the clatter of dishes.

For a few minutes, we ate in silence.

Logan sighed. "Sorry. Didn't mean to ruin the mood or whatever."

"Don't be sorry. That really sucks." I reached for his hand, giving it a small squeeze. "I'm here if you ever wanna talk."

His eyes searched mine for a long moment, something flickering behind them. "Thanks." He cleared his throat. "Baseball will start soon. That'll keep my mind off things. Maybe you can come to a game."

"When?"

"Season starts in February."

"You'll have forgotten about me by then." I dropped my gaze and sipped my tea.

He frowned. "Why do you say that?"

"I don't think I'm very memorable."

His expression softened. "I think you are." His voice was quiet but sure. "I like talking to you."

I swallowed past the lump in my throat. "I like talking to you too."

I found myself opening up to Logan in a way I hadn't with anyone in a long time. His genuine interest and easygoing nature made me feel comfortable. But the other part of me felt scared. Once he found out my secret, he'd want nothing to do with me.

We finished eating, lingering over our drinks as we talked about music, movies, books we'd read—anything and everything that filled the comfortable space between us.

Logan leaned back in his chair. "I have one more thing I wanna do."

I arched a brow. "What?"

He grinned, tossing a few bills on the table to cover the check. "You'll see. Come on."

Outside, the evening had settled into a crisp chill, the festival's lights casting a warm glow against the darkened streets. The hum of distant laughter and music softened as Logan guided me away from the crowd, leading me down a quieter path. The town felt different at night, cozier, quieter, almost dreamlike.

"Where are we going?" I asked.

"You'll like it."

We rounded a bend, and suddenly, the road sloped steeply upward, revealing a massive structure looming above us in the moonlight.

"The tram?" I asked, my voice tinged with surprise.

His grin widened. "Yeah. Trust me."

I stared at the cable car suspended in the air like something out of a dream.

The cool night air nipped at my cheeks as I stepped onto the platform, a shiver running down my spine that had nothing to do with the cold. The tram swayed slightly as Logan joined me, his hand brushing against mine. Before I could pull away, he clasped my hand gently, his fingers warm against my chilled skin.

"I've always seen people in Ferris wheels or cable cars at night in movies, and I've wanted to do this," I said.

"Yeah?" Logan squeezed my hand lightly. "Then I'm glad I brought you."

As the tram began its slow ascent, the world below transformed into a glittering sea of twinkling lights. The town stretched beneath us, a mosaic of golden hues and darkened rooftops, while the mountains loomed beyond, vast and endless against the star-studded sky.

"It's even more beautiful than I imagined," I whispered.

"Yeah, it is. But I think you might be making it more magical."

I smiled. "You're really laying it on thick tonight, aren't you?"

"Can you blame me?" He turned toward me, his gaze locking onto mine in that slow, deliberate way that made my stomach flip. "You're the one who's got me all worked up."

A nervous heat curled through me. I didn't know how to respond, so I just leaned into his side, letting his warmth chase away the cold.

The tram climbed higher, the town below shrinking until it became nothing more than a blur of distant lights. The night stretched around us, vast and quiet, wrapping us in something that felt entirely separate from reality.

Logan's hand slid to my waist, steadying me as the tram rocked slightly.

"There's something about being up here with you ..." His voice was lower now, more serious, rawer. "It feels like anything's possible."

My heart stuttered at his words. I looked up at him, our faces inches apart.

Logan's eyes flicked down to my lips. And he kissed me. Slow. Unhurried. Like we had all the time in the world. Then more intense, as if he was discovering something he hadn't realized he needed.

The world around us blurred. The tram, the town below, the stars above. None of it mattered in that second.

By the time we reached the top, the stars felt closer, the air crisper, the night holding its breath around us. We stepped off the tram and wandered to the edge, where the world seemed to fall away. For a moment, we stood in silence, taking in the faint glow of the town barely visible below, swallowed by the vast expanse of darkened mountains and the endless scatter of stars above.

"Thank you for bringing me here," I whispered.

He smiled, his fingers still tangled with mine. "I'm glad I could share this with you. It's ... special."

I nodded, unable to find the right words. Instead, I leaned my head on his shoulder, letting the quiet between us speak for itself.

Eventually, we made our way back to the tram. As it began its descent, I realized something had shifted, something subtle but undeniable. I was no longer floating in the sky but instead falling in the best possible way.

Chapter Nineteen

The night had settled over the cabin, its crisp air carrying the distant murmur of crickets and rustling leaves. A thin mist curled over the ground, swirling like ghosts between the trees. The world felt quiet, as if it belonged only to us.

Logan and I slipped into the steaming hot tub, the contrast between the cold night air and the warmth of the bubbling water sending a delicious shiver down my spine. I folded my arms over my stomach, suddenly self-conscious in my bikini, but if Logan noticed, he didn't say anything.

I sank deeper into the water, letting it soothe the tension coiled in my muscles. Above us, the sky stretched endlessly, studded with stars that blinked against the inky darkness.

Logan sat beside me, his shoulder barely brushing mine, the heat of his body merging with the warmth of the water.

For a while, neither of us spoke. The only sounds were the rhythmic hum of the jets, the occasional crackle from the nearby fire pit, and the slow, steady rhythm of our breathing.

His fingers found mine beneath the water. The warmth of his touch ignited a spark that shot straight up my arm.

I turned toward him, feeling the weight of his gaze before I even met his eyes.

Our faces were close. Too close. His lips were barely a breath away, the heat between us tangible, electric.

He closed the remaining distance between us, his lips finally meeting mine in a tender and achingly sweet kiss.

Our lips moved in synchrony. The water bubbled and swirled around us, mirroring the whirlwind of sensations that engulfed my body and mind. Lost in the ecstasy of the moment, I allowed myself to be consumed.

When we finally pulled apart, we were breathless, our foreheads still touching.

"Logan..." My voice barely worked.

"Yeah?"

I swallowed, my heart slamming against my ribs. "I really like you. Like—not just as a hookup. And if that's weird, or too much, or whatever, I get it."

Logan smirked. "You think you're that intimidating?" His thumb brushed over my knuckles beneath the water. "Trust me, Hazel, if anyone's freaking out here, it's me."

"It's just … I'm scared. We barely know each other, but I—I feel something. And I don't know if that's a good thing or a mistake. Because I'm a mess, Logan."

"Hazel." Logan's voice was quiet, steady. "You don't have to be scared of this." He squeezed my hand. "We're all just trying to keep our shit together."

"But what if … I mess everything up?" I whispered. "What if I ruin this before it even starts?"

Logan let out a slow breath. "I don't have all the answers. But I know I don't want to stop whatever this is." He traced small circles on my wrist. "And if you want to figure it out together, then I'm in."

I wanted to believe him. But deep down, I knew if Logan found out the truth about me, he'd run.

My chest tightened, a crushing weight pressing against my ribs. I had to tell him. It was better if he knew now, before I let myself fall any deeper. The air thickened. My throat dried. My heart pounded against my ribcage like a caged bird desperate for freedom.

He searched my eyes. "What is it?"

I inhaled sharply, willing the words to come. A single tear slipped down my cheek.

Logan reached for me, his touch featherlight as he tilted my chin up. "Hey," he whispered. "You can tell me anything. You don't have to hide from me."

I hesitated, my gaze drifting towards the distant trees as if searching for words in the shadows. "Logan..." I swallowed hard. And then, before I could stop myself— "I have bipolar disorder." The words spilled out, quick and raw, like tearing open an old wound.

Logan stilled. His eyes flickered with understanding, recognition. "It's okay," he said softly. Not pity. Not hesitation. Just quiet certainty.

I bit my lip. "I know, but ... it's not just that." I exhaled slowly. "I've been through some really rough patches. I'm afraid you might think I'm ... unstable."

Logan's brows knit together. "Not at all, Hazel." His voice was firm, unwavering. "Whatever you're going through, or have been through, it doesn't change how I see you."

I searched his face, waiting for the discomfort, for the shift, for the regret. But there was none.

"I was diagnosed in February," I continued, "and this past summer ... I had a breakdown." My throat tightened, my voice growing small. "I'm in therapy. On meds. But sometimes it feels like a rollercoaster." I hesitated. "I don't want to burden you."

Logan reached out, his fingers tracing my jaw, a touch so light it sent shivers down my spine. "We all have our issues," he murmured. "Who you are is what counts."

I blinked. How was he so calm? Why wasn't he running? Laughing? Making an excuse? "How are you okay with this? Why aren't you scared?"

His gaze flickered. "My sister," he said, looking away for a moment. "She has bipolar."

The words hit me like a weight. The way he said it—not casually, not dismissively. Like he had lived it.

A beat of silence passed.

"I've seen what it can do," he continued, voice softer now, like he was wading into painful waters. "I've seen how hard it can be." He swallowed. "So no, Hazel. I'm not scared."

I opened my mouth, then closed it. I hadn't expected that. "I didn't know."

He nodded. "It's not something I talk about much."

I nodded too, resting my head against his shoulder, feeling the warmth of his arm wrapping around me.

We sat like that, the hot tub's bubbling water the only sound between us, wrapped in something fragile yet safe.

Maybe Logan had done some reckless things this past summer, but that didn't make him a bad person. Not like Jax or Matt had tried to say.

Maybe they didn't understand him.

A short time after, the others returned, their loud, excited voices dispelling the quietness that had settled around us.

Logan sighed. "It was inevitable."

"Maybe they won't come out here," I teased.

But just as I said it, Matt, Aniyah, Candace, and Marcus emerged, clad in swimsuits, breaking the bubble of intimacy we'd just built.

Matt shot me a critical glance, his eyes filled with judgment.

I rose from the hot tub, allowing the water to cascade off me.

Logan reached for my towel and handed it to me.

"Did y'all have fun?" I carefully stepped out of the hot tub, wrapping myself in the towel as I braved the chilly night air.

"Yeah," Candace added, her words carrying a hint of reservation.

"Becca may have sprained her ankle," Marcus said.

I gasped. "Oh my god. No! I should check on her."

"Jax beat you to it," Candace said, a note of irritation in her voice.

I met Candace's eyes in a silent apology and then moved swiftly up the stairs from the bottom level to Becca's room, my feet barely making a sound. The door was slightly ajar. Just as I reached for the knob, voices stopped me cold.

Jax. Becca.

The tension in their hushed tones sent a chill skittering down my spine.

"That's why we agreed to come." Jax's voice came through clearly.

"I know," Becca whispered, her voice taut. "I really think she ran away."

"Hannah wouldn't have done that."

My breath hitched and my stomach turned. They were talking about Hannah. I pressed myself against the wall, pulse hammering in my ears.

"Jax, it's been months, and no one's heard from her."

"Because Logan did something to her. And I can't believe you tried to set him up with Hazel."

A sharp pang shot through my chest. *What?* I struggled to breathe, my mind racing. Jax thought that Logan did something to Hannah?

My fingers dug into the towel wrapped around me, still damp from the hot tub. The warmth that had lingered from Logan's embrace evaporated instantly, leaving behind a bone-deep chill.

Becca's voice wavered. "Hazel will be fine. She's safe. Logan won't hurt her."

Safe from what?

Jax let out a frustrated breath. "Except now she's having freaking delusions. How does she even know about Hannah?"

"She saw her missing poster at the store." Becca sounded defensive now. "Logan wouldn't have told her. He never talks about Hannah."

"Because he's guilty. You've seen how he's been acting. He's hiding something." Jax's voice hardened. "Have you seen the way he looks at me?"

"He's been acting normal. Better than the past nine months. Definitely better than when we saw him during the summer when he was drunk all the time."

Silence stretched between them.

"You really think she made all this up from that poster?" Jax asked.

Becca didn't answer right away. My stomach twisted. "I don't know. She said Aniyah's aware of her condition and that she's been messing with her. But Aniyah couldn't know about Hannah."

"Matt could've told her."

"He's clueless and wrapped around Aniyah's finger." Becca's tone turned sharp, irritated. "I'm sorry. I shouldn't have brought Hazel. But I can't believe you brought Candace."

"I wanted to, Becca. You know why."

"Whatever. It'll never work out."

"I'm not fighting with you again."

"Fine."

Another pause. The floor beneath me felt unsteady.

"What if Hazel tells Logan about Hannah?" Jax asked. "He'd lose it."

I sucked in a breath, my grip on the towel tightening.

"I told her not to mention any of this to Logan."

Jax exhaled. "I've already warned her about him. She can't get close to him, Becca. It's too dangerous. I can't believe we let them go to town alone."

Dangerous? My chest tightened. My thoughts were spinning too fast.

"What if Hazel could do some digging for us?" Jax asked. "Maybe she can help us figure things out."

"What the hell, Jax?" Becca sounded horrified. "Why would you do that to Hazel?"

Jax didn't answer right away. "We only have two days left to figure out the truth."

The truth. *What truth?*

"Becca, do you think ... Hazel actually saw Hannah?" Jax's words made my blood run cold.

Laughter rang out from downstairs near the hot tub. Panic gripped me.

I turned on my heel, heart pounding so loudly I was sure they'd hear it. I slipped away, darting back toward my room, my breath shallow and ragged.

Slamming the door behind me, I pressed my back against it, my hands shaking. My thoughts tangled into a chaotic mess.

They *knew* Hannah. Becca had lied to me.

My stomach twisted violently, a mix of anger and fear surging through me.

Who was I supposed to trust?

Chapter Twenty

Knots twisted in my stomach, each one tightening with the sting of betrayal. Ten years of friendship with Becca and Jax, now unraveled by a single conversation. The walls of my room felt closer, pressing in like they knew something I didn't.

They knew Hannah. Worse, they thought Logan was involved in her disappearance.

A chill settled over my skin. Could I have been so blind to him?

Jax and Matt had both warned me. But if Logan was dangerous, why hadn't they stopped me from spending the entire day alone with him? Why had Becca encouraged me to get closer to him?

Be careful who you trust.

Hannah's words echoed like a sinister whisper in my mind.

Had Logan dated Hannah? What had he done to her? My stomach turned. Had he...?

I clenched my fists, anger rising like a tide. How could Becca and Jax have kept this from me? Was I just some pawn in whatever game they were playing?

Tears burned the edges of my eyes, but I blinked them back. I couldn't fall apart. Not yet. I had to think, to be smart. Confronting them now would be useless. They'd only lie.

A knock at the door made me jerk upright.

"Yeah?" My voice was rough.

Becca hobbled inside, her twisted ankle barely slowing her down, her eyes sparkling. She dropped onto my bed, practically vibrating with excitement. "You won't believe what just happened," she gushed, leaning in.

I forced my face into something neutral, despite the lingering burn in my chest. How could she be so ... happy? "What?"

Becca's grin stretched wide, like a giddy schoolgirl with a crush. "Jax kissed me."

I froze. The words didn't register at first. "What?"

"He kissed me!" she repeated in a breathless squeal.

For a moment, my thoughts were static. Jax kissed Becca? After all the drama with Candace? "What about Candace?" The words felt strange in my mouth.

Becca's expression wavered for a second, before she sighed dramatically. "I know, I know. It's complicated. But you don't get it. Candace ... she's not who she seems."

My skin crawled. *Apparently, no one is.* "What do you mean?"

Becca leaned closer, like she was sharing the juiciest gossip, completely blind to the fact that my world was crumbling. "She's the reason I twisted my ankle. She did it on purpose." Her voice darkened. "She's been trying to come between me and Jax. I can't just sit back and let her win."

A sharp pang echoed through my chest. Win? Like Jax was a prize to fight over?

Becca kept talking, but I barely heard her. Her voice felt distant, like I was hearing it through water.

Becca had lied to me about Hannah.

And now? Now she wanted me to what—support her cheating? To pretend everything was normal? I couldn't do it.

"Becca, I..." My voice faltered. How could I be there for her when I didn't even know who she was anymore?

She grabbed my hand, squeezing it. "I know it's a lot. But I need you. You're my best friend." The words stung. Was I? I didn't feel like her best friend. Not anymore.

As she rambled on about Candace, Jax, and their drama, my mind drifted. Hannah. Logan. Secrets and warnings. Becca and Jax had lied, but Logan hadn't or at least, I didn't think he had. Being around him felt different. Soothing, even.

But isn't that what you thought about Matt, too?

I clenched my jaw, shoving the thought away.

Was I losing my grip? Was I drawn to an evil man?

Chapter Twenty-One

66What is with you?" Becca asked as we settled into the living room.

Laughter rang out, music hummed softly, and the fire crackled, wrapping the room in warmth. But I felt nothing. Detached. Like I was watching it all through glass, separated from the world around me.

Everything felt off.

I took a slow sip of my drink, my fingers curled around the cup like it was the only real thing I had left. Becca's voice was just another sound in the background. Jax's easy grin? Fake. Matt sitting too close to Aniyah, pretending like he hadn't betrayed me? Fake. Candace was missing, and Jax didn't seem to care that he'd done the same thing to her that Matt had done to me.

And Logan ... *Logan*. Calm and chaos, wrapped into one.

Be careful who you trust.

Hannah's warning slithered through my mind, curling around my ribs like ice. Who was she talking about? Jax? Becca? Logan? All of them? The thought tightened around my throat.

Then, a deeper chill settled in my gut.

I'd told Logan.

I had spilled everything to him. My disorder. My past. My fear of unraveling again. And he'd looked at me like I wasn't broken. But now, I wondered why had I trusted him so quickly? I barely knew him. At this point, I wasn't even sure if I could trust the people who had been in my life for years.

A rock dropped in my stomach.

What if he was saying what I wanted to hear? What if he only acted understanding? What if I was just desperate to be seen, and that made me blind?

I rubbed my arms, suddenly cold despite the fire crackling in the hearth. The illusion of safety I'd felt with Logan started to dissolve, leaving only uncertainty in its place.

Had I made a mistake? Had I let him in too fast?

"Hazel?" Becca's voice cut through my spiraling thoughts.

I blinked. She was staring. Waiting.

"I need a drink," I muttered, pushing past her to the kitchen.

Once there, I grabbed the vodka and poured a splash into my cup. The vodka burned going down, but it didn't settle me. I poured another. Faster this time.

Still, the questions wouldn't stop.

Did I imagine the conversation between Becca and Jax? No. No, I heard it.

But ... had I? My grip tightened around the kitchen counter. Had I really?

They were my best friends. They wouldn't put me in danger ... would they? Had I misheard them? Misunderstood? The thought cracked something inside me, an ache that spread like wildfire. If I was wrong, if I had imagined it, then everything was my fault. My mind, slipping again.

The weight of uncertainty crushed me. If I told Becca, she'd brush it off. If I told Jax, he'd say I was crazy. If I told Logan, he'd think I was losing it too.

My thoughts ricocheted, exhausting me. The glass slipped from my hand, clinking against the counter.

I needed air. Grabbing my coat, I stepped outside. The cold slapped me as I opened the door, the shock of it settling deep into my skin. I sank into one of the rocking chairs on the porch, wrapping my coat tight. The rhythmic creak of the chair cut through the silence, steady and sharp.

Out there, under the wide-open sky, the world felt bigger. The stars flickered above me, distant and indifferent, but real.

Not like the thoughts clawing at my skull.

I focused on breathing, willing my pulse to slow. But no matter how deep I inhaled, the fear stayed lodged in my chest like a thorn I couldn't pull free.

And then a memory clawed its way to the surface.

My breath hitched. My fingers dug into the fabric of my coat. The last time I trusted someone this fast, it was Matt.

The night flashed back like a film reel unraveling too quickly. His sharp tone, the way his hands clenched when I pushed for the truth.

"You're overreacting," Matt had said, his voice calm, even. Too calm. Like he wasn't caught. Like he wasn't lying to my face. "I'd never hurt you, Hazel."

Lie.

I had known. I had felt it deep in my gut. The same sickening sensation I felt now. The way his eyes flickered away for just a second too long. The way he kissed my forehead and told me to trust him when I had already found the messages on his phone.

The truth had been right there, staring me in the face, and I had still let him convince me I was crazy.

"Hazel, you need to stop. You're making up stories."

Gaslighting.

"Maybe if you weren't so paranoid all the time, we wouldn't be having this fight."

Manipulation.

The memory crushed my ribs like a weight pressing down, making it hard to breathe. I had ignored every warning sign. Every red flag. And in the end, he had betrayed me anyway.

And now ... Logan.

My stomach twisted.

He had looked at me tonight the same way Matt once had. Soft. Understanding. Safe.

And I had told him everything.

What the hell had I been thinking?

A shiver ran down my spine, not from the cold, but from the realization that I had let myself trust Logan too easily. Maybe Jax and Matt were right. Maybe I was falling into the same trap.

But Logan wasn't Matt.

… Was he?

I clenched my fists, anger and doubt warring in my chest. I wanted to believe Logan was different. That I wasn't repeating history. That he was telling me the truth. But I had wanted to believe Matt, too.

I forced out a shaky breath. I had to be careful. I had to stay in control. I wouldn't be blindsided again. Not this time.

Squeezing my eyes shut, I willed the memory away. Logan wasn't Matt. He couldn't be. But that sinking feeling still gnawed at my ribs, whispering that I'd made this mistake before.

The door opened and closed with a quiet click. My shoulders tensed. For a split second, my stomach twisted with unease until I turned and saw Marcus. The only person I didn't have complicated feelings about right now.

"Mind if I join you?" he asked.

I gestured to the empty chair beside me, relieved I wouldn't be alone with my thoughts anymore.

He sat down, and silence stretched between us, thick but not uncomfortable. "How was the arts festival?" he asked after a beat.

"Good. How was skiing?"

He chuckled, shaking his head. "Aside from all the drama? It was fun."

"Ahh. The Becca-Jax drama?"

"The one and only."

A comfortable pause settled between us, but the question burned on my tongue before I could stop it. "Is Logan a bad guy?"

Marcus turned to me, his brows knitting together. "No. Why? Did something happen?"

"No." And that was the problem. "We went to the festival. Had a great time. We've had a great time this whole week."

He nodded, a small smile playing on his lips. Like he already knew. "Good. Logan needs someone like you."

My heart stuttered. "What do you mean?"

"He needs some stability. For a while, he was drinking too much, sleeping around, not dealing with things. I wasn't sure about this trip, but he's slowly finding himself again."

I hesitated. "What happened to him?"

"Nah, that's not my story to tell."

Frustration twisted in my chest. *Everyone keeps secrets here.*

Marcus must've seen the look on my face because his tone softened. "Look, Logan will tell you when he's ready. He likes you, Hazel. I haven't seen him like this around anyone in a long time."

I looked down, my breath fogging in the cold air. "I'm not sure I'm the girl he needs right now."

"Maybe you're both what each of you needs."

His words lingered, heavier than I expected. Could I really be that for Logan? When I could barely trust my own thoughts?

"I just don't want to get hurt," I whispered. Or be wrong again.

Marcus turned to me, his expression kind and understanding. "I get that. But sometimes taking a risk is worth it. You never know what could come out of it." He paused. "And besides, Logan cares about you. I can see it in the way he looks at you."

I took a deep breath, his words sinking in. Love was messy and risky, full of cracks and sharp edges, but maybe … maybe it was worth the leap. "Thanks. I think you're one of the only honest people here."

He grinned. "Some of them will never outgrow their drama."

We sat in silence again, the stars above a quiet witness. For a moment, I felt a glimmer of hope. Maybe Logan and I could be what we both needed, not perfect but enough.

Marcus stood, stretching. "Come on. Don't want to freeze out here."

The moment I stepped into the warmth, a strange heaviness settled over me. The cabin smelled of pine, alcohol … and something unspoken.

Laughter bubbled from the living room, but it felt wrong. Too loud. Too forced. The glow of the fire flickered, casting long, stretching shadows that made my skin prickle.

Logan looked up. His gaze found mine, and instead of suspicion or distance, he smiled. A soft, easy smile that made my breath catch. Like he was just happy to see me. Like he wanted me there. For a fleeting second, the tension in my chest loosened. But just as quickly, doubt seeped back in. Because how could Logan be so open with me while everyone else warned me about him?

I looked away, sinking onto the couch, the war in my mind far from over.

Even after Marcus's reassurances, that gnawing doubt wouldn't leave me. Not just because of Logan. But because I couldn't tell if my friends were using me or if my grasp on reality was unraveling.

At some point, the conversation shifted to strange, unexplained events, ghost stories, and local legends in the area.

I hadn't realized there were more beyond Logan's story about Eleanor.

Becca leaned forward, her voice animated, eyes bright with intrigue. "People have talked about mysterious orbs and flickering lanterns around here for decades. Could be spirits of Cherokee and Catawba warriors. Or ghostly search parties still looking for loved ones lost in some tragic flood."

Jax smirked. "Or maybe it's just swamp gas. You get your info from Google, Becca?"

Becca groaned, rolling her eyes. "You're such an ass."

Aniyah leaned in, a slow smirk playing at her lips. "They say that people who disappear in these mountains are never really gone. They just … blend in. They're still here, but you'd never know it."

Something about her words sent a cold ripple down my spine.

Jax's expression darkened. "People think they can hide anything in these woods. But secrets always have a way of coming out."

The fire crackled. No one spoke. The room wasn't warm anymore. The shift happened in an instant. The playful edge of the conversation evaporated, leaving behind something else. Something that twisted in my gut.

My eyes flicked toward Logan. He wasn't smiling. His gaze had dropped to the fire, his jaw tight, shoulders rigid. Shadows danced across his face in the firelight, concealing his expression, but a darkness flickered in his eyes.

The tension in the air grew thick and heavy. A silent game of glances passed between the others, like they all knew something I didn't.

Marcus chuckled, the sound too forced. "Well, guess that means we're all screwed, huh?"

A few uneasy laughs followed, but no one relaxed. And I couldn't ignore the way Logan's fingers curled into fists against his thighs. Or the way Jax's words hung in the air, lingering like smoke.

Had his comment been aimed at Logan?

Secrets always have a way of coming out.

A moment later, the conversation continued, but I barely heard it. My focus stayed on Jax, watching him for any sign of what he really meant. Had Hannah been warning me about Logan?

A chill slithered down my spine. I had to leave. "I'm gonna head to bed," I said, forcing a yawn.

Logan's eyes lifted to mine, searching, lingering.

I looked away. I barely made it to my room before my hands started to shake. The faint glow of the bedside lamp stretched long shadows against the walls. The thick and unyielding silence pressed against me.

I hugged the pillow, breathing unevenly. What if Marcus was wrong? What if Jax was right? And what if Logan was keeping a secret bigger than all of them?

A knock broke the stillness.

I flinched. "Yeah?" My voice barely carried past my lips.

The door creaked open, and when Logan stepped inside, my whole body went rigid. My breath caught. My eyes darted toward the window, toward the door, searching for an escape route.

"Hey," he said, his tone light, casual. Too casual. "Just came to check your vent again. Don't want you freezing in here." His lips curved into a teasing smile. "Unless…" His eyes flickered with something unreadable. "You'd rather I keep you warm?"

My stomach twisted. The warmth of his voice, the easy flirtation, normally would've flustered me. Normally, it would've made me laugh. But now?

Now, it felt like a trap.

I forced my fingers to stop trembling. "Thanks." I gave a weak, fragile smile. "But I can manage to stay warm on my own."

His smile faltered, just for a second, but then he recovered quickly, eyes narrowing slightly. "Are you sure? I could always keep you company, you know."

Something inside me snapped.

"I'm perfectly capable of taking care of myself," I said, my words sharper than I intended. "I don't need anyone to keep me warm."

The shift in his expression was immediate. The teasing vanished. Concern replaced it, a flicker of something deeper in his eyes. He stepped toward me. Too close. "Hazel," he murmured, softer now, like he was trying to soothe a frightened animal. "What's wrong?" He sat on the bed beside me, the mattress dipping under his weight.

The air between us felt thin, stretched tight, and I couldn't breathe. I bolted. My back hit the dresser, hands gripping the edge so tightly my knuckles ached. My pulse roared in my ears.

His face changed.

"Hazel…" he said again, but quieter this time. Like he was putting something together. Like he could see the fear in my eyes.

I didn't trust him.

And he knew it.

His jaw clenched slightly before he forced it to relax. "What's going on?" His voice was even, patient, but I caught the flash of unease behind it. "You seem afraid of me. What's wrong?"

I couldn't meet his gaze, my mind spinning. Hannah's warnings echoed in my head: *Be careful who you trust.* Logan was dangerous.

"I—" My voice cracked. I swallowed hard. "Nothing," I lied, but the words felt hollow. "I'm just tired."

His frown deepened as he stood. "You're not acting like nothing's wrong." He took a slow step forward. Not close enough to touch me, but close enough to corner me. "Hazel, talk to me. Just a little while ago, everything seemed fine. What changed?"

What changed?

I'd overheard my best friends saying he was a monster. That Hannah was missing. That Logan knew more than he let on. And I had let him kiss me. Let him hold me.

My throat tightened. I was so, so stupid.

Tears burned my eyes. I wanted to trust him. I wanted to believe the concern in his voice was real, not just another illusion.

"Did I do something?" he asked. "Tell me what's wrong. I'm in the dark here."

"I don't know who to trust," I whispered, barely able to say it.

Silence.

Logan's gaze softened, and he took a step back. "It's okay to be scared." His voice was gentle, steady. "But I'm here, Hazel. I'm not going anywhere."

His words landed like an anchor, pulling me down, grounding me, suffocating me all at once. Was he lying? Or was I too broken to believe him?

"I promise you're safe with me."

Safe.

He thought I was safe with him.

Am I?

The moment his fingers brushed against mine, I flinched. Yanked my hand away like his touch burned.

Logan stilled. Something in his face cracked.

I swallowed back the guilt threatening to choke me. "I'm sorry. Please, just go."

Logan froze, his face falling. Disappointment etched across his features, but he nodded. Slowly, he turned and walked to the door. "Goodnight, Hazel," he said quietly, pausing to glance back. "Sleep well." The door shut softly behind him. And the room felt so much colder.

I wrapped my arms around myself. My breath was uneven, my hands shaking. Had I made the right choice? Or was I pushing away the only person who actually cared about me?

Crossing the room to the bathroom, I reached for the medicine cabinet. I just needed to see the familiar bottle to remind me that I was okay, that I had control.

But when I opened the cabinet, the shelf was empty.

I blinked. Stared. Checked again, as if my mind was playing tricks on me.

No. My meds. They have to be here.

I shoved aside bottles of shampoo, toothpaste, travel-sized lotion. Each item was exactly where I had left it, except for the one thing that mattered.

My stomach clenched. *Maybe I moved the bottle. Maybe I put it in my bag or left it in a drawer.* I was tired when I got ready to go to town earlier. I could've put the pill bottle somewhere else and forgotten.

It has to be here somewhere.

Crouching, I yanked open the drawers, rifling through them with growing urgency. The clatter of the objects inside barely registered. My pulse thumped too loudly in my ears.

Nothing.

I'd taken my meds this morning. I knew I had. Unless … had I forgotten? Could I have skipped it? *No.* I remembered opening the bottle. Tipping a pill into my palm. I hadn't forgotten.

Then where the hell were they? Where could they have gone in the last few hours?

A chill slid down my spine as a new thought crept in. What if I'd thrown them away?

I had done it before in moments of doubt, when I convinced myself I didn't need them. When I thought I was stronger than my own mind.

I lunged for the trash can, flipping open the lid, digging past tissues and wrappers, my hands trembling. But nothing. No sign of the small amber bottle.

Then someone had taken them.

The thought slammed into me so suddenly that I almost rejected it. *No.* That didn't make sense. Why would anyone do that?

I stumbled into the bedroom. Ripped apart my suitcase. Sheets flung to the floor. The mattress lifted and slammed back down. My breath was coming too fast, my chest too tight.

Gone. They were gone.

I pressed a hand to my forehead, a cold sweat breaking out on my skin. I hadn't misplaced them. I hadn't thrown them away. So where were they?

My thoughts raced, colliding with each other. Becca knew about my meds. Matt did too. But they wouldn't.

A pulse of unease shot through me.

Would they?

Becca had been watching me all week, checking in like she knew something I didn't. Matt had warned me about Logan but never explained why. And Jax knew something about Hannah.

My mind reeled, grasping at fragments of conversations, moments that suddenly felt sharper, like puzzle pieces I hadn't realized were part of the same picture.

And Logan—

Logan must have locked me in the bathroom. He'd broken the glass that first night. He'd tampered with the water. He'd closed my vent. My heartbeat roared in my ears. Had he taken my pills, too?

I didn't want to think it. Didn't want to believe it. But hadn't I trusted him too fast? Hadn't I told him everything in the hot tub? Laid myself bare? And only a couple hours later had my medication go missing?

The floor felt unsteady beneath me. My breath came in ragged gulps.

And Becca had pushed me toward him this entire time. Had she known? Had she wanted this? Had they planned this? Had they wanted me off my meds? Or was Logan acting alone?

The possibilities churned in my stomach, twisting into something dark and ugly.

I had to get out of here. The realization hit me hard, like a slap.

My hands curled into fists, my nails biting into my palms. The fear that had choked me moments before transformed into something pointed and intense.

This had to end.

No one thought I was strong enough to handle myself. They were wrong.

I needed answers. And I wasn't going to sit back and let them manipulate me anymore. Logan had the truth, and I was going to get it no matter what it cost.

I was done being played.

Chapter Twenty-Two

I stood at the edge of the lake. The water was unnaturally still, a perfect mirror reflecting the cold, hollow glow of the moon. But something was wrong. The reflection wasn't right. It shimmered, warped, like glass about to shatter.

The air was thick with the scent of damp earth and decay, clinging to my lungs with every breath. The trees whispered, their rustling leaves forming half-words, a conversation just out of reach. A breeze slid against my skin, but it wasn't natural. It felt like fingers brushing my arm.

A pressure weighed on my chest.

I wasn't alone.

The shadowy figure appeared beside me, a smudge in the air, its edges shifting like smoke unraveling in slow motion. It wasn't fully formed, not quite real, but I could feel it.

I tried to move, but my feet were stuck, sinking into the mud like it was swallowing me. "Hello?"

The voice that came wasn't my own. It was mine, but it wasn't. Like an echo from the past.

"I didn't mean to hurt him." The words fell from my lips, automatic. Familiar. But I hadn't spoken them before. Had I?

"I love him. You can't keep us apart." My mouth was moving, but I wasn't in control. A memory that didn't belong to me.

The figure turned. Its form blurred and flickered, like something trapped between two realities. Then it reached for me.

A cold, thin, bonelike, impossibly strong grip encircled my throat.

I gasped. Choked. My fingers clawed at empty air. I tried to step back, but my feet wouldn't move. A wild panic seized me, sharp and suffocating. I tried to scream, but no sound came.

The figure's grip tightened.

The trees bent toward me. The moon cracked in the water.

Then, with a violent shove, the shadow hurled me forward.

I plunged into the lake.

The moment I hit the water, the world flipped. What was up became down, the surface slipping farther and farther away.

The cold was instant, biting, sharp. It tore through my skin like needles, searing through my veins, freezing me from the inside out. My lungs burned, my limbs went rigid.

I kicked, fought, reached, but the water was endless.

The surface wavered above me, the moonlight nothing more than a distorted blur. My arms felt like lead, my thoughts sluggish. The deeper I sank, the more the cold swallowed me whole.

The trees, the shore, the sky gone. The shadowy figure stood above the water's surface, watching. Waiting.

I tried to breathe, but I couldn't.

Wednesday

Chapter Twenty-Three

I jolted awake, my breath coming in ragged gasps. My heart slammed against my ribs, my skin damp with sweat. The room was dark, the air thick and still, but the suffocating grip from my dream lingered. I could still feel the fingers around my throat.

I pressed my palm to my neck and felt no marks. Just a dream. But it hadn't felt like a dream.

Dragging in a shaky breath, I tried to ground myself, but my body wouldn't stop trembling. The nightmare clung to me like a wet sheet, its pieces still sharp and jagged in my mind. The lake. The shadow. The words that weren't mine.

"I love him. You can't keep us apart."

I swallowed hard, a chill prickling up my spine. Those weren't my words. The realization settled over me like a weight of ice. I had felt them, spoken them, but they didn't belong to me. They belonged to Hannah.

A deep dread coiled in my stomach, but before I could process it further, something else registered, something worse.

The sheets beneath my fingertips felt gritty. A sick sense of unease unfurled inside me. Slowly, I swung my legs over the edge of the bed and froze.

Dirt and dried blood caked my feet.

My lungs seized. My pulse pounded in my ears. *What the hell?*

I scrambled to my feet, panic swelling in my throat. My gaze darted to the floor. In the faint moonlight, I could make out footprints. They tracked across the hardwood. My footprints. Smudged with dirt, marred with blood.

No.

My breath hitched. My mind raced for an explanation, but nothing made sense. I couldn't have sleepwalked. Could I?

I tried to recall anything. Any sensation of moving through the night, of stepping outside. But my memories were nothing but fragmented static, disjointed and hollow.

Ducking into the bathroom, I flipped the light on. Too bright. The sudden glare sent a spike of pain through my skull. Blinking past it, I stepped into the shower, turning the water scalding hot.

The blood ran in thin rivulets down the drain, vanishing as if it had never been there. But the tiny cuts on the soles of my feet remained. As if I'd walked barefoot through the woods.

I gripped the sink, my reflection staring back at me with wild, haunted eyes. My thoughts spiraled. I'd been fine, uninjured, when I fell asleep. I had locked my door.

Hadn't I?

I wasn't sure how long I sat on the bed, wrapped in my towel, staring at nothing. Time stretched, my mind a tangled mess of questions and fear.

The first hints of sunlight painted the sky in soft pinks and golds, but the beauty of it didn't reach me. Time stretched endlessly as I sat there, my thoughts tangled and my nerves fraying.

The silence of the house was complete until the soft creak of the front door broke through it.

My heart leapt into my throat. I froze. Holding my breath, I moved to the window, peeling back the curtain just enough to see outside.

Logan was leaving. In the dim light of dawn, his figure moved steadily, his steps purposeful as he walked toward the woods. The sight sent a shiver through me.

Something was wrong.

I watched until he disappeared among the trees, my breath shallow. The fear from the nightmare still clung to me, but now it twisted into something sharp like suspicion.

Had he done something to me last night?

I wrapped my arms around myself, trying to shake away the thought. *No.* Logan wasn't like that. I still wanted to believe that I was safe with him.

I thought about following him into the woods, but a deeper instinct told me to stay behind. If he was hiding something, the answers weren't out there. They were here in the cabin.

Swallowing my nerves, I slipped out of my room. The house was silent. It was the kind of silence that settled thick in the air, making every breath, every movement feel too loud.

I hesitated, fingers resting on the doorknob of Logan's room. A tremor ran through my hands, but I pushed the door open, stepping inside before I could second-guess myself.

The room was cleaner than I expected. Bright and orderly, his bed neatly made as though he hadn't slept there at all.

I paused, guilt flickering at the edges of my resolve. Invading Logan's privacy felt wrong, but I had to know what was going on.

My hands shook as I moved to the dresser, opening drawer after drawer. Clothes neatly folded, nothing out of the ordinary. I sighed, hating myself more with each empty search. Next were the nightstands. Empty again. I swallowed down my frustration. Why was I even doing this? If Logan had nothing to hide, then this was just a massive betrayal on my part.

I turned to the bookshelf.

Among a few decorations and books were framed photos. I picked up one of a younger Logan standing beside a girl with bright, laughing eyes and long, dark hair. She looked familiar, but my mind couldn't place her.

I picked up the next picture, a more recent one of Logan with the same girl, and my stomach dropped.

It was Hannah.

Hannah Foster. Logan's last name was Foster. She was Logan's sister.

The realization hit me like a punch to the gut. Why hadn't I made the connection sooner?

The waitress's words from the bar resurfaced: *Logan's been a mess for a while. He wasn't always like this.*

Jax's warning: *If anything feels off, trust your instincts.*

The words from my dream. *"I love him. You can't keep us apart."*

Hannah was trying to tell me something.

Was Logan mourning his sister? Or hiding something? Had I misread everything?

Had he killed—

No.

I shoved the thought away, but it was already burrowing deep, sinking its claws into my brain.

Jax's voice rang in my head again, louder now. *"Secrets always have a way of coming out."*

Nausea rose in my throat. My stomach twisted, my vision swam, and the room tilted. The sound of my heartbeat echoed loudly in my ears, drowning out the voices in my head. Clammy sweat coated my palms, and a wave of dizziness made me sway unsteadily. The realization hit me like a tidal wave. I was attracted to a murderer.

I had to leave.

My shaky hands returned the picture frame to the shelf, but I bumped another object, a book that toppled to the floor with a dull thud. The sound echoed louder than it should have. I froze, panic flaring as I glanced over my shoulder, praying no one had heard it.

Slowly, I bent to pick the book up, but it was too light.

My fingers trembled as I turned it over. A faint rattling noise made my stomach tighten. Something was inside. I opened the cover, and stopped breathing.

There was a hole in the book's pages. And there were my pills. Tucked neatly inside.

For a long moment, I just stared, as if looking too long would change what I was seeing. I tried to think, tried to make sense of it. My mind raced.

Had Logan really stolen them? Or had someone else planted them here? And what was the point of anyone taking them? To set me up? To try to control me?

Jax's warning looped through my head again and again.

Secrets always have a way of coming out.

This was proof. Proof that something was wrong. Proof that Logan had secrets.

My fingers curled around the pill bottle as I slipped it into my pocket. I carefully placed the book back where it had been. I scanned the room one last time, making sure nothing looked out of place.

Then, as silently as I could, I opened the door and stepped out. The hallway stretched before me, dark and empty. As I closed the door softly behind me, one thought burned in my mind: *I can't ignore this.*

I didn't know the full truth, but one thing was clear. I wasn't safe. Not here. Not with Logan. Not with anyone. And worst of all? I didn't know if I could trust myself.

Chapter Twenty-Four

I couldn't hold back my panic any longer. Clutching the bottle of pills so tightly my fingers ached, I rushed down the hall and burst into Becca's room, throwing the door open with enough force to make it slam against the wall.

"Becca!" My voice trembled as I shook her awake. "Becca, wake up."

She groaned, her face scrunching in irritation as she turned onto her back. Blinking groggily, she glared at me. "What the hell? What time is it?"

My pulse pounded, my breaths uneven. I held up the bottle, my hands trembling. "I—I found them. My pills. In Logan's room."

Becca sat up, rubbing her eyes, blinking hard. Something flickered across her face, too quick for me to catch, before she masked it with groggy confusion. "What?"

"They were *in his room*, Becca." The words spilled out, each one drenched in breathless panic. "I tore my room apart. They weren't there. And now, suddenly, they're in *his* room?"

Frowning, she took in my frantic state. "That's ... really weird," she murmured, her voice measured. "But ... are you sure he put them there?"

I sucked in a sharp breath. "Who else would it be?"

"Maybe you just misplaced them? You've had a lot on your mind this week."

A sharp stab of frustration shot through me. "I didn't forget! I know what I packed. I've been taking them every day until now. There's no way I'd misplace them in Logan's room. They were hidden inside a hollowed-out book."

She exhaled slowly, like she was carefully considering my words. "Okay, okay. Just ... let's think." She reached for the bottle, turning it over in her hands like it held some secret answer. "If Logan did take them, *why*? What would he get out of that?"

The question sent a fresh wave of nausea curling through my stomach. I shook my head. "I don't know. He's been acting weird all week. Hot and cold. Glaring at Jax. At Matt. I think he's the one who locked me in the bathroom. And now this?"

She ran a hand through her hair, her eyes flickering with something unreadable. "Maybe ... maybe he wanted to see what you were like *without* them."

The thought made my blood run cold. I swallowed hard, my throat suddenly dry. "Why would he care?"

"I mean ... Logan's got his own demons. You've seen it. He's ... unstable sometimes."

I stiffened. Logan avoided talking about his sister any time she was brought up. I thought of the way his jaw clenched when Jax mentioned secrets. The haunted look in his eyes. I bit my lip. "It's because of Hannah, isn't it?"

Becca's expression froze for just a fraction of a second, so fast I might have imagined it.

"Why didn't you tell me about her?" I pressed.

She sighed, shifting slightly in bed. "Because it's ... complicated, Hazel."

"Complicated?" I stared at her. "She's Logan's sister. And she's the same girl I've been *seeing* and hearing."

Her jaw clenched. "I didn't want to overwhelm you. You've had a lot going on, and this ghost stuff"—she exhaled sharply—"isn't *healthy* for you. I wanted you and Logan to meet because I thought you could help each other, *not* because of ... whatever this is."

Her words felt like a slap. "You knew who she was this whole time and said nothing?"

She rubbed her temples. "It wasn't my secret to tell. But..." Her voice wavered. "If she's the one you've been seeing, and she's warning you..."

I swallowed, my heart hammering against my ribs. "What if something happened to her?"

Becca's throat bobbed. "Like what?"

I hesitated, the words pressing against my tongue. *Say it.* "What if Logan hurt her?" My voice came out strained, like I couldn't quite believe I was saying it.

Her breath hitched. For a moment, she said nothing. "Hazel ... do you really think Logan hurt Hannah?"

A part of me wanted to take it back. Wanted to rewind the last five minutes and pretend none of this had crossed my mind. But another part of me knew—*knew* that Hannah wasn't just a delusion. Knew that something terrible had happened.

"I don't know," I admitted. "But everything keeps pointing to him. He's been hiding things."

She exhaled, rubbing her arm like she was suddenly cold. "I don't want to believe it. But ... if he *did* hurt her ... it would explain so much." Her voice lowered. "Ever since Hannah disappeared, it's like something in him broke. He doesn't talk about her. He shuts down anytime someone brings her up."

I couldn't breathe. "Then we need to find out the truth."

Neither of us said anything for a while.

I slumped onto the edge of Becca's bed. "What if I'm wrong? What if I'm imagining all of this?"

"You're not. You found your pills in his room, Hazel. That's not nothing."

I swallowed hard. "But what if I'm making it worse?"

"You're not. But you can't let him know you're onto him. Not yet. If he's guilty, he's already on edge."

Her embrace was warm. Solid. The kind that should've made me feel safe. But it didn't. It just made the silence louder.

And somewhere beneath my skin, something sharp and cold was beginning to settle like the moment before a storm breaks.

Chapter Twenty-Five

I wanted to be wrong about Logan.

Wanted to believe that the person who had made me feel safe, even for a little while, wasn't the same person who had been pulling me apart piece by piece.

So, I locked myself away in my room, buried under the weight of my own thoughts. The walls felt too close, the silence too loud. Every voice outside my door sounded distant, like it was part of a world I no longer belonged to.

Lying in bed, my fingers curled into the blanket as I replayed the events of the morning: finding my pills in Logan's room, the unsettling conversation with Becca, the undeniable realization that Hannah was Logan's sister.

A thread of unease pulled tight in my chest. I wasn't just seeing a ghost. I was tangled in her unfinished story.

And then, like a puzzle piece clicking into place, the truth slammed into me.

Hannah wasn't just Logan's sister. She was Jax's ex.

The tension between them suddenly made sense in a way that made my stomach twist. It wasn't only ego clashes or old resentment. Something darker was buried in their history. Something tied to Hannah. But *what*?

Hannah's voice slithered into my thoughts, unshakable. *"I love him. You can't keep us apart."* Her words settled like a cold hand on my shoulder, making me shudder.

Was Logan the one she'd been pleading with? Or someone else?

A shiver ran through me, and I wrapped my arms around myself. The room felt colder, the shadows in the corners darker, shifting like they had a life of their own. My heart pounded, my breath shallow as my thoughts spiraled.

And then a chilling realization hit me: Was this the start of another breakdown?

The weight of that thought pressed against my ribs. Too familiar, too much like before. The last time this happened, I'd felt it creeping in like an unwelcome whisper. At first, it was just a hum in the back of my mind, then a scream I couldn't silence. Sleep had become a luxury, my nights filled with racing thoughts and the certainty that something terrible was about to happen.

I'd lost time. Hours, maybe days. Everything blurred, and I couldn't tell what was real.

One morning, I'd woken up convinced my brother was in danger. I didn't know why or how, but the certainty was paralyzing. I'd tried to call him, but the words wouldn't come out, my throat closing with panic. My mom found me sobbing on the floor, clutching the phone like it was my lifeline.

The hospital stay had been a blur of sterile white walls and muted voices. I remembered the shame of sitting in group therapy, listening to others share their stories while I felt too raw, too exposed, to speak. The fear that I'd never feel normal again had clung to me even after I was released.

I squeezed my eyes shut, my fingers digging into the mattress as I tried to calm myself. *This is different*, I told myself, even as fear clawed at my chest. *This feels different.*

But the thought didn't comfort me.

The temperature shifted so subtly at first that I almost didn't notice. A prickling chill ghosted over my skin, crawling up my arms, settling into my bones. My breath misted in front of me.

The whisper didn't break the silence. It slithered through it, curling around my ears, pressing into my skull like an invasive thought.

"Help me."

My pulse quickened, and I froze. The sound came from nowhere and everywhere at once.

An icy touch, light as breath, skimmed my shoulder.

My stomach plummeted. I jerked upright, heart slamming against my ribs. But there was nothing. Just the shifting dark, swallowing the corners of the room.

Near the closet, the shadows warped, bending inward, like the air itself was holding its breath. Then a flicker.

Light and dark twisted together, struggling to take shape, until the outline of a girl ripped through the space, like she was being forced into existence.

Hannah.

Her hollow eyes snared mine, pulling me into something I couldn't escape. Grief clung to her like mist. And beneath it—rage. Cold, burning rage.

My breath came in short gasps as I pressed myself back against the bed frame, unable to look away.

"I'm sorry," I whispered, though I didn't know why.

The room tilted. The air thickened, pressing against my lungs. The walls weren't just closing in. They were crushing me, burying me under the weight of words I couldn't hear, couldn't understand, but somehow still felt.

A strangled whimper clawed up my throat, my chest seizing. I couldn't move. I couldn't—

Something in Hannah's face shifted. Her expression showed an urgency that sent a jolt of terror through me.

I leapt off the bed and lurched for my jacket. My hands shook as I ripped open the door, stumbling into the hallway. The moment I slammed it shut behind me, I sucked in a desperate, shuddering breath, but the cold still clung to me.

This wasn't a breakdown. I wasn't spiraling. This was real. And Hannah wasn't done with me yet.

I braced myself against the wall, my pulse hammering in my ears. Every nerve in my body screamed at me to run, to get out of this house, away from whatever Hannah was trying to show me. But I couldn't.

Because if Hannah was reaching out to me, it meant she needed something. And if I didn't figure out what, I'd be next.

I forced in a steadying breath, my hands still trembling as I pushed away from the wall. I needed answers. Real ones. No more half-truths. No more lies.

Jax. He had to know something. He had to. And I wasn't going to wait any longer to find out.

I turned and set off down the hallway, each step fueling my urgency. Whatever had happened to Hannah, whatever Logan was hiding was all tangled together. And Jax was right in the middle of it.

I climbed the stairs and paused outside his door, swallowing hard. What if I was wrong? What if this was another delusion? But the thought of doing nothing felt worse.

I raised my fist and knocked. Muffled giggles. The sound of hurried movement. "Jax, it's me, Hazel. I need to talk to you."

A few seconds later, the door swung open. Jax emerged, breathless, sweat clinging to his forehead, his disheveled hair sticking to his flushed face. "What's up?" he asked, his voice slightly strained.

I cleared my throat, awkward under the circumstances. "Um ... I can come back later."

"It's fine," he said, though impatience edged his voice. He stepped aside, letting me in.

Candace sat up in bed, her tangled blonde hair spilling over her shoulders. Her sharp eyes flicked between us, suspicion flickering behind them.

I opened my mouth, then closed it. Hadn't Jax just kissed Becca? *Less than a day ago?*

The thought knocked me off balance. Everything about this group felt too tangled, too messy. Maybe this was normal for them. Maybe nothing meant anything. Were any of them actually telling me the truth?

My stomach twisted. If Jax could so easily switch between Becca and Candace, could I trust anything he said?

I blurted it out before I could second-guess myself. "I know what happened to Hannah."

Jax froze, pure shock registering on his face.

I pressed on, the words tumbling out. "It's Logan. I think he ... he killed her."

Candace's eyes widened. She swung her legs over the bed and pulled on a sweatshirt, like she suddenly needed armor. "What are you talking about?"

I gripped my arms to stop my hands from shaking. "He's been messing with me this whole week. He stole my medicine. He locked me in my bathroom. And I've ... I've been seeing Hannah. She's been warning me about him."

Jax's expression tightened. "Hazel..."

"You told me to trust my instincts," I pressed, stepping closer. "Becca thinks it could be true."

He exhaled sharply, raking a hand through his damp hair. "Becca told me about your ... delusions." He whispered the last word like it might shatter me.

My chest tightened, the humiliation of the word sinking into my skin like a thorn. "This isn't a delusion," I snapped, my hands balling into fists at my sides. "It's real. I—I can prove it."

Jax's gaze flickered. "How?"

"I'll get Logan to confess." The words left my lips before I fully processed them, but once they were out, they felt like my only option.

He stiffened. "No."

"If Logan's dangerous, you shouldn't be around him alone," Candace cut in, her voice rising with alarm.

"I've already been alone with him," I countered. "I'll be fine. I can get him to confess."

"That's insane!" Candace shot back. "What if he hurts you?"

"I have to know." My voice cracked. "You don't understand. I need answers."

Candace's voice dropped. "And what if you're wrong? He'll never forgive you."

I turned to Jax, desperation clawing at my chest. "This is what you want, isn't it? You want me to get close to Logan to get the truth. Becca told me."

Jax flinched, his lips pressing into a thin line. His eyes darted to Candace, then back to me.

A long pause.

"Okay," he said finally, though the word felt forced.

Candace gaped at him. "Are you seriously okay with this?"

Jax didn't answer right away. His gaze dropped to the floor, tension creeping into the room like a slow-moving storm. "I don't want to believe Logan could hurt Hannah," he said quietly, his voice almost breaking. "But ... something's not right."

His words hit me like a weight, and for the first time, I saw the cracks forming in his calm exterior. The doubt, the guilt, the fear.

"Remember when he took us to that abandoned house?" Jax asked. "It's like he wanted us to see it."

My stomach twisted. "For what?"

He shook his head. "It's just ... a place Hannah and I used to go. Why would he take all of us there? And why is he harassing you? It doesn't make sense."

The memory of that house, of seeing Hannah in the attic coming through the mirror, sent a shudder through me.

"Jax," Candace started, her voice softer now, tinged with disbelief. "He's your friend."

Jax closed his eyes briefly, like he hated what he was about to say. "I know." A deep breath. A slight shake of his head. "But if there's even a chance..." He trailed off, jaw tight.

I swallowed hard.

"Hazel," he said. His voice softened, but his unease was unmistakable. "Just ... be careful, okay?"

I nodded, even though my chest was tight with nerves. I had no idea what I'd do when I confronted Logan. But I couldn't back down now. I had to prove it to them, and to myself.

The fire popped and crackled, shadows flickering across everyone's faces as we gathered around the firepit. The warmth against the chilly night air should have been comforting, but instead it added to the strange, uneasy ambiance.

Dinner had been awkward. Forced conversations and small talk that barely masked the tension.

Candace had gotten sick after dinner, and Jax tended to her. Becca and Marcus laughed softly over drinks, and Matt and Aniyah whispered to each other. Despite the semblance of normalcy, I couldn't shake the feeling that everything was wrong.

Logan sat apart from the group, fiddling with the label on his beer bottle, his shoulders hunched. The flickering firelight caught the furrow of his brow, the way his eyes kept darting toward me when he thought I wasn't looking. He seemed ... off. Sad. But it could've just been another act.

I hadn't spoken to him all day, hadn't even looked him in the eye during dinner.

My gaze snapped to the second-story window of the cabin. A faint silhouette stood motionless. My breath caught. Was it Candace? Or ... Hannah?

A chill snaked down my spine. I blinked, and the figure was gone, swallowed by the shadows.

"Hey," Logan said, his voice low, almost hesitant. "Are you okay?"

I flinched at his voice, my stomach twisting. "Yeah," I lied, keeping my gaze on the fire.

A beat of silence.

"Please tell me what I did."

I frowned, startled by the rawness in his voice. "It's not you. It's me."

Logan's brow creased, his fingers gripping the neck of the bottle tightly. "You've been avoiding me all day," he said, his voice cracking slightly. "If I did something to upset you, I'd rather you just say it."

The words almost pulled me in. Almost. Was this guilt? Or was he trying to manipulate me, to cover up what he'd done?

I needed to know.

"Come walk with me," I said.

Confused, he hesitated for a moment. But then he followed me.

We stopped a short distance from the firepit, close enough that I wasn't alone with him, but far enough that no one could overhear.

The moon hung low in the sky, casting a silvery glow over the trees. The air smelled of pine and smoke, the soft crunch of leaves beneath our feet filling the silence.

My heart pounded. How was I supposed to start this? "You haven't done anything," I whispered. "I promise, it's me. Sometimes I see things and hear things that aren't there. It ... makes me do and say things."

Logan turned to me fully now, his brows drawing together. "Hazel, if something's wrong, you can talk to me. You don't have to push me away."

I hesitated. He sounded so genuine. So unlike the image I'd built of him in my mind. "I had a breakdown in June," I said finally. "Everything felt so overwhelming, like the walls were closing in on me. I started questioning everything. Who I was, what I wanted ... It was like my mind was unraveling, and I couldn't stop it."

"I'm sorry you went through that," he said softly. "But you're stronger than you think. You've been trying, right? That's what matters."

"Yeah, I've been trying. But it's hard when I feel like I'm always on the edge, like something's always lurking, waiting to pull me back into that dark place."

"You're still here, Hazel. You're fighting. I see you."

I let out a breath. He sounded real. Honest. And for a moment, I almost let myself believe him. But the pills. My stomach twisted. The doubt crept back in. *He's lying. He's manipulating you.* I bit my lip. *Just say it, Hazel. You need to know.* "I got through it. But ... something tells me Hannah didn't."

Logan stiffened. "What?" His entire posture changed.

"Hannah. I know she's your sister, and I know she was dating Jax."

His jaw clenched, but he didn't speak.

"How can you just ... go on like this, Logan?" I demanded, the words spilling out in a rush. "Like nothing happened? She's gone, and you're pretending everything's fine."

His eyes widened, hurt flashing across his face. "Did Jax put you up to this?"

"No," I said, my voice rising. "I know you stole my meds. You locked me in the bathroom. You made me think I was losing my mind!"

Logan's head snapped back like I'd physically hit him. "What?" His voice shook.

"Don't lie to me! I found my pills in your room."

"You went through my room?"

"They said you were dangerous, but I didn't want to believe it."

A bitter laugh escaped him. "I don't care what they told you. Whatever game you and Jax are playing, it's not funny."

"I'm not the one playing a game."

His expression twisted with hurt and frustration. He let out a slow, unsteady breath, running a hand through his hair. "Hazel, I don't understand what's happening right now." His voice wasn't angry. It was quiet, raw. Like he was trying to hold himself together. "I would never—" He broke off, shaking his head. "I don't know what happened with your pills, but I swear, I didn't take them. I don't—" He exhaled sharply, as if the words were getting caught in his throat.

"Then why were they in your room?"

His brows pulled together. "I don't know, Hazel! I don't even go through my own stuff half the time! Why would I do that to you?"

My chest tightened. Was he lying? Or was I wrong?

But wasn't this what someone manipulative would do? Look wounded? Make me feel like the bad guy?

Logan's gaze searched mine, pleading, confused, breaking. "I don't want to fight with you. But it's clear Jax has put ideas in your head." He turned and walked toward the woods, his shoulders slumped, the silence heavier than any shout, instead of storming off or yelling.

I didn't stop him. Maybe I should have. Maybe I should've gone after him.

But then I heard them. Voices, faint but unmistakable, drifting from the woods. Two people, arguing.

I strained to listen, my breath hitching as I recognized one of the voices. It was Hannah. The other voice was familiar, but I couldn't place it. They were arguing about Jax.

"...I can't believe you're doing this. Jax deserves better!" Hannah shouted.

"Like you're deserving of him," the other voice snapped.

"He deserves someone who's actually there for him, not someone who's always playing games."

"Says the one who disappears when you can't handle life in the real world. You're a joke. And Jax doesn't need your crap. You can't even take care of yourself."

"Oh, here we go," Hannah said. "Making fun of me for being crazy has gotten old. You've always been selfish. You treat Jax like shit. You don't care about anyone but yourself."

The darkness around me seemed to press in, the shadows between the trees thick and impenetrable. I couldn't see who was speaking. No movement between the trees. No sign of people. Only the voices. Echoing. Twisting. Pulling me forward. My fingers curled into my sleeves. What was I hearing?

Was Hannah showing me something? A piece of the past, a secret that had been buried? Or was this just ... my own mind betraying me?

My breath came in shallow gasps. I tried to convince myself that this was just another trick of my brain, another cruel twist in a week of unraveling.

But how could I imagine something this detailed?

The voices rose, tangled in their anger, then suddenly...

Silence. It was deafening. The woods swallowed the voices whole.

I backed away from the trees, my pulse roaring in my head. My mind scrambled for an explanation, but there was none that made sense. Nothing about this made sense.

What did Hannah want from me? And who had she been arguing with?

Chapter Twenty-Six

Pushing open the creaky door, I stepped inside, the echoes of laughter from the firepit fading into the cabin's hushed stillness. The air was cooler here, heavy with a quiet that seemed to press against my chest.

I climbed the stairs to Jax and Candace's room, my steps slow, my thoughts racing. The door was slightly ajar, a faint strip of light spilling into the hallway. I hesitated, then gently pushed it open.

Candace lay on the bed, her face pale and drawn. The soft glow of the bedside lamp bathed her in gold, but it did nothing to erase the exhaustion shadowing her features. The air smelled faintly of sickness, stale ginger, and unease.

"Candace?" I whispered.

She stirred, her lashes fluttering weakly. When her gaze finally landed on me, she offered a small, tired smile. "Hazel? What's up?" she asked, her voice a raspy whisper.

"I just wanted to check on you. Is there anything you need?"

She shifted slightly, wincing as she adjusted the pillow beneath her head. "Aww, thanks. Jax went to get me some ginger ale. Hopefully, I'll be able to keep that down. I think I just need to sleep."

I nodded, my fingers twisting together. I didn't know how to say what was really on my mind. I didn't even know why I was here, really, except that everything felt too heavy, too tangled, and I needed someone to tell me I wasn't losing it.

"What happened with Logan?"

I froze, Candace's question hitting me with a jolt. My throat was dry, my heart pounding.

"I really upset him," I admitted. The words tumbled out before I could stop them. "He was ... hurt. And angry. He walked away, and now I don't know if I made things worse. He thinks Jax put me up to it."

Candace's eyes flickered with concern. "Oh no." She pushed herself up slightly. "Did he confess anything?"

I shook my head. "No. He acted like he didn't know what I was talking about."

"Look, Hazel, for what it's worth, I really don't think Logan is dangerous."

"I don't know. Maybe he's not. All the time I've spent with him, he never made me feel unsafe. He kinda just seems like he's struggling. And if he were dangerous, Becca wouldn't want me around him."

"None of it makes sense. I've noticed the tension between Jax and Logan too. They're keeping something from us. Something big."

I swallowed hard, bracing myself for what I was about to say next. "I overheard Becca and Jax arguing about Hannah. Everyone knows about her. But when I asked Becca at first, she told me she didn't know her. Later, she backtracked and said she didn't want to overwhelm me."

Candace's eyes widened. "Wait." She shook her head, sitting up straighter. "Hazel, that's ... Why wouldn't they tell you about her? That's so messed up."

A lump rose in my throat. "I don't know what's real anymore." My voice cracked. "But I know something's very wrong here, and I'm scared."

Candace stilled. Then, slowly, she reached for my hand and gave it a squeeze. "Hazel, I don't think Logan would hurt you. He's been distant and weird, yeah, but ... if he cared enough to be hurt by what you said, that means something. Just ... be careful. Talk to him when you're ready. But don't do it alone if you're scared."

I nodded, my breath shaky. "Thanks."

As I stepped back into the hallway, the weight of the conversation lingered. I wasn't sure if Candace's reassurances had helped or if they'd only made the knot in my stomach tighter.

I wrapped my arms around myself, trying to shake the memory of Logan's face when I'd confronted him. His hurt expression, the way his voice cracked didn't match the image of someone who had something to hide.

And yet, the fear gnawed at me all the same.

Thursday

Chapter Twenty-Seven

The time on my phone read 6:58. I was waiting for Logan to leave for his morning walk. I needed to talk to him. Ask him about Hannah. Someone had to tell me the truth. I'd stayed up all night, rehearsing everything I wanted to say.

But the moment the door creaked open and softly shut, my stomach clenched. Logan was leaving. This was my chance.

I zipped up my jacket and followed him outside.

As the morning light fought to pierce through a heavy canopy of brooding clouds, the dark gray sky above created a moody atmosphere. The wind seemed to carry shards of ice, slicing through my clothing and chilling to the bone. The remaining brittle leaves on the trees were torn from their branches, swirling in frenzied dances before settling on the frost-hardened ground. Shadows stretched long and thin, cast by the skeletal trees that lined the horizon, their bare branches trembling in the relentless wind.

I kept my distance, my breath barely contained, watching Logan's every move. He walked with purpose, his pace brisk but unhurried, as if his body knew exactly where to go.

What was he doing out here every morning? What if he really did have nothing to do with Hannah's disappearance? What if he did?

Thankfully, the ground was soft, and I made little sound as I walked. My heart pounded, not just from the effort to keep up with Logan's brisk pace, but from the fear of what I would say to him and how he'd react. The ground sloped steeply beneath my feet, and I carefully stepped over an exposed root, praying I wouldn't fall and give myself away.

The trees thinned, and the mist parted. And there it was.

The lake.

Still and impossibly wide, like a sheet of obsidian glass stretched across the earth. The storm-heavy sky hung above it, casting shadows that rippled across the surface. Not even a breeze disturbed it. No birds. No frogs. Just deep silence.

Something inside me lurched. A cold, nauseating realization coiled in my gut.

This was the lake from my dream. The one where I fell into the freezing depths. The one where I became Hannah.

My stomach twisted violently. He knew.

Oh no.

A sudden surge of anxiety caused my heart to race. I'd made a grave mistake in following him.

Hiding behind a tree, I watched him drop to his knees at the water's edge, sifting through the dead leaves. His movements were frantic, unguarded, desperate.

What was he looking for?

I leaned forward for a better look. My foot caught a branch, snapping it with a loud crack. I tumbled to the ground. I froze.

Logan's head snapped up. His eyes locked onto mine, wide with shock and something else. Guilt?

For a long, charged second, neither of us moved. The wind howled between us. The lake was eerily still.

"Hazel." His voice was low, cautious. "What are you doing here?"

My pulse pounded in my ears. My throat was parched. *Think.* I got to my feet. "I ... I was walking." I forced the words out, my voice weak even to my own ears. "I didn't expect to find anyone here."

Logan watched me, an unreadable expression on his face. The distance between us felt like a chasm, filled with doubts and secrets. His gaze flicked away. "Did Becca or Jax send you to follow me?"

My brows furrowed. "What? No. Why would they ask me to follow you?"

His jaw clenched and his hands trembled.

Keep him talking.

I forced a steady breath. "Is this where you go on your hikes?"

"Yeah. It has some ... significance to me."

Leave, my instincts screamed at me. *Go back to the cabin.*

I stumbled backward, the cold air slicing against my skin. But I still needed answers. "What are you looking for? Why are you here at this lake?"

His expression shut down instantly, his walls snapping back into place. "It's nothing. You wouldn't understand."

My stomach twisted. "Does it have something to do with Hannah?"

A shadow passed over his face, a flicker of pain. "Look, whatever Jax or Becca said, you can stop playing games."

"I'm not playing games. I promise." My breath hitched. "And no one's told me anything about her."

"Then how do you know about Hannah?"

I hesitated. "I've been seeing things, hearing things—her voice, her warnings. She's trying to tell me something. Something about what really happened to her."

Logan stilled for a split second and took two quick steps forward. His eyes widened. Raw and undeniable hope flared. "You've seen Hannah?" His voice wasn't angry. It wasn't accusing. It was desperate. Desperate and hopeful. "Where is she?"

"She warned me about you," I whispered. "Everyone did. They said you're dangerous."

Confusion flickered across his face. His brows pulled together, hurt leaking into his voice. "What?" He shook his head slightly. "Warned you—? No. No, that doesn't make sense." His voice rose slightly, desperate. "When did you talk to her?"

I stared at the lake as Hannah's voice echoed in my skull. *"I love him. You can't keep us apart."* I gasped. My breath hitched painfully. "It was you," I choked out. "You took her pills and made her think she was losing her mind. And then you—oh no."

I had to get out of there.

"What? Hazel, have you seen Hannah?"

I backed up another step. "Why did you do it?"

"Do what? Do you know where Hannah is?"

My eyes flicked toward the water. "Why do you keep coming here?"

His jaw tensed. "So I can try to find some clue as to what happened to my sister. I found her bracelet here once. That's all. Have you really seen her or are you just messing with me?"

"I've seen her every day."

Logan's breath hitched. His eyes widened in shock. "What? Where?" He grabbed my arms. His grip was firm but not painful. Still, the sudden contact sent panic racing through me. His gaze bored into me, desperate, demanding. "Hazel, where is she?"

My chest constricted. The air around me felt too thin. I had to leave. Now. "Please don't hurt me."

His hands immediately released me. Like I had burned him. His face twisted with shock, confusion, maybe even pain. His voice was staggered. "Why would I hurt you?"

I swallowed hard, my pulse hammering in my ears. "Tell me the truth. Did you take my pills? Lock me in the bathroom?"

Logan's brows knitted together. "No," he said, his voice steadier now. "Hazel, I didn't take your pills. I didn't do any of that."

He sounded sincere. But could I trust that? Could I trust anything anymore?

The secrecy. The coincidences. The fear. It all swirled inside me like a storm, too chaotic to piece together. But what if I was wrong?

I searched his face, desperate for something, a crack, a confirmation, anything. The morning sun painted the lake in soft gold, casting everything in warmth. But inside, I felt cold. Doubt clung to me like a shadow.

Tears blurred my vision. I had pushed him too far. "I'm sorry," I whispered, my voice breaking. "I—I shouldn't have come here."

His jaw tensed, but his eyes never left mine. Something flickered there. Not anger. Not guilt. Something pleading. "Wait." His voice was quieter now, careful. "What's going on? Where is Hannah?"

His hand reached out, fingers trembling slightly. Like he wanted to hold onto something before it slipped away.

I flinched.

His expression flickered between hurt and frustration. "I swear to you, I didn't take your medication."

A lump formed in my throat, making it hard to breathe. "I just ... I need to go home." The words felt hollow. Going home wouldn't fix this. It wouldn't erase the weight pressing down on my chest, the gnawing feeling that something was wrong with Logan, with Hannah, with me.

"Hazel, talk to me. Tell me about Hannah."

I hesitated, his plea hanging between us like an open wound. "I don't know. I'm ... I'm not okay. And I think you should stay away from me."

His face darkened, not with anger, but with something achingly close to fear. "Whatever this is"—he stepped closer—"We can figure it out together. You don't have to go through this alone."

Tears blurred my vision, hot against the cold air. A couple slipped free, betraying me as they trailed down my cheek. "You don't understand. I'm hearing things, seeing things. I see Hannah in my dreams, except ... I don't think they're dreams. And now I'm drawn to this lake like some kind of lunatic."

He frowned. "Hannah loved it out here. She loved this lake." His voice cracked. "Do you know what happened to her?" Tears pooled in his eyes, threatening to spill over. Either Logan was an incredible liar, or he truly had no idea what happened to Hannah.

I shook my head, backing away. "No. My hallucinations are back. And I—" I swallowed hard. "I have to go back to the hospital. You need to stay away. I don't want to hurt you or drag you into whatever madness is happening to me. It's not fair to you."

He reached out again, hesitant but desperate.

I moved before he could touch me. I turned, my chest aching. I couldn't pull him into this. I couldn't trust myself. "I'm sorry," I whispered, my voice choked with emotion. "Please, just let me go."

"*Hazel...*"

A whisper drifted from the lake. Low. Haunting. Not Logan's voice. I stopped, my breath catching. The voice tugged at something deep inside me, something I couldn't quite grasp.

"*Hazel...*" The whisper came again, curling around me like an invisible hand. "*Don't go.*"

My pulse slammed against my ribs. The lake ... It was calling me. My feet moved before I even realized it, drawn forward by a force I couldn't fight.

"Hazel?" Logan's voice was sharp now, urgent. "Are you okay?"

I continued moving toward the water like it possessed me.

The whisper deepened, more insistent. "*Help me, Hazel...*"

He lunged, grabbing my arm. His grip was firm, his breathing sharp. "Hazel, stop!" His fingers dug into my jacket, anchoring me in place. "You're scaring me. What are you hearing? What's happening?"

I barely heard him. Everything inside me was pulling toward the water. "She needs my help." With a trance-like determination, I tried to take another step, but Logan held me back.

"Who does? Who needs your help?"

The whisper turned mournful. *"Don't go..."*

"Don't go any closer," Logan said, his voice tight with worry. "The water is freezing."

I blinked, the trance wavering, like waking from a dream. My breaths came in short, uneven gasps. "Do you ... do you hear her? She needs my help."

He studied my face. "I don't hear anything. Hazel, who are you talking about?"

"Hannah."

He stiffened. "What?"

I shoved away from him and bolted for the water's edge.

It all made sense now. Why she appeared to me dripping wet, why she lured me here. Hannah was in the lake.

"Hazel, stop!" Logan shouted, his voice filled with panic.

The ground, slick with moss and hidden frost, betrayed me. My foot slipped.

I gasped as I plunged into the icy cold water.

The cold was a shock, a violent awakening from the spell. The instant I hit the water, the breath in my lungs vanished, stolen by the freezing depths. The cold wasn't just cold. It was suffocating, paralyzing, sinking its claws into my bones.

I thrashed, my limbs flailing against the icy vise closing around me. My clothes were too heavy, dragging me down. I couldn't swim. I was going to drown.

My mouth opened in a silent scream, but only bitter, numbing water filled my throat. The darkness swallowed me, the world above fading into a blur of distorted light and sound. I was sinking.

Visions of Hannah flickered in my mind. Her wide, terrified eyes, her hands reaching, struggling, disappearing into the black abyss.

This is what happened to her.

I clawed desperately at the water, my chest burning for air. My fingers grasped at nothing.

Then a splash next to me. Strong arms wrapped around me. A force pulled me upward, steady, unwavering. Logan. His warmth cut through the cold like a lifeline, hauling me back to reality. We broke the surface together, gasping.

Air flooded my lungs, searing against my throat. The world blurred in disorienting motion. Water, sky, Logan's panicked face.

His grip was iron-clad as he swam, dragging me toward shore. I let him. I couldn't fight anymore.

The moment my body hit solid ground, I curled onto my side, coughing up freezing lake water. Every breath scraped my throat raw. Shivering violently, I met Logan's wide, worried eyes. "I heard her,"

I whispered between chattering teeth, my voice thin, fragile. "She's down there. She has to be."

Logan panted, his breaths sharp and uneven. Water streamed down his face, his dark hair plastered to his skin. He looked as shaken as I felt. "You're safe now." He gathered me into his arms. His voice was hoarse, but firm. "I've got you. You're okay."

But I wasn't. I was not okay.

I shivered harder. Not just from the cold. It was the truth settling over me like an anchor, dragging me down deeper than the lake ever could.

Hannah hadn't run away. She hadn't disappeared. She had drowned.

And I was the only one who could hear her calling for help.

My vision blurred, the edges darkening like water creeping in. Logan's voice called my name, urgent now, but it was already slipping away.

Then nothing.

Chapter Twenty-Eight

The moment I opened my eyes, I was met with the low murmur of voices. Muted. Distant. But as my senses sharpened, I recognized them. Jax and Becca.

They were inside the room talking about me.

I stayed perfectly still, my breathing shallow, listening.

"I don't know what's gotten into her," Becca whispered. Her voice was tight, sharp around the edges. "She could've died. Why was she out there?"

"That's probably my fault," Jax admitted. "She told me Logan stole her meds. That she's been seeing Hannah ... that he might have killed her." A pause. "She said she wanted to get Logan to confess."

"And you let her go out there by herself? Dammit, Jax."

"She wanted to prove that she wasn't having hallucinations. She said you believed her about Logan."

Becca let out a long, exasperated sigh. "Yeah, maybe about Logan, but Jax, she's *seeing* things. Which means either she hid her meds or she's not taking them."

A sharp, twisting pain lanced through my chest. Becca didn't believe me. She still thought I was having delusions. I swallowed hard, my hands gripping the blanket. It shouldn't have hurt so much. But it did.

"Logan said she heard voices at the lake," Becca continued.

"What if Logan pushed her into the water?" Jax asked, his voice low, urgent. "Maybe he knows she can't swim."

Becca scoffed. "Why would you think that?"

"Maybe that's what he did to Hannah."

My breath caught.

"Jax, stop," Becca snapped. "Hannah ran away."

"But what if—"

"Listen to yourself. Logan saved Hazel. If he wanted her dead, why would he jump in after her?"

Jax hesitated. "Maybe he felt guilty. Maybe he panicked."

Becca exhaled sharply, like she didn't want to say what came next. "Even if—*if* Logan was involved somehow, Jax, you think his family would ever let anything come to light? If something happened to Hannah, they made sure it disappeared."

A heavy silence settled between them.

Jax finally spoke. "So, you *do* think something happened to her?"

"I think..." Becca's voice wavered. "I think Hannah left. I think Logan's family made sure of it. And I think Hazel is not the person to be dragging into this. Don't let Hazel's delusions wind you up, and don't use her for your own benefit. She's sick, Jax."

The words hit me like a blow. *Sick. Delusional.* The same things I'd called myself during my worst moments.

Jax sighed. "I thought she was doing better. But if she's spiraling again ... maybe you need to take her home. I can get the truth out of Logan myself."

Home.

A lump formed in my throat. They were giving up on me.

Becca's voice softened. "Maybe we need to stop."

"Stop?" Jax echoed, incredulous. "We came here to get the truth."

"*You* came here to get the truth. But Jax, this has gotten bad. Our friend almost *drowned* because of all this."

A beat of silence. Then Jax's voice, rough and raw. "I can't just give up on Hannah. I love her. And she's your best friend."

Best friend?

My fingers curled into the sheets. Becca was Hannah's best friend? Why hadn't she ever mentioned her?

"She *was* my best friend," Becca said, her voice breaking. "Until she left. We haven't found anything, Jax. No one has. Because she doesn't want to be found." She paused. A shaky breath. A sniffle. Then Becca's voice, raw and trembling. "I can't do this anymore." And she started to cry.

I had never heard Becca cry like that.

"I can't keep talking about her. I can't keep hoping she'll just show up. I have to let her go." A pause, then quieter. "And so do you."

Jax exhaled. The sound of someone breaking. "It's not that easy, Becca."

"I never said it was."

The air grew thick with unspoken tension between them.

Finally, Jax spoke. "So, what do we do?"

Becca sighed. "When Hazel wakes up, we'll talk to her. I'll take her home first thing tomorrow. She needs help."

She was going to take me away.

Becca's voice dropped lower. "And as for Hannah ... we have to let her go."

The door creaked, followed by soft footsteps. The sound of them leaving.

I lay there, staring at the ceiling, the room spinning around me.

Becca had been Hannah's best friend. And she never told me.

The weight of that realization sank into my chest, pressing harder than the blankets cocooning me.

I had trusted Becca. I had told her everything—every fear, every dark thought—but she had kept this from me.

Jax, too. He had spent all week telling me to trust my instincts, acting like we were in this together. But the whole time, he'd had his own agenda. He had loved Hannah. He had been searching for her.

And yet, neither of them had told me a damn thing.

The betrayal twisted inside me, sharp and unforgiving. Had they been laughing behind my back, whispering about how sick I was, about how I was losing it all over again?

They thought I was sick. Delusional. A burden. Maybe they were right.

Guilt and betrayal churned together, a tangled, suffocating knot. I thought of Becca crying. Jax, frustrated and exhausted.

And then ... Logan.

Logan, pulling me from the freezing lake. Logan, who looked at me like I was something worth saving.

I had been so afraid of him. And yet, when I needed help, he was the one who was there for me.

My fingers clenched the blanket, the sting of my own mistakes burning under my skin. Maybe I'd been wrong about Logan. But that didn't change the fact that Becca and Jax had been lying to me this entire time.

The door creaked open. My breath hitched, my body tensing. For a heartbeat, I thought it was Becca or Jax.

But it was Logan.

His presence filled the room as he gently shut the door behind him. His shoulders were tense, but his expression was softer than I expected.

"You're awake." A flicker of relief crossed his face as he stepped toward me. He eased onto the edge of the bed. "You scared me."

I frowned, sitting up and pulling my knees to my chest. "I'm sorry."

Logan exhaled sharply, rubbing the back of his neck. "The second you hit the water, I felt..." He trailed off, his voice breaking slightly. "I don't want to lose you, too."

His words hung in the air, heavy with unspoken pain.

My chest tightened. I had accused him of horrible things. I had run from him. Feared him. And yet ... he had saved me. He'd jumped into the water without hesitation.

I looked away, unable to meet his eyes. "I'm so sorry for everything. I don't know what's happening to me."

"It's okay," he said softly, his voice steady, but his gaze intense. He hesitated, then carefully reached for my hand.

I didn't pull away. The warmth of his touch seeped into me, steadying the tremor in my chest. I shifted, making room, and he settled beside me, his arm wrapping around me like a protective shield.

The room felt smaller. Safer.

I breathed in his scent of lemon and oak, but the comfort it brought was fleeting. "Logan, there's something you should know."

He turned to face me, his brows knitting together. "What is it?"

I hesitated, my throat tightening. The words felt heavy, tangled with fear and doubt. "I've ... I've been seeing Hannah all week."

He stilled.

"She's been calling out to me. I heard her voice earlier. That's why I went into the water. She kept saying, 'Help me.'"

For the first time, his face wasn't just guarded. It was vulnerable. "Hazel..."

"I know what it sounds like," I rushed to say, my voice trembling. "But every night since I've been here, I've seen her. I didn't even know who she was at first. Becca told me I just latched onto this missing poster I saw at the store. But I don't think that's all it is. She's been haunting me. I'm certain. It can't just be my mind."

Logan's jaw clenched, and I saw the muscle twitch. He dropped his gaze, his hand slipping away from mine. "Is this—"

"This is real. It has to be." I took a breath, forcing myself to say it. "I overheard Becca and Jax talking about you."

Logan flinched, like I had struck him.

"Jax is convinced you had something to do with Hannah disappearing. He and Matt told me you were dangerous. That's why I went into your room. I found my pills and a picture of you and Hannah. And..." My voice broke, shame burning hot in my chest. "That's why I've been afraid of you. Because I believed them. I'm sorry."

His expression hardened, the flicker of hurt replaced by a brewing storm of anger.

"Jax thinks you pushed me in the water," I whispered. "And ... he thinks maybe that's what you did to Hannah."

Logan shot to his feet, his arm slipping away from me. The warmth that had been there seconds ago was gone, replaced by something colder.

For a long, stretched-out moment, he didn't say anything. He ran a hand through his hair, his entire body tense, like he was physically holding himself back from exploding. Then, at last, his voice cracking slightly, he whispered, "Do you really think I'm capable of that?"

Our eyes met, and I saw something inside him crack. His expression wasn't anger. Wasn't rage. It was betrayal.

My stomach sank.

"I pulled you out of that lake, Hazel," he said, his voice rough, like the words physically hurt to say. "I—" He exhaled sharply, shaking his head. His jaw clenched as his fingers curled into fists. "Do you really think I would've saved you if I wanted you dead?"

The breath caught in my lungs. I wanted to say no. That of course I didn't believe that. But the truth was, I had. Even for a second. And now I could see what that had done to him.

He let out a bitter laugh, low and humorless, running a hand through his still-damp hair. "Fuck," he muttered, running a hand through his still-damp hair, his eyes darting away like it hurt too much to keep looking at me. Like he was trying to erase the moment.

He stood frozen in place, grief and anger battling behind his eyes. Then slowly, something shifted. His jaw locked. His shoulders squared. He turned without another word and stalked out of the room.

"Logan—wait—" I stumbled out of bed, the ache in my chest forgotten as panic took over.

By the time I caught up, he was in the living room. Everyone was there staring as Logan stormed in like a lit fuse.

Jax stood, chest puffed, arms crossed like he'd been waiting for a fight.

"You think I killed my sister?" Logan's voice tore through the cabin, sharp and shaking. For a breathless second, no one moved. The pain in his eyes made it worse, because it wasn't just fury. It was heartbreak.

Then his fist snapped forward, connecting with Jax's jaw in a clean, brutal hit.

I gasped, covering my mouth with trembling hands.

"What the hell?" Jax growled. He lunged toward Logan, but Matt quickly intervened, grabbing Jax to hold him back. "I know you did something!"

"Jax, stop," Becca interjected, her voice wavering with uncertainty.

Marcus stepped between them, gripping Logan by the shoulders and gently pulling him back. "Enough. Both of you. This isn't helping."

Jax hesitated, doubt flickering across his face. "You never wanted me to be with her."

"I was trying to protect you," Logan shot back. "She needed help, and you ignored that. You didn't care. You don't get it." His anger seemed to waver, his fingers flexing at his sides, like he didn't know whether to hit Jax again or walk away. "Hannah is my sister," he murmured, his voice trembling. "I have been searching for her, tearing myself apart, trying to figure out where she is. You—" he pointed at Jax, voice cracking "—were my friend. And you let Hazel think I was a murderer?"

The room quieted as everyone exchanged nervous glances.

"I didn't mean..." Jax trailed off, running a hand through his hair.

Becca hesitated, like she was carefully choosing her words. "Logan, no one's saying you hurt her," she murmured. "We just ... we don't know what happened." She glanced at Jax, at me. At all of us. "Hannah disappeared, and we all have questions. You can't blame us for wondering."

I crossed my arms, the ache in my chest growing unbearable. "But you *did* say that about Logan. I know everything. I heard you two talking. You've been trying to figure out what happened to Hannah and trying to use me as a pawn to get Logan to confess." My voice cracked, but I pushed through. "You believed me when I thought Logan did something."

Jax turned toward me, his expression softening. "Hazel, I was desperate. You said you thought Logan hurt her, and I thought ... maybe you were onto something."

"And you encouraged it," Logan said bitterly. "You planted this idea in her head. You made her doubt me."

Matt sighed. "Maybe part of this is on me. I warned Hazel about you, Logan. I shouldn't have said anything."

Logan turned to Matt, his frown deepening. "You think I hurt Hannah, too?"

"No. I just..." Matt hesitated, glancing at the floor. "You haven't been yourself."

Logan let out a bitter laugh, shaking his head. "You think I haven't been myself?" He gestured wildly. "No shit, Matt. My sister's missing, my so-called friend thinks I killed her, and now Hazel—" His voice broke. "Even Hazel was afraid of me." He swallowed hard, his jaw tightening. "But sure. Go ahead. Keep wondering if I'm dangerous because I 'haven't been myself.'"

"I'm sorry, Logan." Becca bit her lip. She looked guilty, but I knew better. "I never meant for things to get this out of hand. I thought Hazel was doing better. She saw Hannah's poster at the store, and her mind just ran away with all these ideas. I didn't think..." Her gaze landed on me. Not with anger. With something softer. "Did you stop taking your medicine?"

The air left my lungs in a sharp gasp. I shook my head. "No. I didn't stop."

Becca sighed, her expression patient and understanding. "You said you found your pills in Logan's room," she said gently. "Maybe you hid them there yourself and forgot. You've done it before."

Logan shook his head, jaw tightening. "Don't." His voice was quieter now, but no less sharp. "Don't dismiss her just because it's easier than believing her."

Becca turned her full attention to me. "Hazel, you've been through so much lately. Stress can make things feel real. So real you'd bet your life on them." Her voice was soft, careful, like she was trying to talk me off a ledge. Like she wasn't the one who had pushed me there in the first place.

"You don't know that's what happened," Logan muttered. His voice wasn't loud, but the way Becca's shoulders stiffened told me she'd heard him.

Becca pressed on, her gaze locked on me. "Do you remember when you thought the neighbors were spying on you?"

I froze. My throat tightened. "That was different."

"Was it?" She tilted her head slightly. Her sympathy felt like a trap. "I'm not blaming you, Hazel. You've had a rough year. And you've been trying so hard to keep it together."

Logan shifted beside me. "Becca." His voice had an edge. It wasn't loud, but it was enough. A warning.

"You said you've been taking your meds," she continued, her voice soft, coaxing. "But can you really remember the last time?"

"I—" I swallowed hard. I couldn't. I thought I had taken them this morning, but now ... my memory blurred. I could only remember searching for them, not actually taking them.

Becca exhaled, like that settled it. "It's not your fault if you forgot. It happens. And stress makes everything worse."

Jax stepped closer, his voice quieter now. Like they were all in agreement about what was happening to me. "Haze, I don't think you're doing well."

"I know what I saw," I said, but my voice sounded weak even to my own ears.

Becca frowned. "Hazel, stop. You saw a missing poster. That's where this all started, right? You wanted to help, so you convinced yourself she was reaching out to you. That's what your mind does when you're under stress." She turned to Logan, her voice gentle now, like she was comforting him. "I'm sorry she made you think Hannah was..." She trailed off, shaking her head.

Logan's face crumpled. The fight in him seemed to drain all at once, replaced by exhaustion.

"No." I shook my head desperately. "It was real."

"Hazel, please," Becca said, stepping closer. Her voice was so soft, so careful. So condescending. "You're scaring all of us."

Logan shifted beside me again. I could feel his eyes on me. And then, quietly—so quiet it almost didn't register at first—he said, "You're wrong."

The room froze. Becca's lips parted slightly, but Logan didn't look at her. His gaze was locked on me.

"She's not making anything up." It wasn't loud. It wasn't forceful. But it shattered something.

Becca's eyes flicked toward him, her expression freezing for a fraction of a second before she covered it with another soft sigh. "I know you want to believe her, Logan, but..."

She didn't finish the sentence. She didn't have to.

No one believed me. No one except Logan.

I swallowed hard, my gaze darting between their faces. They all looked at me like I was broken, like I was dangerous. And maybe I was.

Chapter Twenty-Nine

The soft hum of the cabin's ambiance enveloped me as I stood in the bathroom, the cool tiles grounding me. Staring into the mirror, I barely recognized the pale, tired girl that stared back. Dark circles clung to her lost, confused eyes. My chin quivered as tears slid down my cheeks.

"If you're real, you have to make them see. I need you to be real." The words came out as a whisper, a plea to the only person who might have answers.

In one hand, I held the small bottle of medication, and with the other hand, I picked out pills, counting them methodically, the rhythmic sound of the pills clicking against each other a fragile tether to stability. This was the only thing I could control right now.

I had no proof of anything. Seeing Hannah. Her voice luring me to the lake. Jax and Becca's conversations. Someone else hiding my pills in Logan's room.

The bedroom door creaked open, and I tensed. But I relaxed when I saw Logan.

"Hey," he said gently.

I paused, the pills still in my hand, my fingers trembling slightly.

His eyes flickered downward, taking in the scene. Worry settled into the lines of his face. "Whoa—Hazel. What are you doing?"

"Counting my pills," I murmured. "I have exactly the amount I'm supposed to have." I snapped the lid shut with finality. "I didn't forget to take them."

"That's good," he said, his tone cautious.

Gripping the counter, I shook my head, frustration and fear knotted in my chest. "Then why do I feel like I'm losing my mind? Ever since I got here, everything's been off."

"I don't know. I'm sorry," Logan said, his voice soft. Hesitant. "Sometimes Hannah had to change meds a lot."

My breath hitched. It wasn't just the meds. It wasn't just me.

Tears welled in my eyes as I looked at him. "I'm sorry I accused you. I'm a mess. I've made a mess of everything." The words broke free, spilling over like a dam had cracked. "I don't want to be like this."

Without hesitation, Logan pulled me into him, his arms wrapping around me like a shield. His heartbeat was steady, anchoring. His warmth cut through the cold that had settled deep inside me.

I sank into his hold but hated myself for it. I had thought he was capable of murder only hours ago. I didn't deserve his comfort. "I won't blame you if you never want to speak to me again," I murmured.

His grip tightened. "I never gave up on Hannah. I won't give up on you."

I pulled back slightly, blinking up at him. "She's your sister, Logan. I'm just some girl. We met and it was amazing. But I can't put you through this. I won't."

"You can't decide that for me."

"I need help."

"Then we'll get you help."

"You don't mean that. You tried to help your sister but couldn't. Now, you're using me as your next project."

"That's not true. I'm not trying to fix you, Hazel. I care about you." His voice was steady. Sure. It scared me how much I wanted to believe him. His next words were almost a whisper. "And you're not just some girl."

But I had already made up my mind.

A restless, clawing urgency gripped me. I had to get out of here. The walls of the cabin felt too tight, pressing in on me. My mind was spinning.

I turned, yanking open my suitcase, stuffing clothes inside with shaking hands. I zipped my bag, gripping the handle like it was the only thing holding me together. I had to leave. If I stayed any longer, I'd drown in this place.

"Please, don't leave like this," he whispered.

My hands trembled over the bag. I wanted to listen to him. But I couldn't. I couldn't let him see me like this any longer. Couldn't let him waste any more time on someone as messed up as me. "I have to." My throat tightened. "I knew I shouldn't have come. The only reason Becca invited me was to play spy for them. Except apparently, I imagined that. They all warned me about you ... and I guess I just—"

"I know Hannah's dead."

The words cut through my breathless rambling like a blade. My chest constricted, my grip on the bag slipping. Slowly, I turned to face him. The room tilted. My pulse roared in my ears.

"What?" I whispered.

Logan didn't move. Didn't blink. His expression was blank, like he had been carrying this weight for so long that saying it out loud had left him hollow. "I know she's dead," he repeated. Despite his steady tone, the pain in his eyes was evident. "I didn't want to believe it, but deep down, I've known. I just ... I couldn't admit it to myself. But I can't keep running from the truth." He sank onto the bed. "I wanted her to be missing ... living her life somewhere on a beach, happy."

I sat beside him, silent. Waiting.

His throat bobbed. "The day she went missing, we had a fight." His voice was a whisper now, hollow. "She wanted to be with Jax, but she wasn't in a good place. And Jax ... you know about him and

Becca. Plus, she and Becca were best friends." He sighed. "She left to cool off. I knew she'd go to the lake because that's where she always went. Or to that abandoned house in the woods. I thought she'd be okay. She and I know this place inside and out."

His hands clenched into fists. "Becca and Jax went after her, arguing the whole way. Jax came back, then Becca. She said Hannah wanted to be alone. Typical Hannah." His voice hitched. "It got dark, and the temps were dropping. I went to the lake. She wasn't there.

I called her phone but she didn't answer." He swallowed hard, blinking rapidly. "She texted me, said she'd be back soon. That she was okay. But then..." His voice cracked. "She never came back. She never answered my calls."

I swallowed, the memory of Hannah dripping wet flashed in my mind.

Logan exhaled sharply. "Her phone was disconnected. Her body's never been found. It's like she just vanished." He reached into his pocket and pulled out a bracelet. "This is all I have left of her." He looked at me then, his gaze dark and pleading. "Tell me what you saw."

I knew what he meant. "Logan..."

"I know, but just ... tell me. Please."

I hesitated, but the words tumbled out. "She was soaking wet. Crying. She kept saying, 'I didn't mean to hurt him.'"

Logan went still. "She was wet?" he whispered. A sharp inhale. His jaw tightened. "Could she have...?" He shook his head. "No. She would never do that."

I swallowed. "What are you saying?"

"She wouldn't have willingly jumped in the lake."

The weight of his words pressed against my ribs. I wanted to believe he was wrong. That Hannah wouldn't have killed herself. Or that someone had killed her. That what I'd seen—what I thought I'd seen—was nothing more than my mind betraying me.

"You can't trust anything I've seen or heard," I whispered. It sounded more like a plea than a statement. "It's not real."

"But what if it is?" His voice was barely above a whisper, but the desperation in it cut through me like a blade.

My pulse kicked up. "Logan," I began, forcing my voice to stay steady, "you can't hold on to this. You can't let what I've seen—what I think I've seen—make you doubt everything. You know I'm not reliable. You know that."

His gaze dropped to the floor, his jaw clenching. "But what if it's not just in your head?" His voice had a quiet intensity to it. "What if it's a piece of the truth? I can't ignore it. Not if it could mean finding out what really happened to her."

A sharp pang of guilt knifed through me. I wanted to tell him he was wrong, to force this all away. But a tiny, treacherous part of me wondered, too, what if

I hadn't just been seeing things? What if there was something buried beneath the chaos in my mind?

"Did you even know the lake was nearby?" he asked.

I hesitated. *No.* But I couldn't say that to him. If I did, it would only fuel his hope. "Logan—"

"Why would you see and dream these specific things?" he pushed. His voice was sharp, frantic. Like he was piecing together something he hadn't wanted to see before.

"I don't know. I can't explain it."

He stared at me, searching for something, anything, that could make sense of what I'd told him.

"I know you're looking for answers," I said finally. "I would be too. But it's not real. And I can't tell you how sorry I am."

"What if—"

"Stop." My voice cracked. "Please."

He exhaled sharply, nodding. "You're right." He ran a hand through his damp hair. "I'm sorry." His shoulders slumped, defeated. "I don't know what's real anymore. I just ... I need to believe there's something. Anything. I can't stand thinking she just vanished."

The pain in his voice made my chest ache. I wanted to comfort him, to promise him closure, but I couldn't. "I don't know what happened to her," I said, forcing myself to hold his gaze. "But I know you can't carry this alone."

"I just wish I could go back," he murmured, his voice was hollow and hopeless. "Make it all stop before it went so wrong."

A small part of me wondered if he had ever allowed himself to say any of this out loud before. I wanted to tell him it wasn't his fault. That whatever had happened that night wasn't on him.

"We'll figure it out," I promised, squeezing his hand. Even though I didn't know if it was the truth.

Logan nodded. Like he wanted to believe me. Like he needed to.

I watched him. His grief filled the space between us. He looked exhausted, like he'd been carrying this alone for too long, and I wondered if I'd just made everything worse. It would be better for me to leave. I'd been set on leaving, but now, I wasn't sure if I could.

Instead, I let out a slow breath and shifted closer to him, hesitating for only a second before leaning my head against his shoulder.

He stiffened slightly, but didn't pull away. His fingers twitched, then carefully, he rested his hand over mine.

"I don't want to be alone tonight," I whispered.

Logan nodded, his grip tightening. "Then don't be."

We stayed like that, neither of us saying anything, just the quiet sound of our breathing.

Eventually, my exhaustion caught up to me. The weight of everything pressed down, but Logan's warmth was steady, grounding. For the first time in days, I let myself close my eyes with Logan next to me.

Chapter Thirty

"Wake up," a voice urged me.

But I couldn't move. My limbs felt heavy and unresponsive.

"Wake up," the voice urged again, more insistent now.

My pulse roared in my ears. I strained, trying to force my body to respond, but my arms wouldn't lift. My legs wouldn't budge.

"Please! You have to wake up!" The voice, desperate and familiar, echoed through the fog that clouded my mind.

I wanted to scream, to cry out, but no sound escaped my lips. Panic surged in my chest. I felt trapped, drowning in the darkness. Why couldn't I move? Why couldn't I wake up?

The voice was closer now, almost in my ear. "It's not safe. You have to wake up before it's too late."

With a burst of determination, I fought harder, my body trembling as I pushed against the invisible weight holding me down.

I gasped, my body jolting upright. My heart slammed against my ribs as I blinked into the dim room, my breath coming in sharp, ragged bursts.

The cabin was silent, but the remnants of the dream clung to me, thick and suffocating. My skin prickled.

I rubbed my eyes, trying to shake off the lingering unease.

Something was wrong.

I swung my legs over the edge of the bed, rubbing my arms against the sudden chill in the air. My mouth was dry. Water. I just needed some water.

As I shifted, my fingers brushed against something warm and damp. I frowned, pulling my hand back, staring at the slick substance on my fingers. My stomach twisted. The scent hit me then—metallic, sharp, suffocating.

Blood.

I reached for the bedside lamp, my hands shaking so badly it took two tries to switch it on.

The second the light flickered to life, my breath caught in my throat.

Blood. Everywhere.

The sheets were soaked. My clothes, my hands, were smeared in it. My vision blurred as my gaze traveled to Logan beside me.

His face was pale, lips parted slightly, chest rising in shallow, uneven breaths. A deep red stain spread across his stomach, his shirt clinging to the wound. His fingers were curled weakly over it, blood seeping between them.

A knife lay inches from his outstretched hand.

And next to it was a gold bracelet. Hannah's bracelet.

"Logan," I choked, scrambling closer. My hands hovered over him, not knowing where to touch, how to help. "Logan, can you hear me?"

His eyes flickered open, unfocused, his expression contorted in pain. "H-Hazel…"

Panic shot through me. I had to stop the bleeding. I had to do something.

I grabbed the nearest blanket, pressing it against the wound, my fingers slipping in the blood. "Stay with me. Please, stay with me." I fumbled for my phone, my fingers shaking too hard to grip it properly. No signal. My breath hitched. "No, no, no. Becca! Jax! Marcus!"

Logan gasped, his eyes widening as he stared past me.

I seized the knife, whirling around, but there was no one.

He groaned.

"Who was it? Who did this?"

His eyes rolled to the back of his head.

"No! Logan!" I had to get help.

Footsteps echoed from behind me. I spun around to see everyone. They all stood frozen in the doorway, eyes wide, taking in the scene—the blood, Logan, the knife, me kneeling beside him.

For a split second, no one moved.

"Oh shit!" Marcus rushed to Logan's side.

Matt was already dialing for help. Jax stood with a shocked expression. Candace and Aniyah both gasped. Becca gasped and her eyes widened. Then her gaze landed on me. She didn't move as she stared at me with a knowing look. She'd already decided what happened.

The realization slashed through me, even as my mouth struggled to form words.

"I—I didn't do this," I stammered, backing away. The knife was still in my hand. My bloodstained hands. I dropped it, the metallic clang of the blade against the wooden floor ringing in the silence.

Becca sighed. Slow. Calculating. Then she crouched down, retrieving the knife carefully, like handling something fragile. Her eyes never left mine. "Haze," she said gently, voice tinged with something too soft, too patient. "What happened?"

My pulse thrummed in my ears. "I—I don't know. I woke up and found him like this."

She nodded, a slow, deliberate motion. "Okay." She was too calm.

The weight of their stares pressed down on me, thick and suffocating. I could see the doubt, the hesitation.

Logan let out a weak groan, drawing everyone's attention back to him.

"We need to get him to the hospital now," Marcus said, already lifting Logan as Matt and Jax moved to help.

I took a step forward, but Becca blocked me.

Her hands were still raised as a subtle barrier between me and everyone else. "Hazel," she said, quieter this time. "Why don't you stay here?"

The others were too distracted, too frantic to see what she was doing. But I felt it. I felt the way she was looking at me. Like I was dangerous. Like I was the only person in this room who had something to prove.

My stomach twisted, nausea rising in my throat. "I didn't do this," I whispered. More to myself than to her.

Becca tilted her head, her expression unreadable. She reached forward, fingers brushing my wrist. "Come on," she murmured. "Let's get you cleaned up."

I flinched.

And that was when I knew. She didn't believe me. None of them did.

Chapter Thirty-One

Logan had been stabbed.

Oh god.

Had I done this? Had I stabbed him in my sleep?

I swayed where I stood, nausea rising fast and sharp, my breath coming in shallow gasps. I couldn't have. I wouldn't.

Would I?

The front door slammed. The sound jolted through me. Marcus, Matt, and Aniyah were gone, rushing Logan to the hospital, leaving only Becca, Jax, Candace, and me in suffocating silence.

But would Logan even make it? Would he survive?

A sharp, suffocating fear wrapped around my chest, pressing down so hard I could barely breathe. I saw him again, pale and soaked in blood, gasping my name. I saw the way his body had jerked in pain, the way his fingers trembled as he tried to hold himself together.

My stomach twisted violently, and I clutched the doorway for balance. What if I never got to say sorry? What if I never saw him again?

"What happened, Haze?" Jax took a hesitant step forward, his expression cautious.

The weight of their stares pressed down on me. Candace stood by the couch, arms wrapped around herself like she was holding herself together. Becca's face was carefully blank, but her eyes—her watchful eyes—never left mine.

"I don't know."

Candace shifted uneasily. "No one else was here."

It wasn't a question.

My pulse pounded in my ears. "Someone broke in," I said quickly, grasping for anything that made sense. "There's no other explanation."

Jax frowned. "Isn't there?"

"There was no break-in," Becca murmured.

A sharp chill crawled up my spine.

Becca stepped forward, her head tilting slightly, studying me. "Hazel, I know you've been watching Logan. Following him. You started to believe he was dangerous." Her voice was gentle. Too gentle.

"I would never hurt him."

Jax exhaled, rubbing a hand over his face. "We know." He sounded ... sad. "We know it was an accident."

An accident?

A cold, horrible feeling slithered through me. They'd already decided what happened.

Becca sighed, smoothing her expression into something unnervingly calm. "We all care about you, but you need to get help. You're not well."

I froze, the room seeming to tilt beneath me.

Was I not thinking clearly? I thought of the knife, the blood, Logan's limp body, the panic in everyon's eyes. The harder I tried to hold on to what I knew, the more it slipped through my fingers.

Becca approached slowly, carefully, like I might lash out. "Come on. Let's get you home."

Home. The word twisted inside me. It used to mean safety. But now it felt like a cage. A place where they'd keep me until I unraveled completely.

"I didn't do this," I whispered, my voice cracking. I turned to Jax, Candace, pleading. But their faces were heavy with doubt.

Jax opened his mouth as if to say something, but he hesitated. His gaze shifted to Becca, and when he didn't speak, it felt like a final verdict.

Becca reached out, and her fingers brushed my arm. A tether. A trap. "Let's pack your things before something else happens."

My stomach clenched. *Something* else. It wasn't an accusation. Not outright. But it didn't have to be.

Tears burned my eyes, but I blinked them back. *What if they're right?* The thought twisted deep, wrapping around my ribs. *What if I did it?*

I had no memory of stabbing him, but my memories were feeling increasingly blurry.

With trembling legs, I followed Becca to my room.

She moved with purpose, controlled, her steps steady, like she was guiding me somewhere final.

I stopped in the doorway, staring at my already-packed bag, trying to ignore the bloody mess in my room. Tears blurred my vision, but I didn't wipe them away. I couldn't shake the thought that I might have actually stabbed Logan circling my head, unrelenting. My knees threatened to buckle, and I gripped the dresser for balance.

I don't want to lose you, too.

Logan's voice echoed in my mind. But he never should have gotten involved with me. I had thought Logan was the dangerous one. But it was me all along.

A choked sob escaped my lips. I pressed a trembling hand to my mouth, trying to hold myself together. But it was no use.

Everything was broken. Jax, Becca, and Candace didn't trust me. Logan might never forgive me. And the worst part? Maybe they were right not to.

I glanced at the window, the pale moonlight filtering in through the thin curtains. For a fleeting moment, I thought about running, just grabbing my bag and leaving without a word. But where would I go? There was no escape from this.

No escape from myself.

I slung my bag over my shoulder, my fingers tightening around the strap. My gaze landed on the mug Logan had gotten me. I traced the design with trembling fingers before stuffing it into my bag. It was stupid, pointless, but I couldn't leave it behind.

Taking a shaky breath, I trudged toward the living room, my limbs heavy, my heart even heavier. "I'm ready," I whispered.

Jax stepped forward, hesitating for only a second before pulling me into a quick, awkward hug. The warmth of it barely registered.

This might be the last time I see him.

"It's okay, Haze," he murmured. "You'll get better. This ... this will pass."

Will it? I wanted to ask. *What if it doesn't? What if this is who I am now?* I nodded instead, though the motion felt empty.

Becca's voice cut through the fog. "I'll call when we get home."

Jax cleared his throat. "We'll clean up here, and I'll let you know as soon as we hear about Logan."

Logan. The name hit me like a fist, knocking the air from my lungs. My throat closed up. He was out there, fighting for his life, and I was just ... leaving. Abandoning him. Hot tears welled up, blurring my vision. *What if he doesn't make it? What if I never got the chance to tell him—*

I clenched my jaw, swallowing down the lump in my throat.

No. I can't think like that.

I forced my feet to move forward, but it felt like I was walking away from something I'd never get back.

But then the air shifted.

The cabin walls felt like they were breathing, contracting, tightening. The air turned sharp and brittle, laced with a sudden unnatural chill that coiled around me and needled into my skin. I exhaled, and my breath hung in the air like smoke.

Too cold.

The overhead light sputtered, then flickered violently, casting jagged shadows that danced across the walls, twisting and stretching like they had minds of their own. The silence pressed in, thick and suffocating, as if the entire cabin had gone still … waiting.

Then the lamp beside the couch lifted on its own. For one suspended beat, it hovered.

Then it flew. It slammed into the wall with a deafening crash, scattering fragments of glass across the floor.

"What the—" Jax's voice was tight, sharp with panic.

Candace staggered back, nearly tripping over the corner of the rug. "What the hell was that?"

"You … saw that?" I asked.

All of them nodded, their wide-eyed stares a mirror of my own disbelief.

I'm not hallucinating this.

The front door burst open. A sharp gust of wind swept through the room, pressing against my chest like an invisible force. Then the door slammed shut with a loud bang.

"What is going on?" Becca shrieked.

"You did this," a voice whispered.

A creaking sound echoed above us, slow and deliberate. I tilted my head back just in time to see the wooden beams groaning under pressure, their dark shadows slithering along the ceiling.

Something was up there.

A flicker of movement caught the edge of my vision. A shimmering figure, just for a second, standing in the corner before it disappeared into the darkness.

"I'm not hallucinating that, am I?" I asked with a shaky breath.

"No," Jax breathed.

Becca clutched her arms around herself, trembling. "Hazel ..." she muttered, her voice urgent and breaking. "We have to get out of here." She ran to the front door, yanking at the handle, but it didn't budge. She let out a frustrated cry and slammed her fists against the wood. "It won't open!"

The lights went out, plunging the room into pitch darkness. The suffocating air pressed in, stealing the breath from my lungs.

"Hazel..." Becca's voice was little more than a whisper, trembling in the dark. "I think this is—"

"You did this," the voice hissed again, louder this time, cutting through the darkness like a razor.

Becca fumbled with her phone, the flashlight flickering on just as the voice stopped speaking. But the beam was feeble, swallowed by the inky blackness. Then, just as quickly, her phone died, leaving us in complete darkness again.

"Damn it!" Becca cursed.

"Mine's not working either!" Candace shrieked. "Why is it so cold in here?"

Before anyone could answer, a wooden stool hurled itself across the room, missing Becca and me by inches. It splintered against the wall with a crack that sounded like breaking bone.

I stumbled back, my heel catching the coffee table. Objects scattered across the floor in a chaotic clatter.

The room pulsed with energy, like a heartbeat growing louder and faster. A gust of wind exploded through the room.

Then, from the fireplace, a roaring ball of flames erupted, hurtling toward us.

Becca screamed. I shoved her out of the way, heat scorching my skin as the fireball flew by and slammed into the far wall. The fire quickly bloomed outward, its tendrils licking hungrily at the wood and wrapping the cabin in an orange, writhing glow.

"We need to go! Now!" I shouted.

Becca nodded, her face pale, streaked with tears. She reached for me.

But then a deafening crack erupted.

A beam splintered and crashed down from the ceiling, slamming into Candace with a brutal thud. Her scream pierced the smoke.

"Candace!" Jax lunged forward, dropping to his knees beside her, his hands immediately scrabbling at the heavy wood pinning her down.

I froze. My instincts screamed at me to run, but I couldn't move.

Jax gritted his teeth, muscles straining as he tried to lift the beam. It wouldn't budge. "Run!" he shouted, voice raw. "Get out of here!"

"I'm not leaving you!" Becca sobbed.

The fire roared louder, heat curling into my skin like claws. Smoke thickened around us, choking out every breath. "We can't stay here!" I coughed, grabbing Becca's arm. "We'll die if we do!"

She hesitated, torn. But then the flames surged between us and them, an inferno swallowing the hallway. She stumbled back. I didn't let her hesitate again. I pulled her.

We ran.

The front door, stuck moments before, now gave way with a groan. The night air hit us like a slap, icy, jarring. We tumbled outside, coughing, gasping, eyes streaming.

At the edge of the clearing, I turned back, and my breath caught. The cabin was a wall of fire. Orange and red lit up the trees, flickering against the dark sky. The smoke billowed thick and suffocating, curling into the stars.

Jax and Candace were still inside.

I grabbed Becca's arm. "They'll get out," I whispered, trying to convince myself as much as her. But the words felt hollow against the roar of the fire.

Chapter Thirty-Two

The cabin burned.

Flames clawed at the sky, wild and relentless, casting flickering shadows that stretched and twisted through the trees. The inferno roared, the air was thick with smoke and heat, suffocating and blinding.

As I stood there watching, I couldn't get enough breath into my lungs.

Oh God. Will Jax and Candace make it out? Do they even have a chance?

"No, no, no," I whispered, the words tumbling from my lips in a frantic plea. "We have to do something. We can't just leave them in there."

Becca rounded on me, her face twisted with grief and fury. "Why'd you pull me out?" she screamed, her voice raw and cracking. "We could've helped him!"

My heart pounded violently, my breath coming in gasps. "Becca ... I—" I had no excuse. No words. Because maybe she was right.

Becca's ragged breaths came in uneven sobs as we both stared at the burning wreckage, waiting, begging for a miracle.

But the flames didn't stop. The fire howled, hungry and merciless, devouring everything in its path.

Seconds stretched, warped into something unbearable.

And then the roof collapsed. A deafening roar cracked through the night as the flames surged higher, swallowing the last of the cabin.

Becca let out a broken cry, her hands clawing at her hair, like she could rip herself away from the moment. "He's gone."

"No—" My voice cracked. I shook my head, hard, tears blinding me. "No. They could've—there's still time. They could've found another way out. Maybe through the back. Maybe—"

"*Stop!*" she snapped, her voice sharp with panic and pain. "He's gone, Hazel. Don't you get it? We have to go. *Now.*"

Her words crashed into me like a wave, but I couldn't move. My legs were concrete. My lungs were caving in.

Jax and Candace can't be gone. Logan can't be gone.

My knees buckled, and I dropped, arms wrapping around myself as if I could hold the truth at bay. A sob tore from my throat, raw and shaking.

Then Becca grabbed my arm, yanking me to my feet. "We need to find help," she said through clenched teeth. Her voice trembled, but her grip was iron. "There's no one out here. We have to get to town."

I nodded weakly, barely processing her words. My gaze lingered on the cabin one last time, as if I could somehow rewind the last few minutes. Undo all of this.

But the flames didn't stop. They never stopped.

The cold air slammed into me as we ran, a sharp contrast to the suffocating heat of the fire. My lungs burned. My legs dragged like they were wading through cement. Branches tore at my arms, stinging my skin, but I barely felt them. I just ran.

The forest was too quiet. No wind. No birds. Just the slap of our footsteps against the earth and our ragged, uneven breathing.

Above us, the bright full moon hung heavy in the sky casting silver light across the trees like it was watching everything unfold in silence.

I had no idea how long we ran before the trees broke apart, revealing the lake. Beneath the moonlight, its smooth surface shimmered, a calmness that felt strangely wrong. Like the world had forgotten how to grieve.

Becca slowed, doubling over to clutch her side, her breath coming in gasps. "I—I can't run anymore," she panted.

I hesitated, my instincts screaming at me to keep going. "We have to," I urged, though my own voice shook and my legs wobbled beneath me.

But Becca didn't move. Instead, she straightened. And when she looked at me, something in her face had changed.

Cold. Hollow. Unrecognizable.

"You," she whispered, her voice razor-sharp.

A chill slid down my spine. "What?" I stammered, taking a step back.

She shook her head slowly, her expression twisting into something like disgust. "I thought Hannah was dangerous. But you..." She took a step forward.

A violent twist wracked my stomach. "What are you talking about?"

She let out a bitter, breathy laugh, a sound that didn't belong to her. "You killed them. Jax, Logan, Candace."

My heart stopped.

"They're all gone," she said, voice void of emotion. "And it's your fault."

My mouth opened, but no words came out. My pulse pounded in my ears. "Becca, no," I whispered, panic rising like bile. "I didn't—"

"Didn't what?" she snapped, her tone growing colder. "Didn't drag us into this nightmare? Didn't make everyone think they were losing their minds because you couldn't handle your own?"

Her words hit like daggers, each one slicing deeper. My breathing turned shallow. "Becca, please," I pleaded. "You have to believe me. I didn't mean for any of this to happen."

Her lips curled into something cruel. "Believe you?" She let out a hollow laugh, the sound devoid of warmth. "We believed Hannah. Look where that got us."

My chest constricted. "What do you mean?"

She tilted her head, watching me like I was something she had already figured out. "Hannah was always causing problems, too," she said quietly. Too quietly. "Hurting people without caring." A subtle, unsettling change flickered across her face. "Just like you."

My breath hitched.

"But I fixed it before she could hurt anyone else." She took another step forward, and for the first time, I saw something gleaming in her hand.

A flicker of moonlight on metal.

A knife.

Chapter Thirty-Three

My best friend stood before me, gripping a blood-stained knife. The same one that had been used on Logan. And she was aiming it at me.

My pulse slammed against my ribs. *No.* This wasn't real. It couldn't be. "Becca?" My voice wavered, my throat closing around her name. "What are you doing?"

"You *stabbed* Logan," Becca said, matter of fact, like it was an undeniable truth. "You set the cabin on *fire*. You pulled me away from Jax, and we just left him to die." Her breath hitched. "*You're* the dangerous one."

The words crashed into me, knocking the air from my lungs. "No! How can you say that?"

She took a slow step closer, her voice dropping to a chilling whisper. "Because I know what you're capable of."

Something caught my eye. A glint of gold on her wrist. A bracelet.

Not just any bracelet. Hannah's.

My stomach plummeted. "Why are you wearing that?" I demanded, my voice trembling. "That's Hannah's."

Becca glanced at it, then back at me. Unfazed. "What?" she scoffed, holding up her wrist. "This is mine."

"No." My breathing quickened. "I've never seen you wear it before."

She rolled her eyes, but the gesture felt forced. "I wear it all the time."

Liar.

Something cracked open inside me.

Pieces slammed together like glass shattering. First, Becca's words about Hannah. *Just like Hannah, you're a danger to everyone around you.*

Then, Hannah's warning to me. *Be careful who you trust.*

My breath hitched.

I remembered the way Becca immediately had blamed me for Logan. The way she had turned everyone against me. It wasn't grief for Logan or concern for me. It was a deflection. A way to shift the blame. A way to make me question myself.

I wasn't the one spiraling.

She was.

"You've been blaming me this entire time," I whispered, my voice trembling but firm. "But it was you, wasn't it? You killed Hannah She was warning me about *you.*"

Becca stilled.

I moved forward, my voice gaining strength. "You stabbed Logan to make it look like I did it." My throat tightened. "You were desperate to turn everyone against me. You knew if I started had more time to put things together, I'd figure out the truth."

Her mask slipped. Just for a second. And that second was enough.

"Everyone believed I would do such a thing," I continued. "Because you made sure of it. You've been planting doubt about me from the start."

Becca's grip tightened on the knife, her jaw clenching. "You are sick, Hazel. You don't know what you're talking about."

But I did. For the first time, I knew exactly what was happening.

"No, I know exactly what I'm talking about now." My voice cracked, but I pressed on, anger flaring in my chest. "You've been manipulating everyone. Even me. You wanted me to think I was losing it, so no one would suspect you."

Her expression darkened. Her calm façade shattered into something cold and raw. "You're wrong," she hissed. "You've been dangerous from the moment you got here. I was trying to protect everyone from you."

"No," I said firmly, finally trusting myself. "You can't make me doubt myself anymore. You've hurt everyone—Hannah, Logan, Jax. And now you want to do the same to me."

Becca's face twisted, her emotions warring beneath the surface. "I *never* hurt Jax. Hannah did. And you took me away from him. And now he's ... he's dead!" Her chin trembled.

I took a cautious step back. "Why? Why would you do all this?"

Becca's expression twisted, her features a volatile mixture of guilt and fury. "I needed Jax and Logan to think Hannah left them. That she abandoned them. That's why I sent those texts to them from her phone." Her breathing was uneven, ragged. "Everything was fine. Until you saw that stupid flyer." She let out a bitter laugh. "Of all the things for you to obsess about."

I stumbled back another step, my heart racing. "Becca..."

"And then you made up that dumb shit about Hannah haunting you. I mean ... what's it like inside your head, Hazel?" Her voice was sharp, mocking. "But you had to drag Logan and Jax into your delusions. I had to do something that would make them realize how unstable you really are."

The bile rose in my throat. "Why did you kill her?"

Becca's face cracked, not with guilt, but rage. "She was dangerous. Even Logan knew. He told her to stay away from Jax, but she wouldn't listen. Said she was in love with him." Her nostrils flared. "Hannah tried to kill Jax. She acted like she was invincible. Driving over 100 miles per hour with him in the car. She wanted to die and take him with her." Her voice sharpened, cracking with emotion. "He doesn't love her. He never did. He loves *me*. But Hannah didn't listen. We fought. You know I like a good fight."

Something snapped in my chest. "What did you do?"

Then, a memory slammed into me. The dream. The shadow. The hands around my throat.

I gasped. "Did you ... strangle her?"

Becca froze, her head tilting slightly as her eyes narrowed. "How do you know that?"

A rush of nausea hit me. My legs threatened to give out. My chest tightened. The world tilted. "I ... I dreamed it," I whispered.

She stared at me. Then she laughed. "You *dreamed* it?" she said mockingly, and took another step toward me. "No, Hazel. You imagined it. That's what you do."

I shook my head. "No. This is real."

"Well, I don't know how you know."

"Becca ..." My voice cracked as I tried to process the lies, the secrets, the violence. I backed away farther and stumbled, my heel catching on a rock. I caught myself, but the distance between Becca and me shrank as she advanced.

"You're just like her. A danger to everyone around you. And just like her, you need to be stopped."

Chapter Thirty-Four

Fear gripped my chest like a vice.

Becca's words twisted through my skull. "I don't want to do this, Hazel, but I have to." Her voice was flat, almost detached. But beneath it, something fragile trembled. Something broken.

I staggered back. "Becca, please," I begged, my voice trembling. "This isn't you. You don't have to do this. We can fix it. We can—"

Her gaze hardened, cutting me off. "Fix it? There's no fixing this. You ruined everything, Hazel." The knife in her hand caught the moonlight, its blade glinting menacingly.

"I won't tell anyone," I rushed out, desperation clawing at my throat. "Please. We can forget this ever happened. No one would believe me anyway, right? They already think I'm losing it."

Becca's expression didn't change. "I wish it were that simple."

Something cold sank in my stomach. "Please. I'll admit myself to a hospital. You won't have to deal with me anymore." I needed to get out of this. Anything to defuse the situation. The icy grip of the wind seemed to tighten around me, the bleak sky a mirror to the desolation I felt.

"We'll tell everyone that I attacked you. The police will come and take me. I know you. I know you aren't evil. You're a good person." Every word, every action, was a gamble. But if I could just keep Becca talking, keep her engaged, maybe I could find a way out of this. Maybe I could save myself from this nightmare.

She tilted her head, studying me, like she was truly considering it. For a split second, I thought I saw the old Becca, my best friend, flicker through.

Then the icy stare returned to her eyes. "I know you're lying."

My heart stuttered.

Her lips curved into a smirk. "Which is a shame." She lunged.

I dodged, barely. The knife sliced my arm. Sharp, hot, blinding pain flared. A strangled cry tore from my throat, but I didn't stop. I turned and ran.

"Hazel!" Becca's voice ripped through the night.

The ground blurred beneath my feet. My breath tore in ragged gasps. My heart pounded, hammering against my ribs like a war drum. Branches whipped at my arms and face, the icy air burning my lungs.

But Becca was relentless. A predator on the hunt.

"This isn't you!" I shouted, dodging low-hanging branches. "We can fix this! Together."

Her footsteps crashed behind me.

I veered sharply, spotting a fallen branch thick enough to use as a weapon. I snatched it up, spinning around just as Becca closed the distance. Her wild eyes locked onto mine.

For a moment, I saw her again, the friend I used to know, but only for a second. Darkness swallowed her whole.

"Stay back," I warned, gripping the branch so tight my knuckles ached.

She laughed. "You think that'll stop me?" She lunged.

I swung with all my strength. The branch slammed into her shoulder.

She cried out, stumbling back, the knife flying from her grip and skittering across the dirt.

I didn't wait. I ran. The pain in my arm pulsed, but I forced my legs to move faster. The ground grew uneven, the wind howling through the trees. I reached the edge of a cliff. The lake stretched below, its surface shimmering like black glass. I skidded to a stop, my heart hammering.

Becca staggered up behind me, clutching her injured arm, her breath ragged. "End of the line."

My eyes flicked to the knife in her hand. "Don't do this," I pleaded, my voice breaking. "You don't have to do this, Becca. Please."

She was on me in an instant, a wild look in her eyes. We hit the ground hard, rolling dangerously close to the cliff's edge.

A tangle of limbs. Of frantic breaths. Of desperation and fury.

I struggled against her, grappling for the knife as her weight pressed down on me.

A sudden, sharp pain seared my stomach. My vision swam, and I let out a scream. I looked down. The knife was buried in my abdomen. Dark blood spread across my shirt. The burning sensation consumed me, sharp and blinding.

Becca leaned in, her breath hot against my ear. "You won't win, Hazel. You never could."

Each breath was a battle. The pain was sharp and unforgiving. My strength ebbed away, slipping from my grasp like water through trembling fingers. The cold of the ground seeped into my bones.

How had it come to this? How could she have done this? How could she be a killer?

Chapter Thirty-Five

A pool of warm blood slowly seeped from my wounds. Pain burned in my stomach where the knife had pierced me, and my limbs felt weak, as if the fight had drained the last bit of strength I had. My vision blurred, but I was still conscious, barely.

I was dying.

"Something always happens on a full moon," Casey had told me.

Casey. A pang of sadness hit me. *I can't leave him. Am I really going to die here?*

Above me, Becca loomed, her breath coming in harsh, ragged gasps. Her hair clung to her sweat-damp face, wild and unhinged. "I'm sorry, Hazel," she murmured.

Her fingers dug into my arms, her nails pressing deep as she dragged me across the dirt. My body jolted with every movement, fresh pain slicing through me like hot razors. My clothes were soaked with blood, the dirt beneath me growing wet and sticky. I felt the cold creeping closer, the sharp scent of damp earth mixing with the metallic tang of my own blood.

The sound of the water lapping against the rocks grew louder as we neared the edge of the cliff. She was taking me to the lake.

A new terror surged through me, cutting through the haze of pain. She thought I was unconscious. She thought I couldn't fight back. She was going to drown me.

Becca bent over, gripping my shoulders tighter as she prepared to roll me into the lake.

I snapped my eyes open. With a sudden burst of pure, desperate survival, my hand shot up, clamping around her wrist like iron.

Becca let out a startled shriek. "What the—Hazel!"

I yanked her off balance, twisting my body, throwing all my weight against her footing. Her boots skidded against the slick ground, and she lost her balance.

And in one swift, chaotic motion, we both plunged into the freezing water.

I sank beneath the lake's surface. A gasp escaped my lips as the icy water hit me, its cold grip tightening around my chest. The cold constricted me, making my limbs feel leaden and my body slow.

Becca's fingers clawed at my arm, trying to pull me deeper. I kicked wildly, my boot connecting with her ribs. Her grip loosened.

I broke free, but the water dragged me under. Darkness swallowed me whole. I thrashed, my hands reaching, clawing, but there was nothing to grab onto. A scream died in my throat as the lake's icy water poured in. Panic surged through me like wildfire, consuming every rational thought. The water wanted me. It wanted to claim me. To bury me alongside Hannah.

No. No. No.

I fought, my lungs burning. My body wanted to give in, to let the lake take me, but I couldn't let that happen. Casey. Logan. I had to fight.

Then the current shifted.

The force of the water dragged me sideways, yanking me away from the deep center of the lake. I didn't know where I was going, only that I was moving. The current carried me, pushing me toward the opposite side.

I slammed into a cluster of rocks near the shallows. Coughing and choking, I latched on. My arms shook violently, my fingers barely gripping the slick stone.

I tried to lift myself, but my body refused to cooperate. My arms buckled, my head dipping back beneath the water.

No. Not now.

With a strangled cry, I kicked off the rock, scrambling forward, dragging myself onto the shore of the lake. My hands sank into the mud, and

I crawled. Every movement sent sharp, burning pain through my stomach, but I kept going.

Finally, I collapsed onto the cold, wet grass, my body convulsing from the cold. I was out of the water. I sucked in air, greedy and desperate. My vision blurred, my heartbeat hammering in my skull. Blood from my wound mixed with the dirt beneath me, but I didn't care. I was alive.

I heard Becca's frantic splashing. Her voice rose, hoarse and furious. "You can't run from me, Hazel!"

I forced myself to crawl farther from the water's edge. My entire body screamed in protest, but I couldn't stop. Not yet. I turned, my pulse spiking. The water rippled violently. She was still out there, flailing, trying to reach the shore.

But her strength gave out, and she slipped under.

She didn't resurface. The water stilled, the ripples fading into the quiet night. My chest heaved as I stared at the spot where she had disappeared, waiting, expecting her to emerge again.

But she didn't.

A numbness crept through me, not from the cold, but from the realization that it was over.

Becca was gone.

Chapter Thirty-Six

The ground beneath me was cold, wet, and unforgiving. My entire body shook violently, my blood soaking into the dirt as pain pulsed through me in waves. The world blurred at the edges, slipping further away with every ragged breath.

I tried to move, to lift my hand, to crawl away from the water's edge, but my limbs wouldn't obey. Overwhelmed by exhaustion, I felt the crushing weight of my body. I was slipping.

Then, in the distance, I heard footsteps and voices.

A flashlight beam sliced through the dark, blinding me for a second. The sound of snapping twigs and hurried breathing reached me, but my brain struggled to connect the pieces.

"Hazel!" a voice called, distant but familiar.

Jax.

I blinked sluggishly, my vision swimming. A shadow rushed toward me, the edges of his figure blurred, but I knew that voice. I wanted to reach out, to call his name, but all that escaped my lips was a weak, broken gasp.

Jax dropped to his knees beside me, his breath coming fast. His hands hovered over me, like he didn't know where to touch without making it worse. "Oh my god, Hazel!" he whispered. "Can you hear me?"

Candace stumbled behind him, her limp more pronounced, her face pale and streaked with soot. She knelt beside him, tore off her flannel shirt, and pressed it hard against my stomach wound.

I screamed, the pressure blindingly painful.

"Shit—Hazel, I'm sorry," Candace choked out. "I know it hurts, but we have to stop the bleeding."

Jax grabbed my freezing hand, his grip firm, desperate. "Stay awake," he pleaded. "We're getting you out of here."

I tried to focus on him, but my head drooped to the side. My lips formed words that wouldn't come.

Becca ... gone.

The thought surfaced, hazy and unreal. Had it really happened? Had she really tried to kill me? Had I really survived?

Candace's hands shook as she pulled out her phone. "No service," she muttered through clenched teeth. "We have to get her out of here."

Jax looked at me, his face drawn with fear, then at the blood pooling beneath me. He didn't hesitate. "I'll carry her." He shifted closer.

"Jax—she's bleeding too much," Candace warned.

"We don't have a choice!" He slid his arms under me, one beneath my shoulders, the other beneath my knees. The second he lifted me, agony ripped through me, tearing a strangled cry from my throat.

"I know, I know," he murmured. "Just hold on."

The movement jostled the wound, sending a fresh wave of dizziness crashing over me. My head lolled against Jax's shoulder, my body boneless, useless.

The forest stretched endlessly around us, the darkness pressing in. Every step was slow and agonizing, the effort making Jax's breathing heavy. His grip on me tightened with every stumble, but he never let go.

I drifted in and out, my consciousness slipping further. "Jax..." My voice was barely above a whisper, but it took everything to say it.

"You're okay," he panted. "We're almost there."

Lies. I wasn't okay. Logan wasn't okay. Becca was ... gone.

My chest clenched, my body shuddering. It should've felt like a relief, but it didn't. Because Becca had been my best friend. Because Becca had killed Hannah. Because I had watched her drown.

A faint glow of headlights cut through the darkness ahead.

Candace let out a sob of relief. "A truck! There's a ranger's truck!"

A flashlight flashed in the dark, a new voice piercing the air. "Hey! What's going on?"

Jax staggered forward. "She's been stabbed. We need help, now!"

The ranger ran toward us, his expression shifting to alarm as he took in the scene. Soot. Blood. Wounds. Three kids who looked like they had barely crawled out of hell.

He was saying something, radioing for backup, checking my pulse, but I was barely listening. My mind drifted, the world fading again.

I felt hands lifting me, my body shifting from Jax's arms to the back of the truck. I felt pressure on my stomach again, heard the urgency in someone's voice.

"Stay with me, kid," the ranger muttered. "We're getting you out of here."

Jax's hand brushed mine as he stepped back, his face etched with guilt, fear, pain.

"I'm sorry," I rasped, though I wasn't sure why.

"Don't," Jax said. "Don't say that. This isn't your fault."

I wanted to believe him. I clutched his sleeve weakly, my breath uneven. "Logan ... is he..."

"We'll find out," he promised. "Right now, we just have to get you safe."

I tried to nod, but sleep pulled at me, dragging me under. My eyes fluttered shut, and this time, I let them. Because for the first time in days, I wasn't running.

I was finally going home.

Friday

Chapter Thirty-Seven

I woke to the warmth of soft blankets, their weight grounding me even as my thoughts swirled in confusion. The sterile scent of antiseptic lingered in the air, mingling with the faint hum of machines. As I shifted, a sharp, searing twinge shot through my stomach, and I winced. My hand instinctively pressed against the source of the pain, fingers grazing the bandages beneath my gown. Tender, but I was alive.

My eyelids fluttered open, and I realized I was in a hospital room. The bright overhead light cast everything in a stark, almost surreal clarity—the pale walls, the muted beeping of the heart monitor, the faint shadow of my IV pole standing guard beside me.

Panic seized me for a moment. Was this a mental hospital? Had the fight with Becca been nothing more than a hallucination, a cruel fabrication of my fractured mind? My throat tightened, and I struggled to swallow the lump of fear rising within me.

The door creaked open, pulling me from the spiral of doubt.

Jax stepped in hesitantly, his silhouette framed by the soft light spilling in from the hallway. Relief crashed over me, sudden and overwhelming, at the sight of him. Alive. Whole.

"You're awake," he said, his voice rough with exhaustion. He shut the door gently behind him and approached my bed. Weariness etched his face, his ash-streaked hair plastered to his brow. But it was his eyes that struck me most. A haunting mix of sadness, guilt, and something heavier. "You look better."

I managed a weak smile. "Are you okay? I thought you—" My voice cracked, the weight of everything catching up to me.

"I'm okay," he said quickly, as if saying it fast enough might make it true. He pulled the chair closer, the legs scraping against the floor, before he sank into it with a sigh. "A little sore, some burns. Candace got the worst of it, but she's okay too."

So, it had happened. The fire, the cabin, the chaos was real. I hadn't imagined it. "And Logan?" I braced myself for the answer.

Jax's jaw tensed. "He's stable," he said, though his tone carried a weight I couldn't ignore. "Physically, at least."

I hesitated, then asked. "Who ... who stabbed him?" Though deep down, I already knew.

Jax exhaled sharply, as if my saying it out loud made it more real. "Becca," he said finally, the name hanging in the air like a curse. "She tried to pin everything on you. But she ... she didn't make it."

The words didn't hit the way I expected them to. Maybe because I was too drained, too hollow to process it all. Sadness flickered briefly, but it was swallowed by something else. Not relief. Not satisfaction. Just ... emptiness.

"And they found Hannah's body," Jax added, his voice cracking with barely contained emotion. "In the lake."

The air in my lungs turned to ice. Tears welled in my eyes, blurring the hospital room into a haze of muted colors. *Hannah.* After all this time. She really had been there, reaching out to me, trying to tell me something. I hadn't imagined her. She had been haunting me, trying to warn me.

He ran a hand through his hair, looking away. "I was so desperate to find out what happened to her that I didn't care who I hurt. I loved her so much, Hazel. I never believed that she would have just left."

I swallowed hard, my chin trembling. "Why didn't you ever tell me about her? Becca never mentioned her either. Not once."

"I don't know," he admitted, rubbing his hands together as if trying to steady himself. "Becca met her in Paris during that study abroad trip. When they got back, Becca told me not to say anything to you. I think she felt bad. She got to go and make a friend when you couldn't. And then ... you and Matt started dating around the same time Hannah and I did."

His lips lifted slightly, like the memory almost brought him comfort. "I fell in love with her. She was ... everything. Fun, adventurous, passionate. But she wasn't well. Logan was right to warn me. I just didn't want to listen. He didn't think I could handle her, but I didn't care. We went to the cabin for New Year's, and that was when everything fell apart. Hannah and Logan had this huge fight. Becca went after her. I thought it was to comfort her, but..." His voice caught. "Hannah never came back." His words lingered, and the pieces started clicking into place.

Hannah disappeared on New Year's. I was diagnosed in February.

The timeline fit too perfectly. My chest tightened.

Becca had been there with me through everything, and had kept telling me to focus on myself, that I needed to heal. She'd steered me away from asking her too many questions, from noticing the cracks in her façade. She'd talked endlessly about Paris, about the art, the food, the adventure. I had hung on every word, wishing I'd been there with her. But not once—not once—had she mentioned Hannah.

Had she pushed so hard for this cabin trip to keep controlling the narrative? To distract me?

To keep me from noticing the lies she had buried along with Hannah?

My stomach twisted as guilt and anger warred inside me. How could I not have noticed? How could I have trusted her so completely? And now ... Hannah was gone. Becca was gone. And I was left to deal with the wreckage.

"I'm so sorry," I whispered.

Jax reached for my hand, his grip firm but gentle. "I'm sorry, Hazel. I'm sorry for everything. I hate that I believed Becca when she blamed you. I hate that I thought Logan hurt Hannah. I hate that I—" He cut himself off, jaw clenching.

"Don't do that to yourself." I squeezed his hand back. "It's not your fault. None of us could have known what Becca would do."

"I should've believed you. Becca ... she was good at making me think you were having an episode."

A bitter smile tugged at my lips. "From your perspective, it probably looked that way."

His remorseful gaze met mine, his grip tightening slightly. "I promise, I'll do everything I can to make sure you're safe. I should have protected you better."

"You can't always protect me," I said gently. "But ... promise me you'll call or come around more. I need you."

A faint smile broke through his sorrow. "You got it."

The door opened then, and a nurse entered with a clipboard and a kind smile. Jax released my hand and stood to the side, giving the nurse room to check my vitals. But even as he stepped away, I could feel his quiet reassurance, his presence a steady anchor in the aftermath of everything.

I had survived the fire, the lies, the betrayal. And as I lay there in the hospital room, I felt a flicker of hope that maybe, just maybe, I could heal. One small step at a time.

Cabin Retreat Turns Deadly, Uncovers Shocking Truth About Long-Missing Teen

By Helen Parker News Reporter

Posted 9:12AM | Tuesday, October 22, 2024

What began as a peaceful lakeside getaway turned into a night of chaos, violence, and tragedy, ultimately unraveling the truth behind the mysterious disappearance of 16-year-old Hannah Foster, who had been missing since January. The night's events left one person dead, two others hospitalized, and a remote cabin reduced to ashes.

The County Sheriff's Office confirmed that Foster's remains were recovered from the lake near the burned cabin, bringing a heartbreaking end to a ten-month search. An autopsy determined she had been strangled the night she vanished, classifying her death as a homicide. The body of Becca Thompson, 18, was also recovered from the lake, with investigators identifying her as the primary suspect in Foster's murder.

A Deadly Night at the Cabin

By Helen Parker News Reporter

Posted 10:02 AM | Wednesday, October 23, 2024

A group of six friends had gathered at the remote cabin for what was meant to be a brief retreat. However, tensions reportedly escalated, culminating in a violent confrontation. Authorities say that during the altercation, Logan Foster, 19, Hannah's older brother, was stabbed and rushed to the hospital with serious injuries. Later that night, Hazel Williams, 18, was found near the lake, also suffering from a stab wound. Both have since been stabilized.

The cabin itself was completely destroyed in a fire that erupted amid the chaos. Investigators are working to determine the cause of the blaze, though foul play has not been ruled out. Witnesses described the night as volatile, with long-buried tensions between the group coming to a deadly head.

The Truth Behind Hannah Foster's Disappearance

By Helen Parker News Reporter

Posted 7:45 PM | Wednesday, October 23, 2024

For nearly a year, Foster's disappearance remained a mystery, with many believing she had run away. However, new evidence recovered from Becca Thompson's phone revealed escalating hostility between the two young women, particularly over Foster's romantic relationship with a mutual friend. Investigators now believe Thompson killed Foster on the night of her disappearance and later worked to cover up the crime, sending text messages from Foster's phone to create the illusion that Foster had voluntarily left town.

"Hannah lit up every room she entered," her grieving mother said in a statement. "We're devastated by the loss but grateful to finally bring her home."

Survivors & Community in Shock

By Helen Parker News Reporter

Posted 7:07 AM | Thursday, October 24, 2024

The investigation is ongoing as authorities piece together the final hours leading up to Thompson's death and the destruction of the cabin. The revelations surrounding Thompson have sent shockwaves through the community. Once seen as a friendly and kind individual, she is now remembered for her role in a betrayal that shattered multiple lives. Those who knew her well struggle to reconcile the girl they once called a friend with the one responsible for such devastating violence.

Hazel Williams remains hospitalized with life-threatening injuries and has not released a statement. Friends describe her as deeply shaken by the events but grateful to have survived.

As authorities continue their investigation, the community is left grappling with the tragic loss of Hannah Foster and the shocking betrayal that led to her death.

One Week
Later

Chapter Thirty-Eight

The invitation to Becca's funeral sat on my desk. It was a silent reminder of a farewell I wasn't sure I could face. Grief and resentment churned inside me, tangled so tightly I couldn't separate one from the other. Attending meant acknowledging the girl I once called my best friend, but also the girl who tried to kill me.

Would it bring closure? Or would it only make everything worse?

My fingers hovered over the invitation, but I couldn't touch it. The mere sight of Becca's name printed in elegant script made my chest tighten. It felt surreal. Funerals were for victims. Not for murderers. Not for the girl who had held a knife to my skin.

A week had passed since the night at the lake, yet it lingered in every breath, every aching movement, every nightmare that yanked me from sleep.

The wound in my stomach throbbed as I shifted, a sharp pull that reminded me just how close I'd come to losing everything. The stitches tugged at my skin, a constant anchor to reality. I was still here. Becca wasn't.

Back home, surrounded by the familiar comfort of my room, the air felt too heavy, too still. As if my body had left the lake, but my mind was still drowning.

Sleep had been elusive, even with the medication. Nightmares crept in when I closed my eyes: the suffocating weight of the water, Becca's twisted expression, the fire consuming everything in its path. I'd wake up drenched in sweat, gasping for air, my hands clutching at the wound as though reliving the fight.

My fingers brushed against the edge of a photograph on my bedside table. A frozen moment in time, two carefree friends smiling as if nothing could break their bond. The image told the story of trust and camaraderie I had believed in so completely. Now it was a cruel lie. My chest tightened as I stared at it, the familiar faces a painful reminder of what I'd lost, and of the person Becca had turned out to be.

But she had been my friend. Once.

I shut my eyes, but that only made it worse. The silence reminded me of the hospital this past summer, the hum of fluorescent lights, the soft shuffle of footsteps outside my door. And Becca sitting at the edge of my bed, one foot swinging casually.

"Brought you something," she said, grinning as she pulled a bag of gummy bears from her purse. "They're technically contraband, so don't rat me out."

I managed to smile, even though my chest ached with the effort. "Thanks," I whispered.

Becca leaned in, her expression softening. "You're gonna get through this, Hazel. And when you do, we're getting the hell out of here and celebrating like crazy. Paris. Rome. Wherever you want to go."

"Paris?" I scoffed. "You just want to go back for the croissants."

"Damn right," Becca said, popping a gummy bear into her mouth. Then, more seriously, she added, "But really. You're not alone, okay? You're stuck with me. Always."

I blinked, and the hospital faded. I pressed a hand to my stomach, fingers curling into the bandages as resentment twisted inside me like a knife.

She'd lied to me. She had murdered Hannah. Stabbed Logan. And tried to drown me in the same lake as Hannah.

A tear slipped down my cheek, landing on the glass of the picture frame. How could someone I trusted so deeply have been so cruel? So heartless?

I would never get the answers I needed. Would never know why she did it. And that realization cut deeper than I'd thought possible.

I found myself in front of my mirror, staring at the reflection of a girl I barely recognized. Pale skin. Hollowed eyes. A ghost of myself.

A dull ache settled in my chest as I traced my fingers along the faint bruises on my arms, the aftermath of Becca's hands. The stitches on my stomach peeked from beneath my oversized sweatshirt, a cruel parting gift from the girl I used to love like a sister.

I imagined stepping into the church, facing her family, seeing the anger on people's faces knowing who she really was. Would they mourn her the way I once would have? Or would they question everything, just as I was doing?

Jax had texted me earlier asking if I was going. All I could tell him was that I didn't know. He responded that he didn't know if he was going either. No one else from the cabin was going. Especially Logan.

I hadn't spoken to him since *that* night. When he was stabbed. When I was attacked. I wanted to talk to him. But I was terrified. What if he blamed me? What if seeing me only reminded him of that night? What if seeing *him* reminded *me* of that night?

The door creaked open, and Casey barreled in like a tiny tornado. "Hazel! Guess what?" His voice was bright, full of boundless energy.

I blinked, startled by the stark contrast between his excitement and the heavy fog in my head. "What is it?"

He held up a handmade card, decorated with mismatched stickers and scribbled hearts. "It's magic," he declared, grinning. "When you read it, you'll feel better."

Something in my chest softened.

"Magic, huh?" I took the card, and glitter stuck to my fingertips. "This is the best magic I've ever seen."

"I know." Casey puffed his chest proudly. "Dad says I should be a professional at making people happy."

"Well, you're definitely hired."

He bounced out of the room, humming a tune to himself as though the world was nothing but sunshine and adventure.

I stared after him, my throat tightening. His innocence felt like a slap. But also a reminder that not everything was ruined. That there was still light, even if I couldn't quite reach it yet. I traced the edge of the card, letting myself hold onto the warmth of his gesture for just a moment.

The sharp chime of the doorbell echoed through the house, distracting me from my thoughts.

"Haze! Someone's at the door!" Casey's voice carried down the hall. "Do you want me to get it?"

"No, I've got it," I called back.

Pushing to my feet, I sucked in a sharp breath as pain flared deep in my abdomen. I gritted my teeth, pressing my hand to the bandages. Every step toward the front door felt like walking through quicksand.

When I reached it, I hesitated, gripping the door knob tightly. A small part of me still expected danger. When I finally pulled the door open, I gasped.

Logan.

A choked, strangled noise escaped my throat, and I grabbed the doorframe, my knees nearly buckling beneath me. My entire body locked up, my mind flashing back to that night, to him bleeding out on the bed, struggling to breathe.

I had convinced myself I'd never see him again. That even if he survived, he wouldn't ever be standing here, at my door.

But he was.

He looked as wrecked as I felt, his features sharper than I remembered, like he hadn't slept or eaten much in days.

Dark bruises shadowed the skin beneath his eyes. His usual quiet confidence had been replaced by something fragile, something achingly human.

But he was alive.

A torrent of emotions—relief, disbelief, a surge of something so raw it physically hurt—crashed into me all at once.

I launched forward before I could think, throwing my arms around him and barely registering the sharp twinge in my stomach from the sudden movement. A sob tore from my throat as I clung to him.

Logan let out a startled grunt but held onto me just as tightly. His grip was firm, steady, like he knew I needed to feel that he was real.

For a long moment, neither of us spoke.

I felt his heartbeat beneath my cheek, a steady, solid proof of life. I buried my face in his jacket, squeezing my eyes shut. "I thought you were—I thought—" I couldn't finish the sentence.

Logan exhaled shakily, his breath ruffling my hair. "I'm okay." His voice was hoarse, raw. "I'm here, Hazel."

Tears burned my throat. "I saw you on the bed," I whispered. "I thought you were dead."

He swallowed hard. "Me too."

That made a broken, watery laugh escape me. I held onto him for a moment longer before pulling back slightly, wiping at my damp cheeks.

His hands lingered on my arms, like he wasn't ready to let go either. "...Hey," he said, giving me a faint, exhausted smile.

"Hey. How are you?" I winced the second the words left my mouth. "Sorry. Stupid question."

A wry smile ghosted across his lips. "Still hurts to sleep."

I let out a soft, hollow laugh. "Same." I grimaced slightly, shifting my weight to stand straighter, only for a sharp twinge to shoot through my abdomen.

His gaze roamed over me, as if making sure I was actually okay. He frowned as he glanced at my stomach. "Are you okay?"

"I'm fine," I lied. "Just sore."

"Hazel." His voice turned gentle, but firm. "You almost died."

I forced a shrug. "So did you."

Something in his expression softened further. Then, as if realizing where he was, he hesitated. "Is it okay that I came?"

I exhaled, tension slipping from my shoulders. "Yeah. How did you know—"

"Jax gave me your address. I hope that's okay."

"Of course. Come in."

I stepped aside, watching as he walked in. His movements were stiff, cautious, like every step still hurt. When he reached the couch, he dropped onto it with a wince, rubbing at his ribs.

I frowned. "You should probably be in bed."

He lifted a brow. "You're one to talk."

"Fair." Carefully, I eased onto the couch beside him, biting back a wince. "So, what brings you—" I paused, a thought suddenly hitting me. My brows furrowed. "Wait. Did you just drive two hours to get here?"

He nodded. "Yeah." He ran a hand through his already messy hair. "I just ... needed to know how you're doing." Our eyes locked, and the intensity in his gaze made my chest feel tight.

I stared at him, unable to process it for a second. He had driven two hours with a stab wound just to check on me. After everything he had been through, after nearly dying, he still came here. A lump formed in my throat, unexpected and heavy. No one had ever done something like that for me.

"I'm ... okay," I finally said, though my voice lacked conviction.

Logan studied me, his gaze steady and unrelenting, like he saw every fracture, every wound I wasn't saying out loud.

After a long moment, his shoulders dropped slightly. His expression softened. "Hazel ... I don't even know how to say this. But ... thank you." His voice was rough, unsteady. Like he'd been holding those words inside for too long.

I blinked, caught off guard. "For what?"

"For finding her. For not giving up. Even when everyone else did."

His words hit me like a punch. I wanted to say something comforting, but all I managed was "I wish I'd found out another way."

"Me too." Logan hesitated. His eyes shone with unshed tears. "I never should've given up on her."

I shifted closer, barely feeling the pain in my stomach. "You didn't."

His hands curled into fists on his knees. "I could've saved her."

I reached out, cupping his face before he could look away.

His breath hitched. His gaze locked onto mine, eyes burning with guilt, grief, everything he had been holding in.

"Logan, don't do that to yourself."

He nodded slowly.

I dropped my hands, giving him space.

His jaw clenched as he swiped at his face, blinking rapidly. He cleared his throat. "Hannah's funeral is Friday."

I froze.

He inhaled sharply. "I'd … like you to come." A pause. "But I understand if you don't want to."

I thought of Hannah. Of the girl who had warned me. Of the way she tried so desperately to reach me. Of the fact that she possibly saved my life.

I thought of Becca.

I looked at Logan. He was asking if I'd support him. And he was asking me to say goodbye to the girl who, in her own mysterious way, had changed my life forever. "I'll come."

Logan's eyes flickered with relief. "Thank you."

I reached for his hand and gave it a small squeeze.

He squeezed back.

Neither of us spoke.

We just sat there, two people stitched together by grief and survival, staring at the quiet, darkened world beyond the window.

And for the first time in days, I didn't feel like I had to run.

Chapter Thirty-Nine

The day of Hannah's funeral arrived, wrapped in a gray stillness that stretched endlessly across the sky. A bitter chill hung in the air, the clouds overhead pressing down like a weighted blanket.

Logan's fingers tightened around mine. I squeezed back, grounding him as best as I could. The tension in his grip mirrored the anguish that seemed to ripple through the gathered mourners.

The cemetery sprawled before us, rows of gravestones standing like silent witnesses to the grief that had settled over the day. Clusters of people dressed in muted blacks and grays huddled together, their hushed whispers and muffled sobs blending into the soft rustle of leaves overhead. The freshly dug grave stood at the center of it all, adorned with a cascade of white lilies and roses.

Jax, Marcus, Candace, Matt, and Aniyah arrived together. Jax looked lost, his usual confidence replaced by a quiet sadness. Marcus offered him a reassuring pat on the back, though his own eyes were rimmed red. Candace, still bearing the marks of the fire, leaned heavily on Jax's arm. Matt and Aniyah stood a little apart, their arms linked.

Even though I had never known Hannah, she had saved me. Her warnings had been the thread that unraveled the danger I had been too blind to see.

The eulogies began, soft-spoken words carried on the faint breeze. Hannah's mother stood first, her voice trembling as she spoke of her daughter's passion for art, her love for adventure, and the bright light she had been to everyone who knew her. Logan stiffened beside me, his head bowing as the tears he had been holding back finally spilled over. I squeezed his hand.

Jax stepped forward next, his hands trembling as he held a folded piece of paper. He recounted memories of late-night talks, spontaneous adventures, and a relationship that had meant the world to him. "I thought..." Jax's voice broke. He swallowed hard, blinking rapidly. "I thought I'd have more time to tell you how much you meant to me, but I was wrong." He stepped back, his head bowed.

When the prayers concluded and the casket was gently lowered into the earth, the mourners began to drift away, their quiet murmurs fading into the background. But Logan and I lingered, rooted to the spot. His hand slipped from mine as he knelt by the grave, his fingers brushing over the engraved headstone.

I didn't know what to say. There was nothing I could say to take away his pain. Instead, I turned my gaze to the grave, to the flowers trembling in the breeze. "You saved my life, Hannah," I whispered. "I don't know how to thank you. I just … I hope you're at peace now."

I held my breath, half expecting to hear her voice, to feel some sign of her presence. But the air remained still, the only sounds were the rustling of leaves and the distant chirp of a bird. Perhaps she was finally at peace, her soul no longer burdened by the pain and secrets that had haunted her.

As Logan stood, I helped steady him, my arm slipping around his waist as we turned to leave. The others waited near the cemetery gates, their faces heavy with the shared weight of loss. Jax approached, his eyes searching Logan's face. Without a word, the two embraced, their grief momentarily binding them together in a way that words never could.

As we stepped through the cemetery gates, the sky above us shifted. A sliver of sunlight pierced through the heavy clouds, casting a soft glow over the freshly turned earth. It was fleeting, gone almost as quickly as it had appeared.

But for a moment, it felt like a whisper of something more. Like a goodbye.

Six Months Later

Chapter Forty

The microwave dinged, and I carefully pulled the steaming bag of popcorn out, the buttery scent filling the air. I opened it with caution, the heat curling against my fingers as I poured the contents into a bowl.

"Is that the kind with lots of butter?" Casey asked.

"Obviously." I grinned, handing him the bowl. He snatched it up and darted off with it, his laughter filling the room.

"I can't believe he beat me at *Mario Kart*," Logan muttered as he slid up behind me, his arms wrapping snugly around my waist.

"He learned from the best," I teased, leaning into him. His warmth was grounding, familiar, a reminder that we'd survived something no one else would ever fully understand.

"Mmhmm," he murmured, nuzzling my neck. His breath brushed against my skin before he pressed a soft kiss just below my ear.

From the couch, Casey let out a loud groan. "Hey, yo! What the crap? We got a movie to watch. Quit being gross!"

Logan chuckled and released me, shaking his head. "Kid's got no respect for romance."

We joined Casey on the couch, the kind of easy banter I hadn't experienced in so long filling the room. I curled up beside Logan, resting my head on his shoulder. The rise and fall of his chest against me was steady, comforting.

It was the kind of peace I hadn't dared to hope for, safe, surrounded by people I cared about. Six months had passed since the chaos at the cabin, since Hannah's haunting presence had shaken us all. Since Becca had revealed the darkness she carried to her grave.

We were rebuilding. Slowly, carefully. But despite the laughter and light-hearted moments, the memories still clung like shadows on the edges of our lives, waiting to pounce when the silence grew too loud.

The sound of Casey's excited commentary about the opening credits of *The Goonies* brought a smile to my face. I let myself sink into the moment, feeling Logan's warmth against me, the buttery scent of freshly popped popcorn filling the air and calming my nerves.

And then my phone buzzed.

I frowned, pulling it from the coffee table. The unknown number flashing on the screen sent a jolt through me. My stomach twisted, but I told myself it was nothing.

"Hello?" I answered.

There was a pause, long and crackling, as if the signal struggled to make its way to me. A faint hiss of static filled my ear.

I waited, telling myself it was just a telemarketer or a wrong number. But a familiar voice broke through the interference. "Miss me?"

My heart stuttered, and a cold prickle crept up my spine. My grip tightened on the phone. "Who is this?"

The laugh that followed was faint, warped by static, but unmistakably hers. "Becca, duh. Who else?"

Memories crashed in—a blur of water, flames, and the dark, twisted look in her eyes. My breath hitched, but I forced myself to exhale slowly. Calm. Controlled. I wouldn't let her, or my mind, win.

It wasn't real. It couldn't be real. Becca was dead. I had seen her sink into the lake, watched the water close over her. Hadn't I?

A smile curled on my lips, even though my pulse thundered. "Nice try," I said, the words deliberate, firm. My thumb hovered over the "end call" button, but before I pressed it, the faint sound of her laugh filtered through again, sending a shiver down my spine.

I hung up, setting the phone down on the coffee table, though my hands trembled slightly.

Logan glanced at me, his brow furrowed in quiet concern. "Who was it?"

I shrugged, leaning into him. "Wrong number."

He studied me for a second longer than I wanted. His brow furrowed, his fingers pressing lightly against my back. "You sure?"

I forced a small smile, keeping my voice light. "Yeah. Just some weirdo."

He didn't look convinced, but after a beat, he let it go, turning back to the movie. He relaxed beside me, his arm pulling me closer, but I couldn't shake the faint hum of static that still seemed to echo in my ear.

Casey laughed at something on the screen, the sound grounding me, pulling me back to the present.

I closed my eyes and let myself sink into the comfort of Logan's warmth. But in the pit of my stomach, I knew something was wrong. And deep down, I knew the truth.

I would never be safe again.

Playlist

Nightmares – Chvrches
Your Mind Is Not Your Friend – The National
(feat. Phoebe Bridgers)
I Know The End – Phoebe Bridgers
I Hope – Gabby Barrett
Bad Blood – Taylor Swift
Seventeen – Sharon Van Etten
Sunoco – X Ambassadors
Everything I Love Is Broken – The Airborne Toxic
Event
The Waitress – Tori Amos
Seven Devils – Florence + The Machine
Monsters – Conner Youngblood
vampire – Olivia Rodrigo
Girl – Tori Amos
Diagnosis – Alanis Morissette
Stone – Whiskey Myers
Safe – The Airborne Toxic Event
Little Talks – Of Monsters And Men
Leave a Light On (Talk Away the Dark) – Papa
Roach
Panoramic View – AWOLNATION
Surviving – Jimmy Eat World
Don't Let Them See You Cry – Manchester Orchestra
this is me trying – Taylor Swift

Acknowledgements

First and foremost, thank you to all my readers. Without you, my dream wouldn't exist.

To all the musicians who helped me through scenes, brainstorms, and tough creative ruts, thank you for keeping the spark alive.

I had always wanted to write a ghost story, but I also wanted to blend it with a deeper exploration of mental health. I wanted to show that even though Hazel is being haunted, she's not losing her mind or imagining things. And I hope she's someone you can all root for.

To my bestie forever, Jennifer, thank you for putting up with my random questions, Simpsons quotes, and chaotic thoughts, and for making me a crocheted potato and ghost. They sit on my desk, staring at me. And thank you Wyatt for all the funny things you say. It gave me so many ideas.

Paige, thank you for your advice, encouragement, and for being on the receiving end of my 3 a.m. ramblings. You're the best.

Shaynna, thank you for reading *Phantom Delusions* back when she was a wee baby draft, for your help, suggestions, and writing days. You helped shape this story.

Lily, thank you for the movie, book, & music recs, the laughter, and our mutual obsession with fictional crushes.

Tiffany, thank you for your support, for listening to me talk through wild ideas, and for our wine walks—your friendship means everything.

Lin, thank you for your endless encouragement.

Ian, thank you for the laughter.

Lauren, thank you for your research help, your insights, and your friendship.

Thank you to Jake for the oh-so-amazing cover! I'm glad you were able to step out of your comfort zone to bring it to life!

Sophia, thank you for helping shape this book from a rough draft into something I'm proud of. Also, thank you for explaining "further vs. farther." It's forever ingrained in me now.

Thank you to Atlanta Writers Club. You have truly changed my life and I'm so happy to have met all the people and contacts.

To my family: Mom, Dad, Patrick, Alison, Morgan—thank you for your support and love.

To my furbabies Ella and Ozzie, thank you for the cuddles and endless laughter.

And last, but definitely not least, Brandon. There was a time in my life when I wasn't allowed to write, read, or do the things I love. But you make all of that possible. Your support is everything. I hope you know how deeply I love you and how much I appreciate you.

About the Author

Carrigan is the author of several young adult novels that make you cry and whisk you to faraway places. Though born in Cullman, Alabama, she grew up in Birmingham and moved to Atlanta at 18. She earned her BA in English and her Master of Arts in Professional Writing at Kennesaw State University. For as long as she can remember, she was always making up stories and characters inside her head, sometimes using her dolls to act out the scenes.

When she's not writing (which is rare), she's spending time with her family and friends, listening to music, playing with her furbabies, Ella and Ozzie, and cheering on her Atlanta Braves.